A Note from the Founder

5th Year Anniversary Edition.

To some that may not mean much but as the Founder of the Ink Slingers Guild, I can't help but tear up when I think about the humble beginnings of our group and how much we have grown.

It means every fortnight I get to hang out with a group of truly amazing writerly folk who genuinely bring me happiness.

It means I do fun writing exercises which help me to improve as a writer.

It means tea. And laughter. Joy and Future.

The Ink Slinger's have helped me become the confident and proud author I am today. I have so much farther to go and I know they will be there for me. And I'll be there for them.

I hope you enjoy our 5th Anniversary Edition. Thank you so much for your support.

Please raise your glass.

To the Ink Slingers Guild!

Cheers and read on!

Love, Lisa

Dedication

For the Artist.

No matter your medium, keep creating despite any opposition or criticism and enjoy the results of your labor as only you can. If others share in your joy, that is the icing on your cake.

The Ink Slingers Guild

Presents

SERENITY RISING

A Collection of Short Stories
~ Special 5th Anniversary Edition ~

Contributing Authors

Nicole DragonBeck

Desiree Matlock

JM Paquette

Alanna J. Rubin

Lisa Barry

Anne Cargile

Dalia Lance

Rhiannon Matlock

Erika Lance

Witching Hour Publishing, Inc.

Witching Hour Publishing, Inc.

ISBN-10:1-943121-18-4
ISBN-13: 978-1-943121-18-2

Ink Slingers Guild crest: Nicole DragonBeck
Ink Slingers Guild crest digital artistry: Desi Matlock
Cover Design: Lisa Barry
Cover Photo Credit: © Ig0rzh | Dreamstime.com - Full Moon Photo
Editor: Courtenay Dodds www.CourtenayDodds.com

Introduction

The Ink Slingers Guild is a group of writers who come together for support and encouragement. We give each other inspiration and the occasional kick in the arse.

This collection of short stories is based on a writing exercise done at every ISG meeting. The exercise is to have three members each pick one word. Members have five minutes to compose a story with the chosen words. As with any creative outlet, members take each other into new worlds the way only writers can.

And the concept of these books was born.

Serenity Rising is the Ink Slinger's fifth anniversary special edition anthology based on that exercise.

The words that were chosen this year were:

- Apothecary
- Satin
- Succulent

Each story is an adventure, sit back and enjoy as the Ink Slingers Guild take you to the **Serenity Rising**.

www.InkSlingersGuild.com

Contents

PART I

Love Potion Sold Separately

By Nicole DragonBeck

Maggie Baker dusted the flour from her hands and pulled the next tray of raspberry filled cupcakes out of the oven. As she spooned vanilla glaze over the warm cupcakes so it would soak in, she smiled at the burly man with the ginger beard waiting patiently for her to finish.

"Sorry, I'll be right with you, Mr. Miller," she said.

"Not a problem, Miss Maggie," the man said. "It's a week until First Days, and you're the best baker in a hundred leagues. Everyone's looking forward to the Festival Feast and I wouldn't want it on my hands if it was ruined or something like that."

Maggie laughed, set the cupcakes on the bench, and came over. He had brought a dozen bags of flour. She paid him, and he tipped his hat then walked out. Mr. Miller passed Old Tom, who came to the town of Quin all the way from the city of White Wall to buy her baked goods. More from Droll, Mundy, and even as far away as Troppers, had been in and out for the past week, and they wouldn't stop coming until the Festival was over.

The Festival itself culminated in a dance on the first day of spring. The whole town was in a fervor of delight. Maggie would prefer to stay curled up in her favorite comfy chair, with a good book and a hot cup of tea. However, everyone expected cakes, cookies, and sweets for First Days. She made sure to see to her own first, so grabbing the basket near the door, she hurried down the street.

The weather was fair, the skies blue, the air fresh. The pink and white ribbons tied in the trees danced in a stiff breeze, waving merrily to all who passed. Down the streets, baskets of bright flowers adorned doorways, windows, and lampposts. Banners sewn with hearts or couples dancing hung on walls.

It was festive, brimming with positive energy, good hopes, and love. Maggie returned people's cheery greetings with a polite smile and a nod, and breathed a sigh of relief when she let herself into the cool florist's shop. The chime of a bell greeted her.

"Maggie, is that you?" a voice called from somewhere in the green.

"Yes!" she called back as she made her way through the rainbow of daisies, carnations, roses, sunflowers, bluebells, daffodils, petunias, and the rare leopard lilies that appeared only for a few brief weeks at the start of spring.

"Oh, I'm so glad you're here!" William, the florist's eldest son, rounded the corner, bouquets under each arm. "Do you have them?"

"Why else would I be here?" Maggie asked, holding out the basket of vanilla cookies with a painstaking white and pink floral icing tracery around the edges.

"Those are beautiful," William said, examining one before taking a large bite. "And delicious."

"Don't eat them all, or you won't have any left for your customers," Maggie scolded.

"Who?" William asked as he took another cookie, eyes wide and innocent.

Maggie rolled her eyes. "Fine, eat them all if you want, but those took me hours to make, and I don't have time to make you more."

"Right, the Festival Feast," William said. "Are you going?"

"The whole town is going," Maggie said noncommittally. "Oh, and I need to pick up the bouquet I ordered for the bakery. The First Days Table looks so bare without it."

"Of course."

He left and came back a moment later with a bouquet of roses and carnations, layers of purple, white, pink, and little yellow chrysanthemums that couldn't help cheer someone up.

"It's lovely," Maggie said, caressing the velveteen petals. "Thank you."

"You're welcome. Oh, I almost forgot. You haven't gotten a corsage yet," William said. "I saved one for you."

He held out a delicate ring of pink and white flowers tied together with silver ribbon. Two tiny silver bells were twined into the intricate bow.

"Thank you William," she said, her eyebrows rising in surprise. "That was very thoughtful. How much do I owe you?"

"It's no bother," he said with a shrug, and smiled. "Consider it a florist's dozen."

Maggie laughed. "Alright."

"I imagine you're busy then?" William said, as he took a cookie, wrapped in sheer white paper, and tied it around a huge collection of flowers with red ribbon. "What can we look forward to at the Feast this year?"

"Um, I thought about apple and pear tartlets, chocolate eclairs, cheese and honey bread, strawberry crepes, spice rolls with caramel pecans..." Maggie continued to list the desert menu of the First Days Festival Feast as he put the cookies in the bouquet, ending by arranging the flowers just so, putting an orange monstrosity with black speckles on the outer petals in the middle, and adjusted the ring of tiny white baby's breath around it.

"That sounds amazing. I'll save room to try it all. Now, what do you think?" he asked, taking a step back to survey his handiwork.

"It's beautiful," Maggie lied.

"It's atrocious," William said, pulling a face at the overdone arrangement. "But that's Dame Manning for you. For someone of such standing, her taste leaves a bit to be desired."

"Oh, that reminds me!" Maggie said, suddenly in a slight panic. "I'm supposed to bring her a cake for her First Days' party tomorrow!"

"Well, I'm sure..." he started. "Okay," he said. "I..."

"Bye William!" she called as she ran out of the shop. "I hope she likes the bouquet!"

~~

After eight hours in the kitchen, the little clock chime told Maggie it was two o'clock in the morning. A beautiful baking masterpiece took up the entire table, seven tiers high, pale blue frosting draping like layers of a silk dress, a line of white marzipan roses arranged in rings around the whole cake. Maggie smiled proudly despite her exhaustion.

Too tired to do anything more than put the dishes in the sink, she left the mess in the kitchen and walked into the sitting room. Sinking into the squishy embrace of the old sofa, Maggie kicked off her shoes and tucked her feet under her. The corsage lay on the table, an innocent reminder that she was supposed to think of someone to give it to. If she waited too much longer, all the boys would already have corsages.

It would be another year of wandering around the Festival by herself, watching couples dancing and embracing under the Kissing Tree. She was too tired right then to mind terribly, but she knew it would hurt at the Festival. She pulled the blanket out from under her and snuggled into the armchair. Her eyes closed and she drifted off to sleep, still troubled by her problem.

Sometime later, in the middle of a dream where people wearing huge corsages stared as she ran through the Festival alone trying to tear her corsage off her wrist as it got tighter and tighter until it felt as though her hand was about to fall off, something moved in the darkness and Maggie's eyes flew open. She sat up, looking around with one eye as she rubbed the sleep out of the other. It was not immediately apparent what had awoken her, until she saw a faint purple glow leaking through the door to the kitchen. Maggie breathed a sigh of relief and her heart calmed.

"Aunt Marigold?" she called out into the dark house.

A stumble, bump, and a crash answered her. Muttering followed and the purple glow intensified.

"Aunty, are you wearing your glasses?" Maggie said.

"Ouch!" The purple glow bumped off the door frame, into the bookcase and tumbled over to the sofa. It landed in an ungraceful heap next to Maggie. "Oh, hello dear."

"Aunty, you can't see when you don't wear your glasses," Maggie chided. "Remember what happened last time you showed up without them?"

That visit had resulted in an entire shelf of plates and teacups crashing to the ground as Aunt Marigold had attempted to walk through the front door, which was actually the door to the fine china cabinet.

"I know, dear, but I lost them on the way here," Aunt Marigold said. "Fortunately, I brought my spare pair."

Digging around in one of the many pockets in her baggy cardigan, eventually Aunt Marigold pulled out a small pair of gold-rimmed pince nez glasses.

"Ah, that's better," she exclaimed, looking around interestedly with bright eyes magnified three-fold.

"Aunty, what are you doing here? It's..." Maggie squinted at the clock. "...quarter past three in the morning."

"Ah," Aunt Marigold said. "Well, where I'm from, dear, it's almost teatime."

Maggie was too asleep to do the math so she just nodded. "So why the surprise visit? Not that I'm not pleased to see you," she hurried to assure her aunt. "It's just very...unexpected."

"Well, I had this feeling you needed to see me." Aunt Marigold arranged herself more comfortably on the sofa, folded her hands on her lap and looked expectantly at Maggie.

Maggie shifted under the piercing gaze. "It's not really anything."

"Then why did you call?"

"I didn't call!" Maggie protested.

Her aunt gave a sweet smile.

Remembering the dream, Maggie frowned and crossed her arms. "You shouldn't go peeking into my head like that. I can't help what I dream."

Aunt Marigold nodded sagely. "Of course not dear. But all the same, you need my help."

Maggie considered the tiny woman beside her. Standing, Aunt Marigold came up to Maggie's lowest rib. She had mounds of curly silver hair piled atop her head, held in place with a variety of bejeweled pins and clips, and bright green eyes. Fine lines appeared at the corner of her eyes when she smiled. Her most eye-catching feature was the glow she gave off.

"I'll make tea," Aunt Marigold said abruptly, with complete confidence the panacea would do wonders in curing her adopted niece's melancholy.

Maggie dragged herself off the couch and followed the old woman into the kitchen. The lantern flared to life without a match and the kettle rose into the air, filled itself with water, and settled onto the already burning hot stove. In moments it was singing.

Marigold turned to Maggie, two steaming cups of tea in her hand and a plate of biscuits balanced on her head. She put these on the table and seated herself, gesturing to the chair next to her.

"Now, spill!" she commanded.

It would not be wise to disobey that tone. Maggie sat and stared into her tea. "I just feel like...like my life is missing something."

Aunt Marigold said nothing, just continued to look at Maggie with an interested, caring expression.

"It's just this Festival thing. I can't think of anyone to ask to wear my corsage." Maggie didn't want to admit her wish for a fairytale courtship. Part of her thought it was puerile, something giggling girls whispered or squealed about together, not for someone who lived in the real world.

"Ah," Aunt Marigold sipped her tea, eyes sparkling over the rim of her cup. "Did all the nice young men die?"

"No," Maggie sighed, and reached for a biscuit. "They're just not my type."

Aunt Marigold raised an eyebrow. "There's an easy way to fix that."

"No," Maggie shook her head at once. "We're not getting into that hocus-pocus of yours."

"Just hear me out. You can do this all by yourself. You don't need me there at all."

"Really?" Maggie was both intrigued and skeptical. Usually Aunt Marigold was a bit of a control freak and wanted to have her fingers in the pies to make sure they came out just right.

Aunt Marigold nodded. "You remember the book I gave you? Look up *Prince Charming*."

She drained the last drop of tea, stuffed half the biscuits into one of her pockets, then stood on the chair and planted a kiss on Maggie's forehead. "Let me know how it goes, dear. And remember to smile."

Maggie offered a weak smile to the empty chair and the fading purple glow. After a moment, she went back to the sofa and collapsed, but try as she might she couldn't fall asleep. She sighed, opened her eyes and stared at the ceiling.

"Fine," she said aloud to the empty room. "I'll take a look, but I won't promise anything."

~~

Maggie went upstairs, her hand on the banister to guide her through the dark. She turned on the lantern on her bedside table. Her bedroom was made smaller than it really was by the sloping ceiling, and the bed took up most of the room. A tall bookshelf took up the rest. Maggie reached up and felt around the top shelf until her hand collided with an object.

Maggie pulled it down. Aunt Marigold had spent many teatimes lamenting how the world was losing the beauty of magic, leaving a dreary, grey slop in its place. *This Book is a last reservoir of fading magic*, she would say. When Maggie turned sixteen, Aunt Marigold passed it to her. Maggie was more practical than that, and besides, she didn't have the knack. The Book had sat up here, discarded and forgotten, until now.

Maggie sat on the bed, the Book on her lap. Its cover was thick, the colors faded, pages yellowed, and smelling of pipe smoke and potpourri. The font was some kind of old Gothic, the kind you had to squint at for several seconds to make out the words.

Maggie turned the pages carefully. The first letter on each page was illuminated. At places in the margins, neat notes were written in loopy scrawl. The familiar handwriting made Maggie smile. She skimmed the spells and rustic remedies, taking in a few words here, a phrase there, reveling in her Aunty's knowledge. Then she found what she was looking for.

The page was bordered by detailed pictures of cupids and frogs with crowns on their heads. According to the Book, the legend of Prince Charming had come about a long, long time ago when a king of a small kingdom in Eastern Europe had died, leaving his young daughter the throne. Many offers of marriage came, but all were offered with strings attached. The princess turned them down, but could not remain unwed forever, so she went to see a witch. In exchange for the princess's first born child, the witch promised to find her a suitable man.

A week later, a handsome, charming man had shown up and introduced himself as a prince of a long lost land. He said he had been on a pilgrimage when he heard stories of a princess more beautiful than all others and decided he must see for himself. When he saw the stories were true, he asked her hand in marriage. The princess refused, but the prince persisted, saying he would stay by her side, defend her to the death, blah blah. The princess eventually gave in and they lived happily ever after, or something like that.

"See your local witch or apothecary for assistance," Maggie read the final line aloud, and sighed.

~~

The next morning, after delivering the elaborate cake to Mrs. Manning, Maggie made her way all the way down Main Street and turned the corner. Burry Lane was short and narrow. Only one building occupied it, at the very end. A little sign proclaimed it *Erika's Exotic Tea and Herb Shoppe.*

Letting herself in, Maggie was swathed in smells which did the name of the shop justice. She wandered the shelves for a short while, taking random bottles down and reading the information on the labels. Moving to the back of the store, she found the till. A tall woman with red hair and red-rimmed glasses stood there. Maggie queued up behind an old man with a hacking cough. The red-head woman smiled and sold him a jar of herbs, explaining how to make a tea in a kind voice. Then she turned to Maggie.

"Good morning, dear. What can I do for you?" she asked.

"Are you Erika?" Maggie asked, twisting the hem of her shirt nervously.

The woman laughed. "No. I'm Donna. Erika is my great-grandmother. And it's Ehr-eeka. Like Eureka, but with an 'ehr'."

"Oh," Maggie said.

"Is there something I can do for you?" Donna repeated.

"I was trying to find someone to help me make my Prince Charming," she explained.

"Ah," Donna smiled. "I'll fetch granny then."

Maggie opened her mouth, but Donna was already gone. She returned in a moment with an old woman, probably as tall as Donna was, but hunched, with creamy white hair piled around her shoulders and a wooden cane. The top was carved into a white rabbit's head.

"Hello, ma'am," Maggie said, dropping into a curtsy.

Erika grinned, showing she had a full set of straight, white teeth. "Morning, dearie. Donna tells me you're looking for Prince Charming."

"Yes, my fairy...well, my Aunt Marigold told me about it...him."

"Well, you've come to the right place," Erika smiled. She pulled a Book rather similar to Maggie's from under the counter and opened it. "Come. Tell me what you want."

"A Prince Charming?" Maggie tried again.

The women laughed, not unkindly.

"Yes, dear, we got that," Donna said. "But what are you looking for *in* your Prince?"

"Oh!" Maggie took a deep breath. She really hadn't thought this through very well. "Well, he needs to be sweet. And smart. But not *too* smart. And he must *not* be involved in sports...what?"

The old woman was shaking her head. "Dear, men must do some sport. Else they get soft round the middle, see?"

Maggie considered the woman's words, and saw she was of course right. "Alright. But he should practice sophisticated sports, like tennis and skiing."

The old woman nodded and pursed her lips, running a finger down the page. She gestured for Donna, who fetched two jars off the shelf, one filled with a golden liquid the other with a grey powder.

"Honey for sweetness, pinch of powdered pig's brain for the intellect." Erika rummaged around in a shallow draw and grabbed some more things. "An old tennis ball and a pinch of snow...what else?"

Maggie thought for a moment, then became flustered. So many things to consider - what if she didn't get them all? What if she forgot something, something *important*? What if her Price Charming didn't turn out like she wanted and she was stuck with a...with a...! Maggie started to hyperventilate and grabbed the counter for support.

"What's the matter, dearie?" Erika asked.

Maggie took deep breaths. "I just don't know if I'm ready for this."

"It's a big commitment," Erika said, nodding. "I don't know that anyone is every truly *ready,* but sometimes you just have to leap in and hope for the best."

Leap in. Hope for the best. Maggie nodded, and Erika smiled.

"Now, what else shall we put into your Prince Charming?"

An hour later, Maggie was handed a crude doll carved from a knot of oak (the best for building a strong, healthy, appealing body, according to Erika). The eyes were gouges in the flat face and the arms and legs ended in stumps. A pouch almost as large as the doll itself was tied around its neck with a piece of gold string, filled with a variety of outlandish ingredients to make her Prince Charming smart, sweet, adventurous, athletic (but not obsessed), charismatic, suave, sophisticated, cultured, tasteful, tolerant, cheerful, personable, witty, considerate, confident, eloquent, just, faithful, gallant, hardworking, motivated, helpful, brave, resourceful, honest, humble, optimistic, punctual, romantic, trusting, understanding, old-fashioned, generous, and caring.

Maggie examined the doll, noting the rough strokes, the lack of facial features and unformed hands and feet.

"He'll have all the right...bits and pieces?" Maggie asked. "I mean, fingers and toes and such?"

"Of course dear," Erika said. "The spell will make him look exactly how you wish."

Then the old woman handed Maggie a small glass snow-globe. Inside, a winged cherub flitted back and forth, a gold arrow in one hand, an elaborate bow in the other.

"Here is your Cupid. Try not to crack the glass. It won't hurt him, but he can get a little stale. Instructions for Prince are on the card in the bag and for Cupid, on the bottom of the globe."

Maggie turned the globe over, accidentally causing the Cupid to bash headfirst into the glass at the top. The chubby creature glared at her, shaking a fist in her direction as his wings fluttered unevenly to righten him. The instructions were written in minuscule print that Maggie couldn't read with her naked eye.

"Will that be all for today?" Donna inquired.

"Yes, thank you," Maggie said.

"That will be twenty-nine gold pieces," Donna said. "Sign here please."

Maggie's jaw dropped. Although the price was more than what she earned in a month of selling pies and breads, parsimony wasn't going to get her a perfect suitor.

She signed the parchment Donna placed on the counter and opened her purse.

~~

Maggie hurried home, the Prince and Cupid in her coat as if she had stolen it. She barricaded herself in the sitting room and sat at the edge of the couch before pulling them out. She held one in each hand, trying not to look at either one for too long. Opening the card attached to the doll, she read aloud.

Congratulations on your purchase of this very special Prince Charming! Place the pouch containing the essence of your Prince around the neck of the effigy and place in a hot fire. As it burns say the incantation written hereunder:

> **Ignis et quod**
> **simul et amore,**
> **convenientibus**
> **et ita factum est**
> **Princeps venustus**

"Ignis et quod, simul et amore, convenientibus, et ita factum est...Princeps venustus," Maggie whispered and looked around hastily, wondering if the Prince would appear despite not performing the spell in the right order. He hadn't.

Maggie tried to read the bottom of the Cupid's snow globe. The print was too small, and she had to fetch a magnifying glass from her room. The minuscule writing became readable.

0) PICK a place where you will not be disturbed or interrupted. Failure to do this could result in less than desirable results. 1) ORIENT the Cupid to the intended target. 2) To reduce risk of injury, POSITION yourself out of sight of the target, around a corner or behind something, such as a large piece of furniture. 3) TWIST the bottom of the globe to release the Cupid. 4) WAIT for a bright flash of white, pink, or yellow light, or rarely, a shower of silver stars. This should take no more than thirty seconds. 5) STEP into the line of sight of the target.

If you run into unforeseen complications, vacate the area immediately and alert the proper authorities.

CAUTION: If using this Cupid with a Prince Charming, make certain the Prince is fully mature before you begin.

"Well, that doesn't sound so difficult," Maggie said, but that meant nothing. She could think of all sorts of terrible things that could happen if this went wrong. Maggie took a deep breath and before she could talk herself out of it, she lit the fire, threw the effigy on it, and said the incantation in a breathy voice. Nothing happened.

"Perhaps I didn't speak loud enough," she said a moment later.

She prepared to read it again, but a loud bang from the fire made her drop the card. A shower of silver stars spouted from the flames. Maggie dove for cover behind the sofa. She was so preoccupied she forgot the second part of the operation. The Cupid was sitting on the table. Maggie scooted out, snatched the globe and retreated to safety. The stars were whizzing around the room, circling the fire. Maggie held up the globe and shook it to get the Cupid's attention.

"Now what I want you to do is..." She stopped when the look on the Cupid's face got too ugly to ignore. "Okay, I guess you know how to do your job. Fly little Cupid."

She twisted the bottom as instructed. The Cupid shot out and fluttered around her head. It took its arrow and stabbed Maggie in the arm with a sadistic glare.

"Ow!" Maggie yelped. "What the...."

The Cupid snickered and flew off. Maggie wanted to peek over the sofa, but the warning, coupled with her imagination, was deterrent enough so she kept her head down. Some scuffling, almost like when Aunt Marigold arrived without her glasses, reached Maggie's ears and she started to look.

"Hello? Is there someone there?" a pleasant masculine voice called out.

Maggie clapped a hand over her mouth, ducking back down.

"Oh, hello! What are you? Little, flying, bug thing..." The voice was interested, intrigued, almost childlike. Maggie imagined a puppy, if a puppy could vocalize. "...what are you carrying...ouch! That stung."

Maggie began inching upwards, holding her breath. Her eyes crested the top edge of the sofa and widened. She froze. A man stood in the middle of the room. Dark hair fell in gentle waves around his ears. A smear of blood on his neck showed where the Cupid had struck. He was completely naked.

The Cupid was fluttering around the man's head. When the winged creature saw Maggie, it waved and dove out the window. Maggie didn't think it could do much harm. At least she hoped so. It only had one arrow. She didn't linger long on the freed Cupid, her attention turning to the man who was busy trying to discover where the bug had gone.

"Hello," he said, catching sight of her. "I'm sorry..." His eyes glazed for a moment, then he fell forward.

Maggie gasped and ran to him. He lay on the floor, face down. She touched him.

"Hello?" she whispered, shaking his broad shoulder with trembling fingers. *Please don't be dead.* "Hello?"

His eyes fluttered and then opened. Maggie was looking into deep blue eyes like the sky overhead just after the sun disappears. She blinked. His face was smooth, and masculine lines in his jaw and cheeks made him look like a sculpture. A muscular torso and well-defined arms supported this comparison. Maggie couldn't pull her gaze away for a long moment, then realized he was still unclothed. Pulling the blanket off the sofa, she threw it over him and stood. He followed suit, tying the blanket around himself like a toga.

"I'm terribly sorry, am I intruding?" he asked.

"No," Maggie said. "Not at all."

"I'm afraid I don't remember how I got here," the Prince said, looking around. "Or much of anything."

Maggie took a deep breath. How on earth was she going to explain this to him? What was she supposed to say? What was she *not* supposed to say? She was a baker, not a bard! She gave up and told him a version of the truth that wasn't too hard to disbelieve.

"You've just arrived in the town of Quin, and judging by the silver sparkles, by some spell or other. I don't know what to do about your memories. I'm sorry." She truly was.

"No worries. I'm sure I'll figure something out," he said.

Confident. Optimistic. Adventurous. Resourceful. Maggie blushed. "I'm Maggie Baker, by the way."

"That is a lovely name," he said, smiling. "Maggie."

Personable. Polite. She smiled back, waiting for him to give his name. Eventually she had to prompt him.

"Well, I suppose I must have one, but I'm afraid I don't recall it at the moment," he said. "What would you prefer to call me?"

"You should pick a name you like," Maggie said firmly. *He was his own person, and he needed to act like it.*

"Of course," he said, and tapped his chin as he thought. "In that case, I choose Charlemagne. You can call me Charle."

Sophisticated. Suave. "Very well. Pleased to meet you, Charle," Maggie said.

"Likewise," Charle said, and bowed. "Is this where you live?"

"Yes. Yes, this is my sitting room," Maggie said, looking around as if she had never seen it before.

"You wouldn't happen to have any clothes for a man here? This spell seems to have lacked the foresight of that necessity." Eloquent. Witty.

Maggie gaped. The simple statement threw the magnitude of what she had done into sharp relief. There was a man, a real, live man here. She thought about what she would do if she woke up in a stranger's house with no clothes on and no recollection of how she had arrived there. She didn't think she would take it as well as this gentleman. She began mentally backpedaling even as she began edging in the direction of the stairs.

"There might be something of my father's left. Upstairs," Maggie said. "Wait here."

She hurried upstairs, and pulled out the trunk with her parent's things in it. She found a pair of trousers and an old shirt with patches on the elbows. Charle took them without recrimination.

"Thank you," he said.

"They're not the most fashionable," she apologized.

"They will do just fine," he said.

Understanding. Tolerant. Somehow, even in the old, ill-fitting clothes, he managed to look dapper. Maggie returned the blanket to its place on the sofa, taking the few moments her face was hidden to let a little of the panic leak out before composing herself.

"What are you going to do now?" she asked, turning to face him.

"I'm not sure," Charle said. "I suppose I shall have to find work, and a place to stay."

Maggie entertained the thought of offering to let him stay here, as she was technically responsible for his plight, but the thought made her cringe, then blush again. Now this Prince Charming was actually in front of her, she just wanted him to leave so she could think without distraction.

"There's a tavern just down the way, called the Red Quill," she told him instead. "I can give you some money for a room."

"That is very kind of you," he said.

"It's the least I can do," she said, more to herself than him.

"I will find a way to repay it," he said as he accepted the coin.

"You'll be okay?" Maggie asked, showing him to the door and trying to ignore the little wiggle of consternation tying itself in elaborate knots in her stomach.

"I've no doubt," Charle smiled. "It was a pleasure making your acquaintance, Ms. Baker. I am certain I will see you soon."

Maggie watched him walk down the street before closing the door and banging her forehead against it. *What in the seven realms of the underworld have I gotten myself into?*

~~

Soon turned out to be in three hours, giving Maggie less time to think than she would have liked. A knock on the door came as she was folding pastry around candied nuts. Supposing it to be another merchant, Maggie received a shock when she opened the door and found familiar blue eyes. There was a dimple in his right cheek when he smiled. He was dressed more appropriately, in modest yet becoming grey trousers and a green vest over an ironed white shirt. He wore black boots, shined and elegantly pointed.

"I believe these belong to you," he said, holding out the clothes she had lent him, fully laundered, dried, and folded in a neat pile.

"Thank you," she said, and held out her flour-covered hands in apology. "You'll have to put them on the chair just there."

"Of course," he said as he did so, then stood in front of her. "Maggie Baker, I've come seeking work."

"Pardon?" she asked.

"Mr. Temmerson, the gracious keeper at the tavern has advised me you are the person in most need of assistance at this time of year," he said. "I'd like to offer my service. I am physically capable of a great many tasks of value to a baker, such as carrying large sacks of flour, as well as being hardworking, honest, and upstanding."

Undoubtedly, because I specified all of that in the spell.
"You mean you're not going to steal anything?" she asked instead.

"I promise to steal nothing from the bakery," he said, a lighthearted glint in his eyes. "Though I will have to make a proviso on your favor."

Despite his forward comment, he remained standing at a distance propriety could not fault. He waited patiently for her response. Maggie couldn't help but smile.

"Well, in that case, you're hired," she said. "The hours are ten in the morning to five in the evening. I can pay you 12 silver pieces a day, and lunch is included."

"Wonderful," Charle beamed. "When do I begin?"

"Right now?" Maggie said, looking into her kitchen which, with flour all over the benches, three bowls of different batters waiting their turn in the oven, and candied nut rolls in progress on the table, looked like a drunk troll family had ransacked it. "Can you wash dishes?"

Charle smiled. "Absolutely."

True to his word, Charle worked hard. He caught on quickly, and Maggie found herself hard-pressed to keep up with him. He kneaded breads, mixed fruits and nuts into muffin batters, and even became proficient at making custard turnovers. He fetched bags of flour, sugar, and butter for her. If she found she needed more cinnamon or apples, he'd go to the market or the general store and come back with precisely what she had ordered.

Every morning, he arrived promptly at ten o'clock and left at sundown. His conversation was sparse and unobtrusive, which Maggie appreciated. Though she preferred to work in silence, she hardly noticed being drawn into conversation by his sweet, somewhat naive questions about everything from the proper shampoo, to the usefulness of a dog, to what fruits were best paired with vanilla or ginger, and the difference between a bakery and a confectionery.

He requested she eat lunch with him and refused to eat if she wasn't going to, no matter how many times she explained that she had to swirl the caramel over the shortbread or it would harden, or custard would curdle if she walked off from it just then.

With a day to spare, Maggie had filled every order for First Days parties, brunches, gifts, and the most important order, the Festival itself. Surveying her spotless kitchen, she felt at a loss. What was she to do with all the extra hours?

"Perhaps you would allow me to take you out to dinner tonight." Charle spoke as if in answer to her unvoiced question.

"Sure," Maggie said, still flustered by his presence. It was so much easier dealing with the idea of a perfect man. Having one in front of her gave her nervous butterflies.

The smile Charle gave lit up the room. "Wonderful!" he bowed his head. "I shall return for you at seven o'clock?"

Maggie nodded.

~~

Despite jitters, Maggie was looking forward to dinner. Charle was an enigma, though she felt she'd known him forever. For the first time in a long time she agonized over what to wear and did her hair six different ways before settling on a modest twist over her shoulders.

"You look lovely," Charle said, making the whole ordeal worth it.

He offered her an arm and she took it, noting how easy and comfortable it was to lean into him as they walked. His pleasant conversation on the weather, the decorations, and Quin's appealing quaintness put Maggie at ease, and she found herself smiling and laughing more readily. At the Red Quill, Quin's one and only tavern, a table in the corner had been set with candles and flowers. Charle held her chair for her before seating himself.

"This is very nice," Maggie said.

Charle smiled. "I'm glad you like it. I wasn't sure what you would enjoy most. Though I would prefer something more meaningful, I took a guess that an elaborate affair would only embarrass you."

She laughed. "Good guess."

Honest, yet considerate and respectful. Maggie thought she should try to stop cataloging his attributes. She tried to observe him with surreptitious glances from under her lashes. Erika had said he would be whatever Maggie's ideal man would be, physically. He *was* gorgeous enough to melt the heart of one of Medusa's statues.

Maggie was fairly certain it wasn't just her. Heads often turned in his direction. Maggie wondered if she should be jealous. Some soul-searching revealed she was not. In fact, she was comfortable about the whole experience. It may be conceited, but Charle was made for her.

Millie, the waitress and proprietor's daughter, spent more time at their table than was really necessary. Again, Maggie didn't mind in the least. Charle looked at the menu, a thoughtful expression on his face as he debated.

"How is the mutton stew?" he asked.

Millie appeared to have trouble breathing. "Fantastic," she managed to get out.

"Is there something else you would recommend?"

She tried to think of something, but could only blink.

"Mutton stew it is then," Charle said. "And some greens, and black bread."

Millie nodded several times too many. "Would you like anything to drink?"

Charle raised an inquiring eyebrow in Maggie's direction. On anyone else the gesture could be construed as demeaning or disinterested, but his whole face belied that. Maggie shook her head. Milli sniffed, then shot a winning smile at Charle before departing.

"So, tell me about Maggie Baker," Charle said, folding his hands on the table.

Refraining from starting with the cliche *there's not much to tell* and playing with the napkin while she spoke, Maggie concentrated on returning his steady gaze. "My parents were Bakers and taught me the craft. I came to Quin after my parents passed away because Darcy was too big. You could get lost there so easily, and not just on the streets," she said. "I like it here. Everyone knows your name. Though the library was far grander in Darcy. New books are rare in a small town like Quin."

"What do you like to read?" he asked, leaning forward.

They spoke for hours over dinner. For someone born last week, Charle had no trouble with stimulating discussion. His interest in the world around him, his plans to see it all, intrigued Maggie. His unique view of the world, untainted by negative experience, was bracing. Somehow they ended up talking about the Goblin Wars and the sympathizers in the Lower Mountlands.

"Yes, but how can you condemn an entire race for the actions of a few?" Charle was arguing. "How would you like it if others judged you only on their knowledge of King Balar the Black, or Harold of the Axe?"

"That's different," Maggie said. "Those are stories of *one* man. Goblins make an art of warfare. The last time they were at peace was when the Mountains were too tall to cross. As soon as they found a way over, they began slaughtering and pillaging those who had never raised a hand against them."

"Have you ever talked to a goblin about this?"

Maggie knew she was losing this exchange, so she switched the subject. "How do you even know about all this?"

"You're not the only one who enjoys a good read," he said. "And I hadn't read any of the books in the library, so I'm finding it quite magnificent."

"You should visit the one in Darcy," Maggie said.

"Perhaps you could take me there," he said.

Her heart caught in her throat. "That would b...b..." she stammered.

Just then Millie the waitress returned and saved her. "Would you like desert?"

Charle didn't blink. "I'm sure we've both had enough of cakes and pies to last at least a month, thank you," he said with a smile.

Millie looked disappointed, but short of tying him to a chair and force feeding him her mother's passable chocolate cake there was nothing she could do. Charle walked Maggie home, in the silver light of stars and a crescent moon.

"I enjoyed this evening," Maggie said, trying to regain the pleasant rhythm of their earlier conversation. *Before she had ruined it.*

"As did I," he replied. He hesitated, then continued. "I noticed your corsage still sits on your mantle. May I assume this means you have not asked anyone to the Festival?"

Maggie shook her head.The intensity of his gaze made her avert her eyes as a warmth flushed her cheeks.

Charle sighed. "You are impossible, Maggie Baker. I shall just have to ask *you* then. Would you do me the honor of attending the Festival of First Days with me?"

Maggie was flustered beyond the ability to speak. She simply nodded.This was the entire reason she had created Charle in the first place, and she had forgotten to ask him.Hehad to askher.None of the other boys is Quin would have done it, simply because it wasn't done. Charle was so determined to be with her that he wasn't going to let that stop him.Maggie didn't know why she felt so terrible about it.

"Thank you," Charle said.

"Of course," she said, and handed him the corsage.

Charle slipped it onto his wrist, and held it up to admire it before taking her hand and kissing it. "Goodnight, Maggie. I cannot wait for tomorrow."

~~

Maggie's sleep was restless. She tossed and turned all night, snippets of dreams visiting her, showers of silver stars that burned her skin and an evil Cupid that laughed manically as she fell, down, down, down...

"Ow!" she said, coming awake as she hit the floor, the blankets tangled around her legs. Grunting in an unfeminine fashion, she disentangled herself and hauled herself back onto the bed.When she remembered what day it was, she fell out of bed with a yelp, on purpose this time.

It was the day of the Festival, and this year she had a companion. Maggie had always looked on the dance with mild but well-concealed disdain. She was going to have to put that aside if she wanted to enjoy herself. For a moment, she fantasized about staying in bed all day with a good book and a cup of hot chocolate, then pushed it away. Charle was wearing her corsage; she *was* going and she *would* enjoy herself.

Maggie spent all day getting ready. She polished her nails, put mud on her face and took a long bath with scented salts. Her hair was twisted with paper to give it long locks. In her closet was one formal dress she had brought with her from Darcy. Maggie looked at herself in the mirror. Aunt Marigold had given it to her on her fifteenth birthday. It was exquisite, blue satin trimmed with lace and tiny pearls. White gloves came to her elbows, and her hair was studded with tiny white flowers.

Despite the extent of her primping, Maggie was ready an hour early, and tried her best to be relaxed. What was a girl supposed to do before a dance? She sat down on the edge of a chair and tapped her fingers on the table, then moved to the sofa and tried to read. When that didn't work, she tried to plan next week's breads but doodled flowers instead. When the knock came on the door, Maggie bolted upright.

Charle stood on the step, in black trousers, a white vest, and a black swallowtail jacket with blue lapels. His smile widened when he saw her. She dipped a curtsy, and he offered her his arm. She took it, heart drumming. The corsage sat on his wrist. On the street, a carriage with two snow white horses waited.

The Town Square was done up with soft lights. The tables were covered with frilly cloths and piled so high with food it was a wonder they didn't collapse. On the pavilion, three fiddlers, a piper, and a drummer played lively waltzes and reels. People were laughing, spinning, leaping and clapping. Others meandered past the tables filled with a panoply of succulent delicacies, fruits, and sweets. Couples lined up at the Kissing Tree, holding hands and swaying to the music as they waited their turn.

Overhead, the gods cooperated and blessed the Festival with a heaven of glittering stars. Charle seemed oblivious to anything except Maggie. They danced, and ate and drank, and stood in the line to the Kissing Tree, behind Missie and Tom Miller. Missie pouted, but no one paid attention.

Charle gazed into Maggie's eyes and leaned towards her. When his lips touched hers, a shock ran through her. She expected to want to fall against him, but she couldn't. The kiss deepened, pushing Maggie further into a confused panic, and she welcomed the excuse to separate when above them, a starry flower of fireworks sprang up with a resounding *pop*. Eyes turned to the sky as more followed, and cries of delight filled the air. Charle slipped his arm around her waist and pulled her closer. He did not try to kiss her again.

After the fireworks came more dancing, eating and drinking. Charle wanted to stay and see the sunrise, but Maggie begged off. She couldn't tell him the real reason, so she gave him the most acceptable one.

"My feet hurt so much, I can't stand for much longer," she told him.

He nodded, then walked her home. At her door, he placed a chaste kiss on her cheek.

"I do not believe I have words to express the quality and quantity of my regard for you, Maggie Baker," he said, holding her hand. "Thank you for this wonderful evening."

Maggie wanted to return the sentiment, but the words stuck in her throat.

"Of course," she said softly, and turned away.

She heard his footsteps fade. Tears sprung to Maggie's eyes, and misery threatened to overwhelm her. She escaped to the security of her room.

~~

Waking the next morning, Maggie found the world had taken on the surreal aspect of a bard's tale of mighty heroes and dragons. It took a moment to remember who she was, then where she was, and the reason for this black pit of melancholy sitting heavy in her chest.

Maggie sunk back into the blankets. It was truly the most enjoyable First Days celebration she could remember, including when she was a little girl in Darcy where the festivities were grander; the fireworks turned into chocolates which rained down as she watched from her father's shoulders, sword jugglers and fire throwers entertained, and she was too young to care about corsages and the Kissing Tree.

Something tainted her delight, something *missing* about last night. Maggie closed her eyes and pictured Charle's face. He was like a distant cousin she only had anything to do with when they got married or died. That felt so wrong she had trouble comprehending it.

What was wrong with him? What had she forgotten to add? Was it aspiration? Was it daring? Was it...? Maybe there was something Erika forgot to mention? Did the relationship have to be consummated to be true? Maybe the Cupid was so outraged by Maggie's indifferent treatment it didn't actually shoot Charle with the magic arrow. That wasn't right either. Charle was enchanted with Maggie. She could see how much he loved Maggie every time he looked at her.

Like a winter swim in the lake, Maggie realized what it was. *She* didn't love *him.* She enjoyed his company, and his conversation. She had gone to the Festival, but only because she was supposed to. If Charle walked out of Quin today or tomorrow, she would carry on with her life as though nothing had happened.

She tried to want him around, gritting her teeth and clenching her stomach to prompt some feeling of loss because he wasn't there. She searched for the hole that was the lack of him. She searched for the idea, the hope, the dream that in thirty years they would be together, silver-haired with a dozen grandchildren. No matter how she tried, there was nothing.

A feeling of despair grew until it was all she tasted, all she smelled, all she felt crawling over her skin. *I just need to give it time*, she tried to tell herself.

How could that be? she wondered. He was a good man with many admirable traits. He was attractive. He was everything a girl could wish for in a suitor. The realization came like a burned hand, a bright flash of awareness which made her jerk away. The lack was not with him. It was with her. The emptiness she sensed in her life did not reflect a void in the world, it showed only a void in herself. It was *her* emptiness, *her* hole to fill. Charle, as wonderful and perfect as he was, couldn't fill a hole she herself had made. She wanted to love him; she just didn't know if she could.

"Whatever am I going to do?" she asked.

~~

An hour later Maggie was back at *Erika's Exotic Tea and Herb Shoppe,* explaining her predicament to Erika.

"Isn't there some way to undo the spell?" she asked at the end.

"A dagger between the ribs works well."

Maggie winced. "That's not what I meant."

"He's as real as you or I, dearie," Erika said. "And he's here to stay. So, are you going to break his heart?"

Maggie bit her lip. "I don't want to. Really."

"Then I suggest a love potion," the old woman said.

"But he already loves me," Maggie said.

"Not for him, lovey, for you."

"Oh." Maggie couldn't think of anything else to say. "How much is that?"

"Forty."

"Forty?!" Maggie said shrilly "What's in it? Virgin unicorn tears?"

"Among other things. It's a tailor made potion, not one of those things you can get for a silver penny which might make someone love you or might make them grow ass's ears. All you need to do is put one of his hairs in it, drink it, and your problem will be solved."

Maggie wasn't so sure about that, intuition telling her that problems had a habit of breeding no matter how thoroughly you thought you'd fixed them.

"I don't know," she said. "Doesn't it come with the Prince?"

Erika produced the paper Maggie had signed, and a large crystal. Placing the crystal at the very bottom of the paper, the disclaimer became readable: *Prince Charming and Cupid; results not guaranteed; love potions sold separately.*

Results not guaranteed. "What if I fall in love with him then find I don't want to love him?"

"Well, there's a solution for that too. You take the first dose, and see what happens. If you like it, wonderful. If you don't, no worries, just don't come back when the effect wears off."

"What?"

Erika clucked condescendingly. "It's a potion dearie, not a heart transplant. Potions aren't permanent, not even a death potion. There are potions for everything, and I mean everything. Every desirable and undesirable condition or character can be simulated with a potion. Charisma, intelligence, foresight, telepathy, forgetfulness, eidetic memory, youth, ingenuity, healing, and many more. Potioning is part science, part art. No two potioners will produce the same potion. People kill to get the recipes of the really great potioners or to get rid of competition, literally. There are some who try to bamboozle others by selling a counter-potion or a cure, but all potions eventually wear out so you just have to wait it out."

"That sounds really complicated," Maggie said.

"It takes a lifetime to learn and master," Erika said. "It's not something to trifle with."

"Of course it isn't," Maggie said, and sighed. "Alright, hand it over."

Erika beckoned her around the counter. Maggie followed the witch into the back room. There were shelves with jars, shelves with little bottles and tall bottles, shelves with boxes and shelves with crates. There were little pigeonholes with vials of powders, herbs, tinctures, essences, extractions, and other things that had yet to be named.

"Sit there," Erika said, and began to dance and shuffle about, gathering this and that and depositing the things on the workbench beside Maggie.

Maggie watched apprehensively.

"Your first time, dearie?" Erika asked. "For a Love potion?"

Maggie nodded, wondering at the overabundance of pet-names. She tried not to think of a couple of children being lured to their doom by a hunched figure using those same endearments.

"Don't be nervous," the witch said, misinterpreting the look on Maggie's face. "It's not painful, and a love potion actually tastes quite good, something like strawberry shortcake."

"Hmm." Maggie nodded and tried to smile.

She sat quietly as Erika hummed and mixed, held up various bottles beside Maggie's face and squinted as she considered, put a dash of one and set the other aside, then double-checked the first against Maggie's skin again.

"Smell this," she ordered, opening a vial under Maggie's nose.

Maggie gagged at the smell of unwashed lavatory and onions.

"Alright, what about this one?"

This wasn't much better, smelling like wet dog and burnt hair.

Only after the eleventh or twelfth did Maggie's nose get a break, when Erika offered a very tiny vial containing the gentle scent of cinnamon on a fresh day. Maggie smiled and the witch put a generous splash of something orange and viscous.

The finished product was a violet color and did smell a bit like strawberry shortcake.

"Now, take this just before bed. And be prepared."

"For what?"

"There will be a slight euphoria that will hit fairly hard, intensify for the first few hours, and then temper out."

"Okay," Maggie said, looking at the innocuous bottle in her hand and handing over her gold. "Do I need to sign anything more?"

Erika clucked reprovingly. "No dearie. Just remember, you must add one of his hairs. It may or may not change color."

Maggie nodded and walked out.

~~

Maggie sat on her bed looking at the potion. It had taken an hour and a half to find a hair she was certain belonged to Charle. Visions of becoming a raving narcissist if she accidentally put one of her own hairs in had made her paranoid and she had examined the hair under a magnifying glass for at least two minutes to be absolutely sure it was definitely his dark chocolate hue, and not her honey brown. Moments after she had added it to the potion, the potion turned a silver reminiscent of the shower of sparkles that accompanied Charle's arrival to the world.

Still, she couldn't bring herself to drink it. The potion was clinging to the side of the bottle with sparkling fingers. It was so tempting, and yet...she knew where trying to solve a problem with a quick-fix would get you. Maggie sighed.

"Aunty, I need you."

When the accident-prone purple glow didn't materialize, Maggie saw she would have to work this one out on her own. Aunt Marigold meant it when she had said she wouldn't stick her nose in this. After what seemed like hours spent musing Maggie came to a decision. A strange, serene feeling filled her eyes with tears, and she sank into a dreamless sleep.

~~

Maggie woke to the smell of frying bacon and toast. Gentle undertones of coffee made her swoon and she fell back onto the bed, burrowing into the delicious warmth of the covers. When she realized someone was in her house, she leapt out of bed and flew down the stairs, pausing to grab the poker from the fire. Advancing with cautious steps into the kitchen, she heard humming. She recognized the song. It had been played at the Festival.

Charle was at the stove. He turned when he heard her put down the poker.

"You must have been exhausted," he said. "You were sleeping when I arrived. I thought you'd like something to eat."

"That's very sweet," she said, looking at the feast Charle had prepared.

"What's wrong?" he asked at once.

Maggie was blunt. "Charle, I don't care for you the same way you do for me."

He looked at her for a very long time, his eyes searching. When they didn't find what they were looking for, his expression fell.

"Was it something I did?" he asked softly.

"No," she said with an earnest look. "You are an amazing person, and one day I hope you find someone who loves you as much as you love them. But that person is not me."

He took a deep breath, squared his shoulders, and gave her a small smile. It made her feel like crying.

"Very well, Maggie Baker, I must respect your wishes, though I do not like them."

Maggie did start crying, and she busied herself serving food onto two plates to hide it, brushing at her cheeks when she thought he wasn't looking.

"At least help me eat this delicious meal," she said.

"As you wish," he bowed.

Maggie wasn't hungry, but she forced bits past her tight throat.

"What will you do?" she asked.

"Perhaps I'll go visit the goblins and write a book about my travels."

"Perhaps it will show up in Quin one day," Maggie said. "I'll look for it in the library."

"You should do that. And look for me as well. I will not give up on you Maggie Baker," he said, bringing her hand to his lips. "I will return one day to win your heart."

There was nothing she could say to make him give up on his dream, and he didn't condemn her for that.

"You are a delightful person, Charlemagne," she said honestly.

"Oh, I've remembered what my name was," he said. "Davenport Amorston."

Maggie blinked. "How did you remember that?"

"It came to me in a dream," he said. "I have hopes that the rest of my past will come to me in time."

What a past it must have been to create the unearthly creature standing in front of me. "I'm sure it will," Maggie said. "But you'll always be Charle to me."

He smiled, blue eyes filled with a sadness tempered by understanding. Then he turned and left Quin forever.

~~

A month had passed since the Festival of First Days. Life returned to a normal routine, though scraps of the pink streamers were still in the highest reaches of the trees, pushed out by the growing green leaves. The day was a beautiful mid-spring day, and the breeze wafting in through the window was filled with the promise of a gentle summer.

I think I'll close the bakery today, Maggie decided.

She went out the front to bring in the day's milk. Beside the white bottles on the front step was a single purple carnation. This had started two days ago. The day before it had been a daisy, and the day before that was a white rose.

The first time it had happened, Maggie was surprised. The second time, she was suspicious. Now she was merely curious. She glanced around, as if the leaver of the flowers might be lurking nearby. They weren't. Taking the milk and the flower inside, she added the carnation to the daisy and the rose in the vase on the table.

Humming, Maggie dismissed the mystery for another day, and baked chocolate chip cookies spiced with cinnamon just for herself, and made a pot of tea. Then she settled into her favorite spot in the corner of the couch. With a contented sigh, she opened one of the latest books to appear on the shelves of Quin's small library, *Seven Shortest Stories including "Shadow Road" and "The Third King"*.

Absorbed in her reading, Maggie failed to notice the shadows lengthening until it became too difficult to read. She got up and lit the lanterns, then took the empty milk bottles out to the front, her head still floating in the tale of the princess who fell for the notorious leader of the thieves' guild.

Maggie opened the door and gasped as a shadowy figure on her doorstep leaped up with a guilty air. She clutched at the bottles as if they could protect her from the intruder, then realized it was only William the florist's son, his hands disappearing behind his back, a trapped expression on his face.

"Sorry, I didn't mean to startle you," he said.

"That's alright," Maggie said, setting the bottles beside the door.

"I saw the bakery was closed," William said, tripping over his words in a rush to get them out. "Is everything alright?"

"Oh, yes. I was just taking some time to read," Maggie replied. "Mrs. Holders got a new shipment of books in at the library the other day, from Darcy and Finndom."

"Oh, good."

They stood there, each waiting for the other to say something.

"Did you need something else?" Maggie finally prompted.

William looked around as if the answer sat somewhere nearby, then smiled sheepishly and pulled his hands out from behind him. He gestured with the sprig of periwinkle he held. "I suppose you were bound to catch me sooner or later."

Maggie blinked. "You're the one leaving flowers?"

William shrugged, then nodded. Maggie thought he might be blushing, but in the twilight it was difficult to tell.

"Would you like to take a walk with me?" he said.

"Alright," Maggie said, more out of courtesy than actual desire.

They walked down towards the square. The street-lanterns were being lit, emitting golden circles like fairy rings. The two looped around the square, crossed the bridge over the small lake, and came back up. The last of the sun's glow faded, and the first stars came out. They talked, about the weather, how Farmer Hollings' tomatoes were faring against the hornworms, and the family that had moved in from White Wall next to the Smiths.

"She has quite a green thumb," William told Maggie. "My father has started buying her daffodils and petunias. We might have competition soon."

"Everyone in Quin buys flowers from your store," Maggie asserted. "They won't change just because someone new comes into town."

William smiled. Then they were back at Maggie's door.

"Thank you," William said. "I enjoyed that."

"So did I." Maggie smiled.

William held out the periwinkle he had twisted in his hands whenever the conversation had stalled.

"Dame Manning is throwing a birthday party for her niece next weekend," William said. "It's supposed to be even bigger than the First Days Festival."

Maggie laughed. "I heard. Always trying to outdo everyone, that one is."

"Do you think you might attend?"

"I haven't decided," Maggie answered.

"Would you perhaps consider going with me?"

Maggie thought about it. The answer surprised her for a moment, and then she wondered why she would be surprised. "I would."

William gave her a look, almost as if he expected her to laugh and withdraw her acceptance. When she didn't, a smile grew on his face.

"Then I'll pick you up at two o'clock?"

Maggie nodded, and his smile grew wider. He touched his cap, and walked down the street with his thumbs hooked in his pockets. Maggie watched him go, but when he reached the bend, she turned towards the door so he wouldn't see her watching if he looked back. Out of the corner of her eye, Maggie saw him pause, and glance over his shoulder. She couldn't help it.

She turned back and smiled at him.

About Nicole DragonBeck

Nicole was born in California one snowy summer long ago, the illegitimate offspring of an elf and a troll. At a young age her powers exploded and she was banished to the wilderness of South Africa because her spells kept going inexplicably awry. There she was raised by a tribe of pygmy Dragons and had tremendous adventures, including defeating a terrible Fire-Demon that had been tormenting a sect of Dwarf priests. In gratitude they taught her the arcane magic of writing and the rest is horribly misinterpreted history. She reads as much as she writes, is obsessed with dragons and Italians, enjoys cooking, listening to music and can often be heard fiddling on a keyboard or guitar. She currently lives in Clearwater, Florida, is a member of The Ink Slingers Guild and is working on several novels, all of which have at least one mention of a dragon. She lists friends, music and life among her greatest influences.

Connect with Nicole online:

www.nicoledragonbeck.com
facebook.com/nicolebeckauthor
twitter.com/DragonBeck

The Threads That Bind

By Desiree Matlock

"But, you've never left me behind before." Fourteen-year-old me spoke barely louder than a whisper.

The shop door tinkled as my mother opened it with an arm dripping in bangles, her back to me. The bright sunshine poured cheerily through a large pane window. An open sign stirred slightly in a cool breeze as a pigeon cooed somewhere. It was all far too cheerful for what was happening. My mother was headed out without me.

"Why can't I come with you?"

My mother looked perturbed as she turned back around toward me. Her brow furrowed and her eyes scanned me, unable to meet mine. She worried the keys in her right hand. Her other hand stayed on the shop door.

"Look, Auntie Gemma will take good care of you. Won't you, Gem?"

My aunt, whose psychic reading shop I thought we were just visiting for a few days, answered back, "Sure, yeah." She sounded a little lackluster, and it was honestly not helping with the rising panic. My mom pursed her lips at her sister. "I mean, of course."

"Where are you going, mom?"

"It'll be fine, Annika. Just keep hanging out here with your auntie Gem. You're good at this kind of work." My mother turned, whipped out the door, gone in a flash of blue jeans and too much skin.

"Is she coming back?" I asked Gemma, believing as all children do that an adult would know everything.

"You betcha. In no time." Gemma hugged me awkwardly and her clothes flowed around me, slightly smothering. "Have you ever known Leena to lie to you?" I heard the loud sound of our Chevy as it started up and pulled away from the curb outside.

"Lots." Too many times to count.

I wake up under the halon glow from the back alley's lamplight, exhausted. I am so sick of having this dream. Why do I keep having it? I pull myself out of bed in the dark, cross the back room to start a cup of tea, and then wander over to lean against the doorway to the front room. I spend a moment staring intently at the same door from my dream, flashing red and blue by the light of the sign next to it, switching out "PSYCHIC" blue with a large red hand in outline. It has nothing new to tell me.

I pull myself out of my reverie as the kettle whistles, and turn toward the counter to choose my tea. Something to relieve tension, help me sleep. I let it steep and breathe deeply, hoping for dreamlessness. I head with it to my bed by the back door, the door Gemma walked out four years after her sister.

...

I know exactly what she is about to say by the way she hugs herself, the downslope of the mouth, the longing in her eyes. She pulls a picture from a pocket, slides it across the table to me. It shows her at prom in an updo and a ridiculous fluffy dress with a boy about her own age. I scan the photo for a moment. And then I wait.

She looks around for a moment, blonde hair bobbing. Same story, different day. This one longs for a man. Seven years at this shop, and I've seen all the kinds of people I will ever see. They've all been there, haloed in the bursts of flickering neon advertising a psychic. Gemma would have called us what we are, but only a sprinkling of people even know the word magrama, least of all understand the art of the weaver's magic. Psychic works.

This girl has nothing new to offer me. I wait, knowing. The ritual needs to play out, because without the ritual, no coin. No coin, no food. No food, no me.

"So how does this work?" Her timid voice barely crosses the table, and I learn what spell she needs.

I light the candle, place it in the center of the tablecloth, smooth a wrinkle in the satin as I pull my hands back along the cloth, fingers feeling each ridge and slope of thread. It soothes me. I am done looking at her for now. I stare at the wrinkle instead, as I reach the edge of the table, where the imperfection suddenly vanishes. My hands move to smooth the fringe at the edge, below her sight. My ritual has begun.

"I will ask you to be open, I will ask you to close yourself to the sounds, smells, and sights of the world for a moment - just a moment. Retreat into your inner world until you're certain of the exact, perfect way to say what you wish for. Once you know it, speak it at once." The child across from me shifts in her seat, pulls at a thread on the seam of her skirt. Foolish to pull at threads. Unlucky.

She settles back into her chair, closes her young unvarnished eyes, and takes a breath. She calms. She's seventeen if she's a day, this one. I marvel briefly at how we can be so vastly different. I am not all that much older than her. But a few years won't change the complete lack of resemblance in our lives. Her years have been soft with privilege, brushed leather, taffeta, and satin pantyhose that get replaced instead of mended. Probably came down into the city from Calabasas or Desert Springs. She's worn shoes without holes, eaten ice cream on weekends. These rich girls all get ice cream on weekends.

I stop myself from following the trail of such bilious thoughts, partly because I know that bitterness is never true, partly because it might affect my work. Whatever I think of her, I will help her. This little doe is the customer and I could bilk her, but I won't. That would be puerile, petty. Whatever I think of someone, I always earn my coin.

I release the acrid feel of discontent, let it go through the fingertips, pinching and pulling at the warp of the tablecloth. This one round silk cloth holds many of my worst emotions. If I didn't release them before I started, they'd muddy my work.

A skinny brunette waits outside the door, nervous. Her eyes scream disdain, she has no interest in mumbo jumbo. Although with her flowing skirts you would think she'd be the one in the seat across from me. Her style is called 'bohemian'. She wears a peasant blouse and a drawstring gypsy skirt without the essential pockets. Everything about her is a gorja affectation of gypsy, all loose flowy flowers. But, styles come and go, this one, too. When I look past that, she's actually pragmatic. Magic was pulled away from her at a very young age, ripped from her by brutality. I feel a kinship with her for having once bourne magic. But now she coats that ability in dulled senses, and logic over love. I'd rather read the brunette. Of course, I'm not quite gypsy either, but I'm not pretending anything.

The brunette turns away from me, staring across the street now, toward the bodega on the corner. I look back at the ingénue across from me. She squirms in her seat a little, somewhat discomfited. Probably my eyes are unsettling her. I'm told that they're quite piercing. A little discomfort never hurt anyone. It helps you grow. I treasure that I have been uncomfortable as much as I have.

Before my mother deposited me here, I traveled by night, slept under stars when I got tired, stared into the night sky until I could see beyond it. I've mended my own clothes and made my own living. No one with a comfortable life ever looks beyond the visible into the truth of things. Once you've seen beyond the world's appearance, past time, distance, things, it stops mattering. Beyond that lies a realm where nothing exists but the truth, and truth only gets simpler until there is possibly only one truth left. At that point, even the ties that bind us become inconsequential.

This blonde seated across from me continues to breath softly. She is thinking longer about this than I'm used to and my thoughts have wandered. I study the photograph again, musing about that dress. The world she lives in is like the silly peach taffeta; it looks like a fancy poofy thing. But once you see through it, the real dress is underneath. And the real dress is leaner, simpler, with a smooth, obvious shape to it, and clear cut lines. The threads all make sense. That true dress underneath is always simpler, better. Truth is like that. Live with that true world, and you too could listen to the future as I do. There is no real difference between myself and anyone else. I simply look past the poof to the satin underneath.

I stroke at the threads of the round tablecloth to return myself to now, to this moment. She opens her eyes and her lips part to speak, haltingly, timidly. I am certain now that I know what spell to weave.

"I want you to make Jimmy realize that he loves me. Not her." I look down at the picture and see that the person in the poofy dress is not the girl across from me. It's another blonde, stamped with the same mold. Probably a cousin. Foolish of me, not looking hard enough.

I turn to pull red cotton yarn and strong purple wool strands from shelves behind me, draw them on the table. The spell she asked for would need green, brown wool, and some clay red. But I'm not doing that spell. Even if I were strong enough to do such a spell, he would be miserable, and make her miserable as a result. I may only be in this girl's life for a few more minutes, but I won't ruin it by trying to give her what she asks. Love and other realizations must come from within, and must not be spelled. But I can give her what she wants in other ways.

"Is that what you desire? For Jimmy to love you?" The girl nods.

I reach and pull her hand toward me, palm up. She frowns, misunderstanding, and adds quickly, softly, "Please don't tell me my fortune. Knowing it might make it change, worsen it."

"All right. But, what if it were better?" She shrugs, sighs. I notice a small braid in her hair, even and tight, and it warms me toward her some. I smile lightly. "I'm not reading your palm, I'm just starting the spell. But if I do see something, I'll tell you only what needs knowing. Deal?"

She nods. Her gaze wanders to the flame, and I see that she would rather do things that way. Whatever makes this easier, makes it easier for me to focus. I place the ends of the two woolen threads into her palm, run them down her hand and loop them loosely around her forefinger and her heart-finger. Then I turn her hand over. I grasp and pinch the threads together, bind the first knot in the series that begins the spell. Her eyes widen as she feels the magic. I calm her by slightly smoothing the strands against her skin.

"Watch the candle's flame while you speak about him. Start with his name and work your way through everything you know about him until you're sure you've exhausted everything. Include all of your own feelings and thoughts about him."

As she begins speaking, I start weaving the two threads. Colors and textures, my thoughts and hers on how things should go with Jimmy, all begin to blend together, woven into a single thought. I pull and work the ideas together, binding them to her, to the two woolen strands between us, the balls of yarn spinning loose, rolling farther away as I pick up speed. Now I'm adding a few thoughts on the emotions I've seen her display, small winces and tremors, and I shift them to steady hands, steady breaths, steady mindedness. I imagine her freely speaking with him, laughing with the boy in the picture. I imagine them engaged in strong friendly conversation. As the bit of weaving in my hands begins to draw to a close, I work the red into it more and more. These are strong woolen threads, and they'll help the spell stick.

"Stop!" I say, and she immediately stops speaking. Her eyes have fluttered closed while she was speaking. No matter.

"It is done. Here." I take a pair of golden scissors from the drawer, snip the threads loose, open her hand, pull the threads from her fingers gently, and then knot the beginning of the work to the end in one smooth twist. I close her fingers to her palm, over the small woven wool knot in her hands. It looks a little like a lumpy, irregular friendship bracelet, but we both feel the magic in it.

"Do not unravel this. Return home, place it under your pillow for the night and get a good night's rest. Speak with him tomorrow. Any words will do, but you must do the speaking for this to work. I've done what I can."

She thanks me, draws a twenty-dollar bill from a pocket, places it on the tabletop and leaves abruptly. She nearly jumped for the door. I suppose she didn't want the magic I'd made her to seep back out of the knots. It doesn't work that way.

The bells of the door tinkle her exit, clearing away any cobweb remains of the spell.

...

I return the purple for communication and the red for courage to their shelves. This time, I used none of the soft pink that I use for love. This girl does not need to love him any more than she already does. Besides, courage is her true hindrance to happiness.

I hesitate, wondering if now is a good time, then decide to go ahead. I pull out the silver silk thread, impossibly tiny. I pull gold to match, and a thicker black spool, along with its opposite, white.

I lay them out onto the table before me. I am reading my mother, not casting, so I simply decide this spell will be to look for her again. I knot the beginning of our time together, our life. I wrap it around my wrist and make it snug to ground it. All things, including knots and lives, need a foundation.

Silver for memory, my mother's untamable hair and tired eyes that look like mine. Her hands on the steering wheel as we drove the highway. Her morning coffee and crosswords with Aunt Gemma during our visits. The way she chain-smoked. I have a few dull spots, but there are still several lasting memories of her, and they stretch through the knots I pull and twist into place with my fingers. To me, her memory is an endless silver stretched thin by time, but still strong. I decide to add the gold strand, to strengthen the bond of love we had, to hold it forever in time, but then the spell takes over from deep within me and the color needs to change. Abruptly, the silver and gold threads fall loose from the knot, pulling down. The truth I weave gets dark and the black thread gnarls, clogged and confused, patternless. I grab at a new color off the shelf, and now a grey confusion forms, woven into the blackness, a man's hand pulls my mother away by the arm, she yells at me. I see glimpses of the alleys, needles, clouds of smoke, and billowing faded curtains with too bright light outside, the years between us fade into the grey haze. Finally, I end the knot with one tiny perfectly square knot of pristine white. Found. Simple. I look down upon the knot, trying to figure out what it's telling me, what truth it holds. I see a lot of blackness, a drug haze, grey deeds, but thankfully it still ends in a bright moment, the single knot at the end of the spell. Whether that ending is her return or her death, or something else, I still can't tell. I am too clouded on the subject of my mother to see her properly. And I will try to still my mind so I understand, so I can glean more from the knotwork when next I try this.

It's exhausting, so I walk into the back room where I live, to place this spell beside the others, under my pillow, and I wish. I wish for knowing how to help my mother. I wish for the stillness of mind to see it.

Seeing beyond the magical rituals to the truth means that my spells are less effective when I do them upon myself. For one foolish moment, while my hand is still touching the spell I just worked, I wish for another with magic, someone kind and who wants to help me. Then I shake it off and return to the front room with the spell safely finished.

...

In the night, I hear scrapings at my window, a tree branch they sound like. I'm not perturbed. I feel no threat to myself. But, in the morning I find many of my threads missing. A deep blue cotton, several silk threads in earth tones, a wool slate-colored thread, and a nearly invisible thread in clear white that I sometimes use to represent long distance travel. Ooh, and the periwinkle blue thread that I feel represents a cool sunrise. Someone has robbed me of the threads necessary to magic up a rather nice camping trip by a clear blue lake somewhere remote and wintery, but perhaps that's because I keep my nature threads together and this person seems to have simply chosen from a single section of my wall of available threads and dashed out... Perhaps they had no idea how magrama works.

If they did, they'd know that the threads are nothing special. There is no magic in them, only in the weaver and the spelled. Everyone holds magic. It's called life, élan vital, spirit. There is no difference. Magic is just a small release of a boundless, endless supply we all have, can all reach. My threads will get the thief no closer to their own magic.

I do a full assessment of the damage and find that a candle is missing as well. So what? I got it on Amazon. I could get more. Oh damn, one of those yarns was a rather expensive alpaca wool in undulating peach and gold tones. Oh well, it was rarely useful, seeing as it related only to the color and shape of orgasm in my mind. Few people had ever asked me to help them in the bedroom, and none were women. There was a head scratcher for you.

I recall the noise in the night. Whoever it was, I'd felt no ill will toward me, in fact I'd felt no intention toward me at all. Whoever it might be, they were no danger to me, or my hackles would have risen, even in my sleep.

Two weeks pass without incident after, the usual smattering of customers and return clients. I get some bars for the back window on the shop, and forget about the theft. It's Los Angeles, and I'm not the only person robbed in the night. Whoever it is does not return, or if they do, the bars stop them. And I stop worrying, until I find the stolen bundle returned to me a little worse for wear. They are left by the metal gate I unroll when I unlock in the morning, two Tuesdays later.

Looking down at that sad little pile of threads, I see that several are shorter. Someone has tried to spell cast with it. The return of the threads probably meant they'd failed. Or realized that they held no actual magic. I feel badly for them. But, who here would be practicing magrama? My mom left, and Auntie Gemma was abroad studying with the masters of the art. Their parents were dead. I took a moment to look back through my memories of the people I met in childhood who even knew of magrama, and wondered who I might see again soon.

...

The bells tinkle and I come out from my room in the back of the shop to find a sinewy black-haired young man with too many years in his eyes, but a smile on the lips. I smile in response and gesture at the table.

"Sit, please. Tell me what brings you here today."

"Oh, I'm not here to be read." His eyes sparkle with mischief and plans.

I seat myself. "So? Sit. Please. Tell me what brings you here today." I smile, but it's a touch colder. He seems a little unhinged, or excited. I hope for the latter.

"I thought we could share a shop. You have more space here than you need, and I could bring in herbs and tinctures. I am an apothecarist these days. We don't clash."

"Why should I want an herbal shop in my place?"

"Aren't you a little lonely yet, Annika?" His hands splay across the table from me, relaxed, graceful. Familiar. My alarms go off. I don't quite recognize him...but I do. He acts like a friend, not a stranger.

His words are true, as well. I am lonely. "Do you know me?"

He sits across from me, touching the tablecloth, looking at it closely. "Do I still? I see so much anger." His eyes wander the threads between us, then he looks up at me. "Things must be rough. Let me help."

He pulls a few herbs from his vest. Sage comes out, and he draws it closer to my candle, not quite touching the flame, until the sage catches. We both watch it smolder for a moment, then he blows softly through pursed lips, and smoke wafts between us. Just barely does the acrid smell reach me before he dips the smoldering sage into the candle's soft wax, pulls it deftly out once it's fully coated, and grinds the sage into the warm wax before it hardens. He holds a perfect ball of wax and sage between his fingers, which he places on the table and then rolls about briefly under a flattened palm. I feel the anger in the cloth between us release into the wax. He then holds the wax between his sure fingers, smooth yet tough, and blows on it. It shifts to a solid white. He finds a small purple pouch on his belt, and the ball of wax goes in there. The feeling now is a peaceful one. Nice. Familiar. Clean. Romany caravans of beat up RVs come to mind, the sound of sparkling brooks and laughter, and an image flashes of sneaking sodas at night. And I remember.

"Fenn! You've grown. You've changed."

"As have you!" His eyes smile at me; calm emanates from him. He looks me over. Our friendship, though ten years past, was strong. A good one for the brief times that my mother and I had traveled with his family. I reach my hand over into his.

"How is your uncle Jino? How is it you aren't traveling with the rest of your family?"

"Jinoquio has lost his way, Anni. Switched over to easier money." His head hangs.

"Drugs?" It had always been something he flirted with, but it shocked me to think of the travelers quitting magic.

He nods. "I was given a choice, since I was of coming of age at the time of the changeover. He told me that a man could decide for himself. And so I decided. It seemed fine until I had to say goodbye to my sisters." His eyes roll up to the ceiling, and he wipes his face with embarrassment. "Then I changed my mind, cried, begged Jino to go back to the old arts, and..." he sighs deeply. "I got voted out. Weakness. Oh well." He shrugged and I placed a hand on his while he continued, "I was sent off to start out on my own. Jino did not tell me where to go, so I came to you. Someone else not quite traveler, but not quite gorja."

"Come. This calls for tea."

"What does?"

"The beginning of us sharing a shop." I stand, walk to the front, flip the sign on the door so that the word "open" faces us, and head into the back room that serves as my apartment. Fenn follows me, smiling. I start a kettle going. We had always both enjoyed conversation over beverages growing up. Since I had no soda, tea would have to do.

I don't ask Fenn about the theft and return of my supplies. If he needed them, it must have been for a reason. But my gut tells me it wasn't him, and I can tell that this deep-rooted feeling comes from the part of me that sees truth.

...

A few weeks later, and his few possessions are starting to spill from his suitcases. A simple hammock is hung in the corner of the back room. He prefers it to the cot I slept on before Gemma left. His possessions take up little space. Honestly, neither do mine. Most things are my aunt's, and all the furnishings are hers. True, she had been gone for years now, but the place wouldn't have been as homey without at least the feeling of someone else here.

Already our toiletries commingle by the sink, which feels positively suburban to me, and I chuckle to myself when dressing in the morning. He's shown no interest in romance, but Fenn steps right into other manly roles. He lifts things, helps me with anything difficult, heavy, or on a high shelf. The empty section of the front room is already full of his bottles and jars and boxes of herbs. I send everyone who walks in with baggage to clean up over toward him. No one is better at soothing the pain than he is. I admire how well he calms people, helps them find peace.

Another few weeks go by, and we have a real routine going. He sends me anyone who wants to change their future or find their path. Sometimes he watches me while I spell. I can see it fascinates him. Having him there makes my work stronger. Changing the future was already my strongest spell. I do it well.

We each are better suited to different brands of magic, and between Fenn and I, business is booming. It feels like my spells are easier to do and stronger. We're getting a name for ourselves here. I like the idea that the business will be able to sustain us indefinitely, but Fenn buys a delivery truck, cleans it up, and gets it tuned up. I know what that means. He'll want to leave eventually. With or without me, it's a problem. I like having him here, and so I don't want him to go. But I can't leave. And if he asks me to come with him, I'll have to explain why.

When there are no visitors, we sit and talk. Sometimes about old times before my mother left me, sometimes about movies we've both seen, places we've never been but want to go. Sometimes about spells, what the threads mean, what the herbs do. It is nice to have someone to talk to.

...

There aren't many customers today. Since I'm bored, I am weaving a small reading for myself, lightly looking into my own future, but nothing much is coming up. I think because I'm too conflicted about whether to keep waiting for my mother or not. I can smell tea brewing from the back room. A beam of afternoon sunshine is coming through the front window. It's a lovely day out.

As I end the attempt at a spell, the bell tinkles. The bohemian friend walks in and smiles at me. I don't know what I was being so critical for before, she looks perfectly friendly.

"I like the new plants." She points at a potted garden of hen-n-chicks that Fenn set up by the front door. California isn't a great place to grow things, and neither of us has a particularly green thumb, but succulents will grow anywhere.

"Thanks."

"They are together now, you know."

It takes me a moment to realize she's not talking about the plants. "The blonde and the prom date?"

"Yes, Lindsay and Jimmy. Your spell worked." She's coming closer to her real reason for being here, and begins rubbing her own arm nervously.

"How nice. I'm glad for her." The girl doesn't turn around to leave, nor does she speak, so I continue, "Would you like a reading?"

"Of course not. I'm fine with life being the way it is. And there's nothing you can tell me about myself that I don't already know." But she shuffles a little closer to me.

"A truer statement never was. I can't know what isn't right there to know." I point between her eyes.

She looks nervously away for a moment. Then she sits and she speaks. "I came to ask you to do something."

Fenn comes up from the back room at this point, to bring me a cup of tea. When he sees the girl, he turns to go back into the back room. I urge him over instead. "Thanks, it's okay. Bring the tea. She's not a customer, she's the friend of a customer, asking a favor."

Fenn turns and puts the tea down in front of me. He reaches his hand out. "Fenn. What's your name, friend of customer of Anni's?"

"Connie."

Connie looks back at me. "The favor?" she asks. I nod my head, prompting her to speak what she wants.

"I need you to remove the spell. I feel bad that Linds manipulated him into love. I keep worrying that someday he'll come out of the spell and leave her... and it won't be until after she's saddled with babies."

I sigh, and smile. I take her hand. "I left no spell on him. None."

"But...how? It worked."

"The only part of the magic that was a spell, I cast on your friend. And she came in willingly. I boosted her own strength, her own courage. That's all."

"How did you know it would work?"

"I saw the only path to the future she wanted. She needed to let him know how she felt. I cannot do what I do for someone who is not physically here. And anything I do needs to be possible. I cannot change what cannot be."

Connie looks at me, relieved. "Honest?"

"Honest. You're off the hook, and so is she. If you ever see her grow a conscience about trying to spell him, you can let her know, too."

"Thanks." She turns to leave.

"Are you sure you wouldn't like a reading?"

"Oh no. I'm fine." She tucks a strand of hair away, and nervously scratches at her neck.

Fenn takes over as she stands. "You look stressed. Would you like a little lavender sachet to calm your nerves?"

"Got any patchouli?"

"I do. That's not the right herb for you, though. Something subtler, I think."

"Okay." She walks over to his counter, stares down at his panoply of wares spread out in a display case, the same case that I used to keep tarot cards in, despite that no one ever bought them. He wanders his herbs, finding her the right blend, and sends her out the door with a simple spell for composure. Maybe he adds a few extra things in there, maybe he doesn't. But she is smiling and relaxed as she leaves.

He looks at me. "Did you see what I saw?"

"Yes. If you mean that Connie has magic."

"I mean, everyone has some magic, but she's like us. She could do this."

"She doesn't want to look at what hurt her. I understand the feeling."

"You do?"

I turn back toward the back room. "How about some toast to go with our tea, Fenn?"

...

At night, he sleeps enveloped by a linen hammock in the corner of the back room. Now, when my dreams awaken me, I have his calm, even breath to lull me. The white of the linen looks peachy pink by the halon lamplight in the back alley and reminds me of the alpaca that was stolen and returned. His shape through the cloth is fascinating to me, long and angular. When he stirs, it stirs with him and I can almost feel the coarse linen moving.

When I was a girl, and we stayed with his family, I would creep out of bed to go find him so we could play cards or sneak sugar, but tonight I find myself wanting to slink over there for other purposes. I am scared by the way I'm feeling about him, and I stay awake watching him sleep the dreamless sleep of the pure. My bed feels like an empty and achingly lonely place for the first time I can recall. I am uneasily realizing that I must have cared about him this way for a long time. When exactly did I start feeling this way? I met him when I was eight years old, and I didn't feel this then. A specific memory is hard to find, but I can recall my cheek against his damp shoulder, my eyes closed, his long fingers smoothing my hair. When was that? Was that some time down by the creek?

How is it that my usually clear memories are so hazy on this?

In the morning, I am up before him, coffee fresh and ready when he rises with the sun. He lumbers out of his hammock, yawns, stretches. I throw a shirt at him.

"What?" His arms open, hands up in plaintive response.

"Nothing." I turn hard, feet rooted to the spot. I am behaving like a child and it vexes me further. "Nothing except I'm puzzled how I could possibly have forgotten you for so long. We were so close."

"Much happened, Anni. We parted ways, lost family."

I sigh. "But how could I forget?"

Fenn's eyes cloud over. "Anni, I know it's not a nice thought, but what is your mother's magic?"

"Magrama, just like me, just like Gemma. We use yarns, threads, any line of any kind. You know that."

A line creases his brow, and it perturbs me how hard he's trying to be patient. He asks again, slowly and calmly, "But, what was her talent specifically? What could Leena do better than anyone? What is your mother's greatest talent?" His eyes are plaintive.

My mouth goes cold and metallic at the thought. "No. She couldn't have."

He takes my hand in his. It is cool, calming to the touch. "Things happened. Things I think perhaps you don't remember. And you never did strike me as forgetful, Anni."

I shake my head, "No, I mean she quite literally could not have. Drugs cloud the soul. She lost the ability long before she would have wanted to make me forget anything."

He pulls me into an embrace, ever so patiently coaxing me. "Maybe she had help. Perhaps she found someone stronger to help her. You've seen how our spells are each getting stronger in the other's presence. Who was around when you lost her?"

"Only my Aunt Gemma. But she left years ago, which is why I have the shop now. She went to Arabia to study under the original masters. She hopes to learn..." My voice fades off.

"Maybe you should ask yourself how many years that could take? Are there even masters in Arabia? Is there even still an Arabia?" Why had I never asked myself any of this?

He holds me by the shoulders, pulls me back to look at me, eyebrows raised, willing me to realize for myself. And I do. My mother Leena's greatest talent lay in wiping memories, and her sister Gemma's talent was making people believe fantastical lies. It's how she got this shop in the first place. Her with all her cons. It's how she read people more often than not, making things up instead of working real spells.

What lies had she told me? Where were my aunt and my mother? And how would this affect my plans to stay or go? I close my eyes against the questions, willing myself to remember the forgotten. I pushed hard for the memory, and felt something I hadn't felt before. The missing piece of my life; there it was, there were its coarse edges. Perhaps I'd felt it before and willed myself not to believe it.

"They used magic on me." He nods. Tears fall, but they fall onto his shoulder, strong and muscular beneath me. He hugs me tightly to him, as if hugs can keep the past from sucking. "How could they?"

He nods and I can feel it against my ear. "Shouldn't have done."

"No. Definitely shouldn't have done."

As I lean against Fenn, reeling from what I've just recognized, a blue cotton thread comes to mind, long and winding. A river, a lapping shore. Slate grey wool. And I wonder why I am reminded of the stolen supplies at this time of all times. Too many threads, too many spells.

"I need to leave, need to get far away from this place where their magic would be strongest. Once we're somewhere clean, I need to work my way out of the spells that linger on me."

"Why do you think I have a truck now?" I smile at him, tears in my eyes, and he kisses me lightly on the forehead. I kiss his shoulder. Here is my home. I look up into his eyes, and he lightly, carefully touches his lips to mine for the first time. It's magic to me, but he pulls away, bashful about it.

We pack the front room into the truck first, leaving all woven things behind. I gather the little pile of chaotic work I've made casting about for my mother and bring them to the front room. There still remains the white square knot that simply won't go away, no matter how many spells I weave looking for her, or how black they get. It's bad luck to pick apart old spells, even when they don't work. It's hard for me, but I leave those knots behind as well.

All my threads and yarns are packed tightly in baggies and tape, in order to keep them from tangling while we travel. It's not that we're worried about magic leaking out, because the strands bear no magic themselves. It is just such a pain to detangle them.

Fenn's dry herbs are all tightly sealed and separated by cardboard in boxes, the tinctures and oils are in blue glass bottles carefully wrapped in tissue paper and packed into plastic crates from the dollar store. We are careful when packing them. Again, there is no explicit magic in them, but they're quite viscous and stink if they break. Plus, everything of his is expensive to replace. Much more so than my threads.

Then we pack our back room up. Fenn and I are both experts at arranging things in small spaces, stemming from childhoods as travelers of different kinds, and the work goes quickly. It's amazing how little I actually own once I remove myself from Gemma's shop. Not really much more than Fenn does, and he came with only what he could carry. The only thing of my aunt's that we take with us are some camping supplies.

We organize the truck so well that there is space to pull things out that we might need, and even room to sleep if we need to. We both admire our work, sweaty with the labor once it's all done.

It's sad that I have to close the doors. I turn off the neon lights, and I lock up the shop for the last time. Fenn holds my hand while I hide the key to the shop in the loose brick, the spot where my family will look if they show up.

I hold out hope that I am wrong, that I'll find no duplicity, and that I'll come home to find my mother returned. Despite that, my spirit lightens at the idea of leaving this dead end behind.

Our magical shop has become mobile. We are travelers again. We both relax as the road unfurls.

...

As night approaches, Fenn and I camp in a state park in the desert, surrounded by Joshua trees, still frustratingly close to Los Angeles. California is huge. But, it is lovely to be under a black sky and stars again. You can never see the stars from deep in the city, and I realize I haven't seen them in seven years. A full third of my life spent under a haze.

We're staring upwards together. The desert is dry and vast, but I feel happy here. I am reminded of someone I may have been in a previous life. Perhaps a nomadic soul, watched by ancient boughs of wizened trees. But here and now, I am heady with our first night out on our own path. We eat pantry food after getting a small campfire crackling at our feet, and we remember old songs to sing around it. I snuggle up against Fenn. After a particularly raucous attempt at remembering all the lyrics of 'Raggle Taggle Gypsies', I realize I feel young for the first time in years, like a weight has been lifted from me.

I pull his head down towards mine in the middle of a laugh and kiss him. He tastes clean and solid, smells musky and strong. His tongue curls toward mine and I melt. My eyelashes and his flutter against skin rushing with warmth. I pull myself closer into his lap, falling deeper into the kiss. The world swoons around us, and I pull in a breath, drowning in him, in the stars above. He pulls us both down onto the hard-packed desert floor, and his kisses intensify. We are twined together, holding one another as though lost without the love of the other. I weep a single tear of joy, full of the longing I haven't spoken, and he groans as it falls down my face, joining with our mouths. His eyes open wide suddenly, and he pulls back. He seems startled, and I can feel him tremble as he realizes that I love him.

We separate our bodies and he looks sideways at me. "This has to be your choice, my love."

I rise, and he rises after me. I take a deep breath, and start setting up the tent. As I'm pounding the pegs into the ground, he's started helping. He walks to the truck, brings out a small velvet bag and only one bedroll.

"Do we need two sleeping bags?" he asks, eyes pleading to know what I want. I nod, my face flushing. He looks momentarily sad, but he heads back to the truck and pulls another sleeping bag out, laying them side by side within our tent. I follow him into the tent. As he turns to zip the tent closed, I crouch beside the bags, unzip them both all the way, then zip them together.

I stand and hold his hand, and look into his deep eyes. They go on forever, simple, true. This one has never lied to me, and it's easy to see in his eyes.

I walk backwards onto our bed, and he walks with me, a grin growing across his features. We are both smiling now. I start to remove my clothes and he takes his off, too. We're standing naked before one another, and it feels not one bit embarrassing, because it's pure, real. He turns for a moment, finds the velvet bag he brought into the tent, and he stops, holding it.

"Do you trust me?"

I look into his eyes, searching for meaning. He takes my hands, and I feel the velvet of the little pouch between us. I see nothing sneaky in him, but I worry. Could I be blinded by love as I was with my mother? I make the choice to trust.

"I trust you," I say, "but what are you planning here?"

"I cannot tell you, I can only show you." He pulls a small blue bottle from the pouch and breaks the dusty wax seal on it. It smells strange, a little crazy. A mix of what? Myrrh, rosewater, rosemary, and is that sage again? He anoints my shoulder blades, my wrists, the backs of my ankles, and my temples. I feel an odd sensation of being lifted out of cloudiness, of my old memories reorganizing. Then, he reaches between us and swipes some in a place I've never been touched in living memory. The surprise shows on my face, I'm sure.

"You'll understand soon, darling." He looks a little sad for a moment. Now I'm shaking, but he's calm with purpose. He throws the emptied bottle aside and pulls me to him. He kisses me lightly, repeating, again and again, "It will be okay, Anni." We climb into our small, uncomfortable bed and forget everything but one another. The waves of my emotions crash onto his shore.

The act bonds us, and it doesn't hurt me. I briefly wonder how that could be. As soon as we're done, the memories come crashing in, and I cry out. I pull him to me, angry that he would use this, our first time together, to break the spell. But I understand it could have been no other way. I realize what he's done for me, all in a moment, and I cry harder, this time with exalted happiness.

"It will be okay, Anni, I promise." He kisses me softly.

"I love you," I say.

"Love," he answers, in both explanation and declaration. "Love." He brushes the hair from my face, and kisses me softly on the cheek. Then we both fall deeply into sleep, and I dream of my mother again, this time from the beginning.

...

I screamed in the night. Sudden pain, violation. The smell of cheap beer on warm breath, panting, yeasty from beer. I scrambled in the dark, my breath was uncontrollably shallow with panic as I realized there was a stranger on top of me, his weight crushing into me. My hips were pinned. I yelled, and no one responded. I hacked at him with my hands, scratched at his face. I kicked hard, and he yelped. I wanted to sob, but instead I scrambled out from under him while he cursed. I ran outside of the RV to suddenly brighter light from patio lights strung here, there, and everywhere. I had fallen asleep during a party while waiting for my mother. My eyes adjusted and I ran. Legs flying under me, I slammed straight into Jino. His stupid anchor tattoo flashed past as he pulled back to smack me hard. Black spots swam before my eyes as I fell backward onto my ass with a thud. I couldn't understand. Hadn't he heard me scream? I'd thought that Jino would help, maybe because the tattoo had always made him remind me of Popeye, and wasn't he supposed to be the hero?

I realized suddenly how foolish I was. 'Uncle Jino' had to have known. Nothing happened around here without him knowing. I ran the other way. I yelled for my mother. I found her sleeping on a plastic beach chair by the campfire, drunk or high, again.

I clung to her as she protested through her stupor. She was still in her hot pants and that pale pink bikini top she'd been sunbathing in during the day. I tried to explain quickly, aware of my disheveled state.

"Calm down, honey. It's no big deal." Had she gone crazy? I looked at her, saw in her eyes that she'd done this to me. She waved her hand.

She started blurting out a half-assed apology, not for what happened but for not letting me know about it first. Her explanation was slurred and fell out of her sloppily, like the hair that fell over her eyes. I realized that she was telling me that she'd traded me to Jino, sold me to wife for a man I didn't even know. My peripheral vision went black as I went numb with hate.

"Screw you, mom. You're useless. Useless!" I called her a terrible name and stared her down. "As long as you love drugs more than me, we're done."

I saw her realize I meant it, saw past that to her deep and lifelong fear of my stronger magic sitting right behind. And behind that to her self-loathing. All in a flash. I could even see that she knew I saw through her. Her lip trembled and she switched gears. "Ungrateful child! You've always been a pain in my ass. Haven't I fed you? Clothed you? Good riddance, you little shit." Her eyes showed deep pain for an instant before the drug haze clouded her back up again and she slouched back down into her stupid plastic chair.

It was pointless to stand here and yell. Jino would come stop me, make me go back in that RV if I didn't move. And my *mother would do nothing. The intensity of the hatred I suddenly felt pulled at my gut, acid built behind my throat. I push it back. My mother had betrayed me beyond repair.*

I backed away from the fire, ran out into the dark. The ground sloped away and grew cold, and then I was knee high in the creek. The sound of the babbling water cleared my head a little and I sat down in the water. I let it run past me. The cool water pointed out how much I hurt down there, but felt cleansing. I put a hand over my mouth to stay quiet as I sobbed and gasped for air.

I heard Jino calling for me to come back, laughing. Panic overtook me, stopped my sobbing. I needed to find shelter of my own now. I was completely alone. Except for Fenn. Fenn!

In a last desperate attempt to find a friend, I ran to him. I threw myself at him, soaking wet and cold. He wrapped his young arms around me and hurried me into his camper on the back of a rusting pickup and pet my hair, calmed me. We sat on an untidy pile of his clothes, and his soft shushing eased my tears. He never asked what happened. As soon as I would let go for a moment, he just locked the camper door against his family, and returned to letting me hold onto him. Finally, he fell asleep and I listened to his breathing, wondering what I was going to do.

Once the sun came up, my mother lured me outside to talk, grabbed me hard enough to bruise on top of bruises, hauled and shoved me into her beat-up old Chevy, and we drove straight through for the hundreds of miles to the shop. If she had stopped, I would have run. We didn't speak.

When we arrived there, I was hauled into the back room. She tied me to a chair, wrists and ankles. Together, they spelled a knot around me as I fought and squealed in outrage. Aunt Gemma's eyes became everything I could see, my whole world. My mother's voice droned, hummed, lulled. My thoughts went from angry to dull to nothing at all, and I felt the memory of my pain unwinding like so much chaff, falling from my head. I screamed at myself to wake up, but instead... I forgot everything and a calm, coiled feeling came over me.

I dreamt of nothing. When I woke up, I was sleeping on the cot in the back room, and didn't even realize there was anything at all to remember.

"How'd you sleep, Anni?" Gemma asked from the kitchen area. My mother was packing. Was it time to go already? We'd only been here a few days.

...

We're in the truck again, driving north. The trees are becoming less sporadic and greener. It smells of recent rain, and I'm nearly giddy with it. Life is suddenly so much more more-ish.

"I don't want to go back," I declare.

"Obviously. We are never going back if you don't want to," Fenn said.

He looks at me. "I made that blend of oils right after it happened, you know." His hands tighten on the wheel. "Do you remember?"

I nod. I run a hand behind his neck, comforting him. I slip the soft cloth of Fenn's collar through my fingers and run my palm down his shoulder. It soothes both of us. I nod again.

"Do you feel like you got it all? Like you remember absolutely everything now?"

I feel around for holes, and there are no more missing patches. "Yes. I'm sure I do. The memories beg to be heard again, rambling in my mind, piling pell-mell on top of one another newly every time I think of them, but they make a whole." He nods, smiling sadly.

I add, "I can almost admire a spell that strong."

I can understand her wanting me to forget about the burlish man who took my childhood from me. I can see how my mother would find it easy to spell me, tell herself she was helping me, rather than just protecting herself from her own consequences. But the worst part is that she took so much of my memory of Fenn. For seven years, he didn't know what happened to me. He must have worried so much. I look at him, worrying freshly for him now, even though it's pointless. The past is the past. Regret holds no truth.

He's starring ahead at the road, but it's as if he's reading my thoughts when he says, "I didn't know where you'd gone. It wasn't until Gemma showed up looking for her sister that I was able to put two and two together about where you were. When I broke free of the family, I spent months looking for you. I knew we needed to undo things together."

"Gemma... What happened to Gemma?" I still didn't know. That one probably wasn't a spell, just lies from a person very used to duplicity.

"When she was told to return with you, and why, she refused. She tried to spell Jino." It surprises and touches me that she would try to protect me. But maybe it was done to protect herself.

"She always sucked at dangerous spells," I said quietly.

"Well, Jino didn't need magic. He's got my cousins as thugs. Including your -" He pauses, unsure how to say it, "-husband." His face showed he instantly hated his choice in words as much as I did.

"Nu-uh, definitely not my husband. My attacker." It feels atrocious, even to say it. But it purges something to confront it head on.

"Sorry. Of course – you're right. You never actually married him, did you?" He sounds disgusted with what he is having to say. "Leena just traded you...like a possession. Probably a long time before, actually. Some of the older traditions are dying too slowly." His hand reaches across the bench seat to mine. Clasped hands and I feel whole. Strong.

"What did they do with her?" I feel an urgent need to know everything at one go.

"Gemma? I don't know. But there are two choices. She either ran off, or got hauled off. She might be dead for all I know. I'm sorry, Anni."

"You aren't responsible." I fall into deep thought.

"Where's my mother?" I ask, even though I am pretty sure that Fenn won't know where she is.

"She left about three months after she came back from dropping you off with Gemma. Before she did, she wouldn't talk to me about you, or I'd have taken off to find you."

"You couldn't. Jino wouldn't have let you."

"I could have tried."

"You could have been dead. Not worth it." I muse on what I've learned, then ask, "Why didn't you tell me all this before?"

"You like being you, right? You know how memory spells work...anyone telling you what happened, and your head might as well get an ice pick through it."

"I'm stronger than that, Fenn." I am pretty sure I'd have gotten through it in one piece if he had just said something earlier. But then I remember how deep Gemma's spell had been, and realize he's not wrong.

"I couldn't risk it. There was only one way to break the spell."

"True love and a little counter-spell." I undo my seatbelt and scoot across the bench, cuddling into his arms. "Thank you, Fenn."

He kisses me on top of the head. "Of course."

...

That night, we spring for a lodge in the mountains with a great view, and the bed feels deep and soft after a day in the truck. The innkeepers are definitely not parsimonious about their thread count. There is a cedar porch looking out on a forest the deep green of trust. My fingers run over the tight, silky sheets on the bed, reveling in the luxury. We enjoy ourselves for hours, and it's better this time. This feels like a honeymoon. I want to take a long soak under the stars after, so Fenn and I sneak out to the closed pool area and find the hot tub. After a moment, I figure out how to get the bubbles going. We climb in.

The water is fantastic, bubbles all over. Almost perfect, but I am still working my way through my memories. The slate grey comes back into my mind. Fenn is the only one here to listen to the words that I need to speak. "I wish I didn't, but I still hate her. I hate her for spelling me instead of living with her sins."

"I get it. Hate sucks, but it's better than not knowing."

"You're right." After a moment's thought, I add, "For now. But, I will need to get past it. Don't get me wrong, I'm happier for knowing what happened. But I'm not back to the truth yet. Hate, regret, pain, these aren't the truth. The truth is never ugly like that."

Fenn smiles. "I like that thought." He lays his neck back against the edge of the hot tub, and relaxation overtakes both of us.

I calmly recognize now that the blackness in my mother-finding knots was my own anger, that the grey was the forgetfulness. For a moment, I chew on the thought of that one white knot that always lay quietly at the end of the spell. The white knot of forgiveness, of peace before I set her aside forever. I hadn't realized before that the spell was about both of us, not just her.

"It will get better," he says, looking over at me.

"I know." I smile at him.

"You never have to think of her again."

"Actually, I do. I think she's back at the shop."

His eyes widen in surprise. "How can you know that?"

"Slate grey wool." I pause for a moment, then explain further, "I'm willing to bet it was her. No, I'm sure of it. She broke into the shop a few months ago. Stole the color she used when she spelled me. We each feel differently about each color, each material. Slate grey speaks to me of cool stone or maybe clouds. My mother used it for forgetting. A little while before you came to me, she stole it, probably trying to undo the spell. Which means she's either at the shop, or holing up somewhere nearby. She doesn't give up easily once she decides to do something."

"Well then, why didn't it work? You didn't remember anything when I showed up."

I speculate on it for a moment before speaking. "Drugs cloud everything. Her magic is certainly too muddy now even to undo an old spell. She needed my aunt to help her before. And she's burned every bridge in her life to anyone with any real punch. She'd be oblivious to that, of course. She'd try. But until she realizes what she's done, owns up to her life, looks at it head on..." I shrug and the water bobs with my shoulders, "there's no way." I slip into the water a little deeper and wiggle my toes.

Fenn sighs, pulls his hair back out of his face. "That shows remorse, Anni. We can't ignore that. We need to go back. Put her in rehab, maybe." I look at him, admiring how ready he is to change course to do what's right. So different from his family. I realize that it is a trait we have in common.

"Unfortunately, you're not wrong. But it can wait until tomorrow." I smile serenely up at the stars, having that last white knot to look forward to before I forget my mother forever, this time intentionally. Perhaps now that I had the whole story, I would cast a proper spell in her direction to help her along. Perhaps I wouldn't.

I reach out and snake my fingers through Fenn's without looking as I push away from the edge to float freely. The stars above us are winking through the black. My hand feels lovely twined with Fenn's and I am glad this is the only kind of knot I've made with him. No spellwork between us. Even the ones he cast were only to clean things up, pull me closer to the truth. And they worked. I am able to clearly look past the here and now to our future. For the first time in all of my years, it's easy, and I like what I see.

About Désirée Matlock

Désirée Matlock presently lives in a beach town with her beau, twin daughters, two cats and a dog, where, whenever she gets two seconds to rub together, she writes by a window overlooking a lake. She loves to travel and play the piano, although never at the same time. She won't bore you further with the mundane details of her simple life unless you visit her blog.

Connect with Désirée online:
www.DesisTwoCents.com

Memory Games

By JM Paquette

"Ante up," Seth said, the deck of cards held loosely in his palm. He could feel the aces stacked carefully at the bottom, dexterous fingers itching to deal them in at the right moments. He looked to the woman seated at his left. "Wren?"

The elf shifted on her stool, face pensive as she pushed long black curls behind elongated ears. Seth knew it was her way of distracting the other players while she calculated her next move. Her lips curled, a slow sexy smile that crept across her face as she looked across the table to Walker, the stocky man adjusting himself on the opposite stool, no doubt the thought of all that glorious elven hair running riot over his limited mental faculties. Seth suppressed a smirk. Wren could always get her way when she smiled. He could even remember when that trick had worked on him.

But that had been years ago. And now it was time to play. "Are you in?" he prompted.

The lovely elf turned her gaze to him. "I wouldn't dare miss it," she breathed.

Seth nodded. "Name your wager."

Her eyes never leaving Walker, Wren spoke carefully in her honey voice, "I wager my first sexual experience."

Seth felt the blood rise in his face, unable to stop himself from remembering his one night with Wren so long ago. He certainly hadn't been her first, but he could only imagine how amazing that memory must be. Walker stiffened in place, and Seth could practically feel the excitement and greed emanating from the man.

"Accepted," Seth said, fulfilling his duty as the dealer and sealing the spell. He turned away from Wren and his own memories of that silky hair falling onto his chest to face the halfling sitting across from him. "Frankie?" The small creature cocked her head, a green floppy hat covering most of her face. She was kneeling on her stool in order to keep the table at a comfortable height.

"Of course I'm in!" she exclaimed excitedly. "Hmmm. Ok. Get this, guys. I wager when I got my wings."

Seth stared at her, eyebrow raised. "But..." He peered more closely at his old companion, seeing the loose fitting jacket in a new light. They'd shared more than a few drinks over the years, and it was true that he was typically in his cups around her, but Seth was fairly certain he'd have noticed if the halfling could fly. "But you don't have wings, Frankie."

The halfling gave him a wide-eyed stare. "I don't? Then what the hell do you call these?" She slid her jacket off her shoulders, wiggled her shoulders a little bit as if stretching, and then unfurled two colorful butterfly wings. The ambient chatter in the inn stopped for a long beat as everyone stared at the panoply. Even Walker stopped lusting after Wren to take in the curiosity sitting next to him.

"What is that?" someone asked in the silence.

"It's a halfling...with wings!" another voice observed, this one slurred with drink.

"Yeah, yeah, I know. It's weird," Frankie admitted, standing up on her stool and taking a slow turn so that everyone could get a good look. "I'm a butterling now," she announced to the crowd before taking a bow. "Tell your friends!"

"But...how?" Seth managed to ask, his mind sorting through a dozen magical spells and curses that might be able to do such a thing.

"Well," Frankie began, and Seth wondered if he had made a mistake in asking. Once Frankie Miggs started talking, she often had a hard time stopping. "There was this dragon, and he had me in this big golden cage, and he kept saying he needed a new muse..." The butterling paused, as if remembering herself, and then shook her head. "Actually, ladies and gentlemen, you'll have to wait to hear the story another time." She doffed her hat, revealing a shaggy mane of brown hair, and then bowed again, this time in the formal court fashion. She flexed her shoulders and the wings folded up. The bar patrons lost interest as she shrugged back into her jacket, and she knelt back on the seat. "I'm in."

"But..." Seth didn't want to let it go. "Was it a spell then?"

"Nice try, Seth," Frankie said sweetly, "but if you want to know, you have to win the pot."

Seth nodded. If he played his aces right, he'd win all of the memories being wagered. "Fair enough. Accepted." He turned to Walker. "You in?"

The big man nodded, dark eyes back to Wren. "I wager my first kill," he said in a low voice.

Seth tried to keep the grimace from his face. Some memories were worth winning, but he had no interest in seeing one of Walker's victims. He imagined there were some who would relish such a prize, but he wasn't one of them. He sighed. It was the nature of the game, he supposed. Sometimes everything in the pot was useful and worthwhile, and sometimes there were some random things in there that he didn't need or want. Then again, players probably felt that way about some of his memories. "Accepted," he agreed, feeling the magic tingle as it made its way to him. Dealer always had the last spot, and the last opportunity to fold if he wanted.

He thought about the pot: sexytime with Wren was appealing, but he had memories of his own experience with her. He could pass on Walker's murder memory. But the story of those wings...Seth grinned. He couldn't resist a story like that. Sure, Frankie could tell him about it one of these days, but hearing the story and gaining the memory were very different things.

"I'm in," he told them. "I wager the recipe for invisibility."

Wren raised an elegant eyebrow. "How would you know how to make an invisibility potion?"

"You'd be amazed at the things I know, sweets." He winked, and when she rolled her eyes, he added more seriously, "My father was an apothecary. I learned from him."

Walker was looking at Seth with sudden interest. Seth could practically hear the gears whirring in his head as the big man tried to figure out how he would betray them all. Fortunately, the magic bound them to their word. Whoever won gained the memories wagered; the other players lost them. Players could complain and argue, but they generally forgot what they were arguing over in the end anyway. It was the only way anyone would survive long enough to play this special variety of poker.

Seth's fingers draped across the aces on the bottom of the deck, and he wondered again how sentient the magic was, if he could get away with cheating. He'd never tried, and he'd never seen the consequences of someone cheating. Then again, maybe those people had simply played, cheated, and gotten away with it. The thought annoyed him. He was an excellent cheater, dexterous with the cards and charming enough to deflect suspicion. In an ordinary game with people who didn't know him, he cheated as often as he could. It was one way to pay the bills.

But this was a game organized by magic, the deck enchanted with spells that Seth didn't quite understand. And after seeing those wings attached to poor Frankie's back, he reconsidered. Maybe this wasn't the right time. Besides, he liked knowing how to make the potion, but there were other memories of other lessons. He may not even lose the knowledge in the end. It was a wager worth making.

"Accepted," the three players acknowledged, and Seth felt that odd tingle of magic in his skin again, something sealed.

"Ok," he said, laying the cards out, cutting the deck, and truly shuffling the cards, his winning hand disappearing into the hands of fate. He let Wren cut the deck again, and then dealt each player two cards. He checked his hand - the nine of cups and the nine of diamonds. A decent hand, to be sure. He laid the cards face down on the table and looked at Wren.

"Check," she said, knocking on the table and glancing to Frankie. The halfling looked at her cards, began grinning madly, and happily said, "Oh yes. Check. Totally staying in this one." She knocked on the table and glanced to her left. Walker had already laid his cards down, his face inscrutable, and he grunted, "Check," and knocked on the table.

Seth nodded. "Check," he agreed, and knocked. Everyone was staying in for this game. "Three cards out." He laid three cards face up on the table: the squire of hearts, the seven of hearts, and the nine of hearts. Seth kept his face neutral as he spied the nine, bringing his pair to three of a kind. He was definitely in this game. The other players nodded, forming hands in their heads as they took in all of those hearts.

Wren bit her lower lip as she considered the cards, another move calculated to distract her fellow players. Seth grinned as Walker moved in his seat, rocking the stool back on two legs and then bringing it back down with a bang. Wren looked up. "I raise." She looked directly at Walker. "The man I killed in the alley that night...after learning his secret." She knocked on the table, then looked at Frankie.

Frankie also bit her lip, but the gesture had a very different effect as she cocked her head, expression manic as she lifted her cards to look at them again, glanced back at the cards on the table, and then nodded, a broad grin on her face. "I will match," she said. "Ummm..." She looked up, as if trying to remember a memory of equal value. "Oh! Ok. That wizard who fell into that portal that one time. He used to grow all those plants, succulents he called them. I wonder what happened to those plants after he left? Never mind. I wager what he told me before he slipped." She looked up to see three faces nodding in confused agreement, and then she knocked on the table.

"Match," Walker said, face blank. "The man who told me where Tristan's diadem is hidden...before he died." He knocked, and they all looked at Seth.

Seth wanted to scowl. That was a cheap bet. He knew Walker wouldn't willingly give up a valuable memory like that so early in the game. Likely, he'd already retrieved the diadem and sold it. It was a useless memory. Seth wasn't one to judge though. He was betting memories of things that he had multiple copies of, all those years of learning the potions alongside his father. But there were some interesting things to learn in the pot. And he had a good hand.

"Match," he said, considering a worthy memory. Useful information seemed to be the cost of this round. He smiled. "The combination code to access Abernathy's warehouse on the river Massa."

"How do you know that?" Walker asked.

"A lovely lady was kind enough to share that information with me," Seth replied, remembering the warm touch of Mrs. Abernathy's breath on his skin as she whispered the numbers to him while they lay on satin sheets. "And I didn't have to kill her afterwards."

Walker scowled, but Wren and Frankie grinned. Seth knocked.

"One card," he announced, flipping it out and over on the table. The queen of hearts. She was lovely, but she did nothing for Seth this round. He wondered if anyone else had the missing hearts to make the flush. He looked to Wren. The elf was looking at Walker, and then at the cards on the table. She pushed her hair behind her other ear, stretching as she did so to accentuate the shapely lines of neck and shoulder. "I'm still in," she said. "So...another memory." She paused, then looked at Seth. "How about my favorite sexual experience? Can I do that even though I already wagered my first? They are not the same thing."

"Oh sweets," Seth chided, "I don't mind. I will remember it for you." He looked to the others. Wagering similar memories was always up to the players. If they accepted it, fine, but any one of them could refuse. Frankie looked vaguely amused, then nodded. "I accept." Walker was practically licking his lips in excitement, though Seth wondered what would happen if the big man won, only to find himself in possession of a memory of Wren having sex with Seth. Somehow, he didn't think that would go over very well in the long run. "Fine with me," Walker agreed, though he gave Seth a curious glance. Wren knocked on the table, moving the play to Frankie.

"Does this mean I have to wager something sexy?" the halfling asked.

"Please don't," Walker said before Seth could shake his head to signal no. Images of the halfling's sexual exploits were not something he wanted to have to think about. Ever.

Not that he had never slept with a halfling before. They were small and delightfully limber. But he knew enough about Frankie Miggs to know there were some things he did not want to know. "But something important to you," he suggested, hoping that Wren felt that way about her memory with him. He assumed it was him. Who else could it be?

"Hmm," the butterling considered, face twisted in thought. "Something important...Ooh!" She clapped her hands together in glee. "How about that time I became Consort to the Fairy King of the Western Isles?" She gave them a placating look. "It was after I got the wings, of course, during the Great Cheese War of--"

"Do you mean the fabled Western Isles?" Wren asked. "The ones in the myths?"

Frankie nodded. "Oh yes. They're real. Totally real. My ship crashed on them, actually. And then the fairies were going to kill us all to keep the secret, but then I--" she cut herself off. "But you'll have to wait for that," she whispered conspiratorially. "If you win." She looked at her cards again, then considered the four laid out face up. "Which you won't." She knocked on the tabletop.

Walker leaned back on his stool again, hands folded across his chest as he considered his own wager. He opened his arms and pushed up his sleeves as he set the legs down again, hands landing palms down on the table top. "I might, little fairy," Walker said, "and I wager my first lesson with my own blade."

Seth gave him a look. "What, when you were five? How do you even remember that?"

"I was six," Walker replied levelly, "and I remember every moment of the afternoon spent hacking into stumps and wooden blocks. My father taught me." He glanced around the table. "Accepted?"

When everyone nodded, he knocked on the table. Three faces swung to face Seth. "Fine," he answered. "I'm still in. I wager the first book I ever read."

Walker laughed. "It has to be something important, Seth. Nice try."

"I may have learned to make potions by watching my father," Seth said, "but everything he did was recorded in books. Reading is everything to an apothecary." He paused. "Actually, reading is everything to a person who wants to learn anything. I read every book I can get my hands on."

"It's true," Wren agreed. "He borrowed every book in my library when he stayed in Firene for the winter. I accept."

Frankie nodded, and after a moment, Walker nodded too. Seth knocked.

"Final round," he announced relishing the intensity of the moment. "Last card." He flipped the top card: the nine of staves. Seth stared at it, then allowed a small scowl to cross his lips, a tiny bluff. He gestured to Wren. "Last round. You in or out?"

Wren considered the cards on the table, then shrugged. "Staying in," she decided. "But I raise. A lot." She looked at everyone at the table, a slow grin playing across her lips. "I wager my first society party." Seth paused, letting that sink in. Wren's coming out party, her official presentation to elven society--that was huge. She must have a wonderful hand or she was bluffing her little heart out. Seth considered the cards again. He had four of a kind--a solid hand in any game, but did she have the eight and ten of hearts? Could she be that lucky? He decided that she wasn't. If she had the winning hand, she wouldn't need to raise so much. He nodded in acceptance of her bet. She knocked on the table.

Frankie looked at the cards on the table, peeked at her cards again, back at the table, then at her cards again. "So, flush beats straight, right?" she asked, biting her lower lip.

"Every time," Seth told her.

"Nah," the butterling shook her head. "I suddenly think my cards aren't going to win after all." She knocked, then laid her two cards face up on the table. "I'm out." Seth stared at them: the seven of staves and the seven of diamonds. With the cards on the table, Frankie had a full house.

"But..." Seth started to say, but Frankie held up her hands.

"I know! It's a great hand! But I can't win this game. I know it." The butterling sat down hard on the stool, face even with the table. "But this one," she nodded at Walker, "he isn't going to win either."

Walker smiled, the first true smile Seth thought he had ever seen on the man's face. "I'm still in," he said. "I wager my best night so far. Ever." The big man knocked.

Seth gaped. Leaving it open like that allowed the magic to choose. Even if Walker had a night in mind that he intended, the spell that bound the game could choose another, something it deemed even more fitting to the words. There was no way Walker would bet like that if he thought he could lose. Which meant he would win. Either he had the hearts to make the straight, or he would cheat. Seth had watched his hands moving from his sleeves to the table and back again. If the man was swapping cards, that's when it had happened. Seth hadn't seen it, but that didn't mean it hadn't happened. Walker was good.

Seth considered. If Walker was lucky, it meant Seth would lose his memories. He debated if that would be so bad. If the man cheated, Seth would find out if what happened to someone who swapped cards during a memory pot. Either way, it was worth it to stay in.

Besides, there was a memory he had been trying to get rid of for a long time now.

"I'm in," he said. "I wager the very last time I saw my father."

Neither Wren nor Walker said anything, only nodded. Seth knocked on the table. He felt the magic swell around him, and then fade to a low tingle.

"Time to show your cards," he announced. "Wren?"

The elf flipped her two cards: the queen and knave of cups. With the table cards, she had two pairs. A decent enough hand, but not nearly enough to beat Seth's four of a kind. She hadn't even beaten Frankie's hand, had the halfling stayed in. She looked across the table to Walker.

The big man grinned, then slowly flipped his card. The first was the eight of hearts; the other was the ten of hearts. The bastard had the straight. Wren groaned, leaning back on the stool. Seth flipped his cards, and Wren groaned again, seeing that she had lost to both of them.

Seth reached out to touch Walker's cards, pushing them in the center of the table with the rest of the cards. "Straight," he announced. "Walker wins."

Walker stood, about to say something, but then a number of things happened at once. Frankie had been sitting down, seemingly oblivious to her surroundings, when she suddenly dove aside, narrowly avoiding a blast of energy aimed right at her back. "Get the freak!" Someone in the bar shouted and two people moved towards the table with ill intent. The spell continued across the table, smacking Seth hard in the chest. His body froze, the magic paralyzing him. "You missed it!" another voice screamed. Bar patrons scattered and dove for cover, but Seth could only follow the rest of the commotion with his eyes. Frankie's dive had taken her under the table, where she had apparently kicked Walker's stool at him. The big man stumbled as the wood hit his knees, and he took a step backwards, impaling himself on the drawn sword of another patron. Walker looked as surprised as the burly man standing behind him, and he jerked when the man, clearly intent on capturing Frankie, yanked the sword back and pushed him down. Walker said nothing as he fell, but one hand went to his sleeve, and Seth watched as two cards fluttered down from inside his sleeve--the knave of cups and the three of hearts.

Walker had cheated. Not that it much mattered now. Seth tried to move, feeling the magic starting to wear off. His fingers began to wiggle. To his left, Wren had crouched half under the table, face hidden under all of that glorious hair. She had drawn her dagger, the long blade ready if anyone decided that she needed to be part of the fight. She glanced at Seth, saw that he was frozen, and with a smile that was half consideration and half satisfaction, she pushed him backwards. He fell hard on his back, legs up in the air in the seated position he had been in, but at least his head was out of the way of any more spells. From the floor though, all he could see was the lowest edge of the action. He saw Frankie Miggs dart to her feet to his right. She shuffled a little bit, and then she was standing on top of the table, arms waving around as she recited some magical words. Seth thought he heard her say "puerile panoply parsimony popeye" in the midst of her spell, and he scanned his memory for anything that may use those sounds. Most magic didn't require so much alliteration. There was a loud bang from across the room, and smoke drifted across the ceiling. Apparently, Frankie's variety of magic was something Seth hadn't learned about. He wondered if his tongue was up for the challenge.

A pair of booted feet that probably belonged to the man who had stabbed Walker paused when Frankie turned in that direction.

"You sure about this?" the halfling asked, the challenge making her voice hard.

"Umm..." The boots started backing away. "Never mind," the man said, steps getting bigger as he moved out of sight. "It's not worth the trouble."

"That's right," Frankie told him as he fled. "I'm not worth the trouble. And you tell everyone else you meet that Frankie Miggs is not worth the trouble!" She stamped her foot as she said the last, and then made a satisfied humph noise.

The rest of the bar seemed to resume normal operations after that. Such skirmishes were common enough, especially around high stakes poker. Seth waited another moment, and then he could move again. He rolled to his knees and sat up. Frankie Miggs sat on the edge of the table, booted feet swinging in front of Seth's face. She glanced at the still form of Walker lying on the floor, two men, clearly employees of the inn, already walking over to remove the body.

"I told him he wasn't going to win," the butterling commented. "He should have listened to me."

"I think he cheated," Seth said.

"Did he?" Frankie asked, but something in her face said this wasn't news to her. "How fast fate catches up to you sometimes."

Wren stood up, straightening her hair and her long dress. "So..." She considered Frankie and then Walker, eyes scanning the big man with disdain. "Did he die because those men decided to attack you? Or did he die because he tried to cheat?"

Seth shrugged, getting to his feet. "I don't know," he admitted. "But I think the game is void." He looked at the two females. "I still have my memories. Do you?"

Frankie nodded. "Damn." She shook her head. "I've been trying to forget that whole dragon thing for years now."

Wren smirked. "Maybe next time."

Seth looked at the elf. "Maybe next time you shouldn't be betting those memories you want to keep." He flashed her his charming smile. "Though if you'd like to add another memory to wager, I'm in town for a few days."

Wren returned the smile, but without interest. "I think I will keep my memories as they are and find another way to entertain myself tonight." She nodded at them. "Good evening."

As the elf left, Seth gathered up the cards, retrieving the originals from where they had fallen under Walker. They had landed next to a viscous liquid that Seth didn't want to identify.

"You wanted to lose, didn't you?" asked Frankie, her face serious as she watched him clean up the game.

"Why would you say that?" Seth put the deck of cards back into his pouch.

"Because some people play this to steal knowledge," she said, "and you aren't that type. You'll steal, sure, but knowledge is something you value, and you won't play just for that." She gave him a long look. "That means you play to forget things. And that means you play to lose."

"Maybe I just play to find out what I can get away with," Seth commented.

"Maybe," the halfling hopped off the table, "but it won't work."

"What, getting away with things?"

"No, I'm sure you will always do that. The forgetting won't work. Believe me, I've tried. Every time I try to forget, it's always there. Memories of the memory. I can't tell you how many times I've tried to forget that damned dragon. But I don't think I ever will."

Seth nodded. "I know." He had lost the memory of his father seventeen times already, and each time, it seemed like the memory only got stronger, more vivid in his mind. Seth was starting to wonder if the whole game was rigged, some kind of spell that didn't take the memories you wanted to wager, but reinforced the ones you wanted to lose.

"It was good to see you, Frankie," he said, waving to the little halfling as she started to walk away.

"You too, Seth."

"Hey, is there any way you'd just tell me how you got those wings? I really want to know."

The butterling considered, scratching her shaggy hair under the hat. That mop really was atrocious, Seth thought. He should buy the poor thing a haircut and a brush. "Buy me a drink?"

"Of course."

"And no funny business," she snapped. "I know your type. Get a few drinks into a girl and sweet talk her back to your place. Or her place. Whatever place. Well, I don't have a place! Well, I do have a place, but not here, and you're not coming to it!"

Seth nodded, smiling as the familiar flow of Frankie's words washed over him. "No funny business," he assured her. "Just a few drinks and some good stories."

The butterling nodded, then sat down at a table, her back to the wall this time, her voice serene as she began to recount her adventure. "So where was I? Oh, that's right. So, we were trying to find this treasure, and we found this dragon instead. So there I am, face to face with the great beast when...."

Seth leaned in to listen. Memories were good, but sometimes, stories were better.

About JM Paquette

JM Paquette hails from upstate New York, so she misses the snow, but not the shoveling, and now lives in Florida, where she hates the heat, but not the beach. She has an embarrassingly large comic book collection that is only shamed by her ever growing horde of cheesy romance novels, and she openly admits to being both a fantasy enthusiast and a roleplaying aficionado—both of which have earned her solid stamps on her Geek Card. She lives in Clearwater with her husband, her daughter, her big-boned dog, and a cat who occasionally appears at mealtimes.

Connect with JM:
Facebook.com/AuthorJMPaquette
Email: authorjmpaquette@gmail.com

Return to Renwick Hall

By Alanna J. Rubin

The impressive visage of Renwick Hall stared back at me. When I was a boy it felt like home, but sweet memories had turned bitter as tragedies befell the family. I strove to leave it behind, but fate had other plans.

*****

Three Weeks Earlier

I had ridden for the last three days and pulled my horse to a stop as we arrived at the top of the hill, granting me a view of the estate from which I tried so hard to run away. There it was, sitting with a pond in front and woods to the back in its normal stately manner--a silent spectator to all who came and went. The stories it could divulge if it could talk, having been home to three generations of our family. Over thirty windows looked out across the land, bearing witness to the night. Its stare was oppressive and I felt the weight of every stone as I had drawn closer. Destin whinnied and shifted suddenly as if he sensed my dark mood. Or was it the eeriness that emanated from the stillness of the night surrounding us? I patted him on the neck to try and soothe his spirit and gently whispered, "easy boy," into his white-tipped ear. He shook his head in response as if he understood me. We had been each other's friend for several years and I would not wish to take another on a journey.

As I looked up to take in the view of my future prison, I noticed a candle in the west wing of the house, second floor, and third window from the end. My old room. It brought a smile to my face. Mrs. Leighton, the head housekeeper, used to light a candle and placed it in my window when I was a boy so that I could always find my way home. It was a comfort that some things remained constant. That candle, on more than one occasion, lent me the strength I needed to return home. Tonight, I needed that strength more than ever.

We approached the estate at a leisurely pace, neither of us anxious to make it to our destination. We arrived only a few hours before dawn and all of the servants were asleep. I stabled Destin myself and made my way into the house through the servant's entrance. There was a candle on the shelves next to the door. One was always placed there to ensure that any late comers would be able to find their own way-- another sign that, even after all of these years, practices had not changed. Lighting the candle, I walked through the house without any hesitation, its layout as fresh in my mind as the day I left seven years ago, allowing me to swiftly make my way to my room, but when I arrived, I felt a moment's hesitation.

The last time I was here, this room was a safe haven. Would it feel like a prison now, same as the rest of the estate? If I could not face my room, I most certainly would be unable to tackle the challenges that lay before me. This was the first step into a role that I had neither asked for nor desired. Opening the door, I walked in and felt a sense of relief. The room had not changed, my sanctuary. Quietly, I walked over to the candle in the window and picked it up. The exhaustion of my journey was finally starting to take its toll. I placed the candle on the bedside table, removed my boots, and, as I lay back, extinguished the light hoping that a few hours of sleep would restore the energy I would need to undertake tomorrow's duties.

The morning light streaming through the windows roused me from my sleep, but it was a bit longer before the knowledge of my current surroundings penetrated the warm sleepy haze that always accompanied the first moments of waking. I groaned and rose slowly to a sitting position. There was no water in the basin so that I might wash my face, nor did I expect there to be. I hadn't informed anyone of my arrival. That was what I preferred. When I was on my own, I did not cause a fuss. I had managed for myself and I wanted to hold on to that for as long as possible. Walking over to the window, the scene before me, with white clouds scattered across a blue sky, the green hills dappled with wildflowers, brought a feeling of serenity to the day. It instilled within me a sense of calm. I looked down at the pond in front of the estate and longed for an opportunity to jump in, carefree like when I was a boy, but the servants would be awake by now and I would never make it out unseen. No, I'd put this off long enough. It was time to face my future.

Retying my cravat and straightening out the rest of my clothes, I felt as presentable as I could be under such circumstances. I walked out of my room and quietly closed the door behind me. From the hallway, I could hear the bustle of the day. Servants scurrying about, cleaning the rooms, although there was no one about that they knew of to cause them to be so diligent. It was sheer pride in their work that kept them going. As I walked over to the landing, I ran straight into Mrs. Leighton. She had not changed, with her gray hair and her sharp brown eyes that still conveyed that nothing would go unnoticed. She even still smelled of cinnamon. Clearly, her love of cakes and pies had not changed. "Oh," she exclaimed in surprise. "Master Forsythe. I mean...Sir Grayson, you startled me. I did not expect you for another week."

I gave Mrs. Leighton a bow. "My apologies. I found that I could arrive earlier than previously indicated."

"No apologies necessary, Sir Grayson," she said nonchalantly and I cringed at the use of the title.

"Master Forsythe suits very well. No need to use the other." When she called me Master Forsythe, it felt like a term of endearment.

"Nonsense. You are a Baronet now and should best get used to it." Her refusal, though said in a motherly tone, felt like a punch to the gut. "Now let me have a look at you." She backed up a step and took in my appearance. "My goodness how you've grown. You're every bit the man I'd always knew you'd grow into. Your mother and father would be proud to see you now." The unspoken words hung in the air and I perceived her pause as she tried to regain her composure. "I am most sorry," she said solemnly.

"Thank you," I replied.

But Mrs. Leighton did not wish to dwell on it and continued, "Now, your attire needs a bit of sprucing up, but otherwise, you cut a fine figure with your dark hair and blue eyes. Ever so handsome." Mrs. Leighton beamed. She could not have been more pleased if I had been her son. She was the closest person to a mother I had growing up, since my own had died in child birth when I was six years of age. Her opinion carried a lot of weight with me and I was glad that I pleased her. However, she did not stop there. "You'll be bringing home a Lady Forsythe before we know it." Again I cringed. Marriage was the furthest thing from my mind.

It was a good time to change the subject. "I wrote a letter to Father's solicitor and instructed him to meet me here directly. He should arrive late tomorrow."

"Very good sir," she replied. "Is there anything else you require?"

I was going to answer no, but then said, "I would very much like to take a bath. Would you be so kind as to send word downstairs so that one may be drawn?"

"I'd be delighted," she said with a curtsey and then was off. It was a marvel how quickly she could move considering her age. In some respects, coming back was like traveling in time to happy moments such as these, and I allowed myself the pleasure of nostalgia. It would be a little while before the bath was ready, so I decided to visit my father and brother. They were not difficult to find, hiding behind a large tree, but I felt a mixture of sorrow and dread as I approached. When their gravestones came into view, a wave of loss and sorrow crashed upon me. For the first time since being informed of their passing in a tragic stage coach accident, it felt real. In front of me were the final resting places of Sir Henry Allan Forsythe, loving father, and George Maxwell Forsythe, beloved son. Both died the twenty-first of May, the year of our Lord, 1813, now at rest next to my mother and little sister Margaret, who died of fever only one year after mother had lost her life bringing her into this world.

Never had I thought that I would lose my family in such a manner, but fate had other ideas and now I found myself thrust into the position of Baronet. A position for which I never envied my elder brother. Tears began to sting my eyes as the full force of their loss began to take its toll. I had not seen them these past years, but always took comfort in the fact that they were there. Letters passed between us that kept our bonds strong. Now those bonds lay irrevocably broken and worse, I was alone. How could I hope to live up to the name of Forsythe? How could I stand strong without my family by my side? This was not supposed to be my life. I had not been trained for it as George had, so what hope did I have of keeping my family's honor intact? There was no answer and I felt hollow.

I could bear to be at the gravestones no longer and moved to return to the estate when something moving in the distance caught my eye. It was a woman on a horse. Immediately, my attention was fixed. She kept her seat well and was an admirable rider, but there was more to it. The beauty in the way her blue dress flowed behind her as she galloped ahead created an artistic picture that pushed all other thoughts from my mind. For the moments she was within my sights, my heart felt lighter, but she was gone all too swiftly and my melancholy returned. Walking back towards the estate I found myself wishing for a way to have kept her with me.

The bath, though a little cool as I had remained at the graves longer than intended-- did my spirit a service. I felt a bit revived and set out to inspect the property. I began with my father's tenants...*my* tenants, I corrected myself and when I arrived at the first home, I was appalled. It was in terrible condition. Even on first glance, I could see that the roof needed patching and a window replacing. How could Father let this happen? How could George? I decided to knock and see if anyone was about. An older woman opened the door, but I had a difficult time discerning her age. No doubt the years of sun exposure and hard work had taken their toll and had weathered her beyond her years.

"Can I help 'e?" she asked, looking at me distrustfully.

"My name is Grayson Forsythe," I said, intentionally leaving off my formal appellation. Her eyes grew wide with suspicion when she learned of my identity and took in my appearance. Although she could not have been expecting me, a

Forsythe on her doorstep should not have been a surprise. Our family's approach, though unorthodox, had always been to take a personal interest. Grandfather had taught us to understand the value of hard work, as our family came from such a background. It was our great grandfather, Admiral Forsythe, who had earned our fortune and been awarded with a baronetcy. We reaped the benefits of his labors, but had never quite dispensed with the ungentlemanly propensity toward labor, which, I'm afraid, was frequently frowned upon by those in our acquaintance. However, no wealthy family would truly shun another of equal or greater fortune, it would be detrimental to their social circle, and so our eccentricity was overlooked. For me, such two-faced behavior still rankled, although Father and George never seemed to be bothered by it. Nevertheless, the Forsythe family history and work ethic were widely known, so the question was, why was this woman in such a state? I thought the better of asking her the meaning of such a greeting and decided to carry on is if all were normal. "I've come to see if I could lend any assistance with the repairs to your home." Her look of suspicion morphed into something else. Was it shock? I could practically knock her over with a feather.

"'E would?" she asked, clearly confused and I nodded in answer.

"Thank 'e, Sir Grayson." I began to protest her use of Sir, but she did not give me an opportunity to speak as she continued rapidly, "We'd be most grateful. 'E see me husband doesn't have much time after working the fields to do any mendin' to the cottage."

"Then I am glad to be of service," I said and promptly set about my task. The time passed pleasantly enough and I found myself enjoying the physical work. A satisfaction not easily found in the city and even less tolerated than when one is in the country. The sweet smell of orange blossom wafted in the air, which began to penetrate my obliviousness to the rest of the world around me when I heard a knock coming from below. I peered down from the overhang and was shocked to see it was her. It had to be. The blue dress was unmistakable and so was the set of her shoulders, but why would she be here and what business could she have with my tenants? My curiosity got the better of me and I made my way down from the roof in time to see her give Mrs. Pritchard a basket of apples that were sure to be the most succulent food her and her family had eaten in a while. I was touched that this woman would take such an interest in their welfare, but the question of *why* plagued me.

"May I be of assistance?" I asked.

The mysterious woman turned around and said with a start, "Grayson!"

Instantly, I realized that she was none other than Rosalie Winthrop. "Rosy...I mean, Miss Winthrop. What a pleasure it is to see you again." She blushed, creating a striking contrast between the pink hue of her cheeks and the cream tone of her skin. Both appeared to even greater advantage by being set against her chocolate brown hair, which was perfectly framed beneath her bonnet that was tied with a matching blue satin ribbon. Her crooked smile, which I remembered so well from when we played together as children, had added to her sweet looks then, but now added to her beauty in a way I could not express. I suddenly felt an intense rush of nerves. Miss Winthrop was clearly no longer the little girl with whom George and I played. She was exquisite, but what did she make of me? I tried to glean the answer from her face, but to my utter frustration, could not.

Unable to ascertain the answer to the question foremost on my mind, the initial reason for my alighting from the roof came back to me. "What brings you here?" I asked. She looked a little taken aback by the question, so I hoped I did not come across too abrasive due to my disappointment from the lack of confirmation of her thoughts from our encounter.

After a short period of time, she said, "It is the least I could do. I've been visiting the tenants since I returned from school and providing whatever fresh food that I could afford."

Never have I been more astonished or felt greater admiration. "But why?" I could not help but ask.

Rosalie appeared confused by the question. She looked around as if trying to find her answer and then said, "Renwick Hall has been as much my home as Father's or Uncle's." It was as if she solidified the reason for herself as well as to answer me.

The knowledge that she considered the estate home provoked a grin. The silly look on my face seemed to prompt her to take in the full extent of my appearance. "What have you been up to?" Rosalie looked amused by my disheveled and, most certainly, dirty appearance.

I made sure to stand tall to show her that I was not ashamed and replied, "I've been mending Mr. and Mrs. Pritchard's roof." Her look of amusement changed to one of happiness.

"You've done a good deed. I'm afraid that..." she trailed off as her smile faded and brow furrowed then continued, "no, some things should not be said."

"Come now, you may say anything you wish."

Seeing that she was uncomfortable, I gave her a look to encourage her to speak and at length she said, "That is very kind of you, but it's just...what I mean to say is that I do not wish to speak ill of the dead."

"Your sensibilities do you credit, but you may speak your mind to me." I meant every word. I was certain that she would have nothing but the truth to tell me.

"Very well, if you insist," she said, still a bit reluctant. "I'm afraid that George's aversion to exertion of any kind beyond that of attaining his own comfort had not changed since we were children and was a greater vice yet when it came to aiding the tenants. The only difference between now and then was that you were no longer here to push him and plague on his conscience. Without your influence, his true nature took root."

"That cannot be so, it was part of his duty to assist his tenants." I said it wishing to find a glimmer of the man I hoped my brother to be, but her assessment was true and I knew all too well George's tendency toward slothfulness. The pained look in Rosalie's stormy green eyes spoke volumes.

"But Father, surely he would not have wished such neglect." I looked at her in askance.

"I'm afraid that according to my uncle, your father too had little interest in offering assistance to them." I felt ashamed. How could they shirk their duties thusly? There had to be some mistake and yet, I could not refute the evidence in front of my eyes. Some cottages were in better condition than others, but as we walked the tenant properties it became clear that the neglect was not isolated. I felt a deep sense of shame and embarrassment as I came to this realization. I no longer wondered at Mrs. Pritchard's reaction as to seeing a Forsythe upon her door step. The saying "heavy is the head that wears the crown" was true, but what happens when that crown has been tarnished? The residents of one cottage after another that we visited looked upon me with shock and some with disdain. I started to feel ill, but I knew it was nothing that an apothecary could cure. Somehow I had to regain their respect.

Rosalie broke our silence. "I'm sorry to have been the one to bring you such tidings."

She indeed looked distraught, a situation that I could not let stand, so I endeavored to dispel her discomfort. "I'm not. I am most fortunate that it was you. You are a delightful bearer of bad news." I took her hand and kissed it. All other feelings faded into the background. For that moment, there was only Rosalie and I felt like the luckiest man alive when she graced me with another perfect blush.

Alas, all moments come to an end as did this one when she said, "I must be going." The world came rushing back, but I took solace at the perceivable hesitation in taking her leave. "My uncle will be wondering where I got off to." As she began to step away, I did not wish to let her go. She made my most recent revelation bearable. With her departure, I felt as if I was losing some of my strength, but our parting could not be avoided. She curtsied and I bowed, then watched as she expertly mounted her horse and rode away. Her orange blossom scent remained to keep me company for a few precious seconds more.

*****

The next afternoon the solicitor arrived to go over the affairs of the estate. He was a portly gentleman, with blonde kempt hair and smelled of cigars.

"Thank you for coming," I said as I led him to my study. Once there, he did not waste a moment of time to dispense with the business at hand and his tidings were not what I had expected. "This cannot be," I said in shock as I looked from one paper, that he had given me, to another.

"I'm most sorry to say it, but I'm afraid it is." Mr. Andrews's expression was most dire and it made the case presented on paper more real.

"How could they be so irresponsible?" I asked, even though I knew he could not answer. My father and brother had so neglected the estate it was only producing barely a quarter of the income it once had.

"There's more," Mr. Andrews said and I did my best to brace myself against the impact. If it was even possible, the look upon his face told me that this news was even worse.

"Say it," I said. "There's no point in hesitation now."

"Very well, Sir Grayson," he responded as he nodded his head. "It's your inheritance - There's only two hundred twenty-one pounds and six schillings left."

I felt the blood rush from my face. There was well over twenty thousand pounds to our family fortune when I had left. "How?" was all I could utter.

"Your father took to gambling and your brother to spending beyond their income." Mr. Andrews's comment was said so matter of factly it was as if a great weight had been dropped on my chest.

"What am I to do? With what is remaining and the paltry income now produced by the estate, it is not enough to rectify the rampant neglect *and* pay the wages of the staff." I had not wanted any part of this life but as I was faced with its pending fall, I felt myself clinging to it. This was our family's legacy and I could not bear to see it perish under my watch.

"You have three options," the solicitor said as he started collecting his things, "sell the estate; mortgage it to fund repairs; or marry a woman of fortune. Whichever course of action you choose, you must do it quickly. With the current state of affairs, Renwick Hall will fall into debt in a matter of months."

After Mr. Andrews left, I remained in the study. Shock soon gave way to anger. How could they do this? What had they been thinking? How was I to fix this? I was pacing back and forth in an agitated manner. These questions swirled, but one struck me most severely, *did I want to*? The weight of the responsibility pressed upon me and the spacious room suddenly felt small and confining. I burst out through the closed doors as if the room were on fire and went directly to my horse. Mrs. Leighton called after me as I stormed off, but I ignored her. I had no patience for anyone and I was sure the stable boy felt the sting of my brevity as I paid him no heed. Mounting my horse, I proceeded to make my escape and slowed only once as I passed by their graves and my anger seethed, prompting me to push onward at a gallop in an effort to outrun the tumult of emotion that threatened to overtake my senses.

The sun was low in the sky before I slowed, my breathing ragged from the exertion. I felt a pang of remorse for Destin who was sure to be feeling the exhaustion much more keenly than I, and stroked his neck in a calming manner in way of an apology.

It was not long after we stopped that I heard a rider approaching from behind and to my surprise and delight, it was Rosalie. "Miss Winthrop," I said still a little out of breath, "what brings you here?" For truly, there was no reason that we should end up in the same place. I had ridden with no destination in mind.

"You," she said forthrightly and then seemed slightly embarrassed. She continued, "That is to say, I was coming to see you at your estate and as I drew near saw you ride off in a hurry. You looked distressed, so I followed to make sure you were well." I was struck by her sincerity and the effort with which she engaged to seek me out. She was truly a remarkable woman with a spirit that seemed to bolster my own. For, indeed, I felt stronger the longer I was in her company.

The procession of my thoughts caused an awkward pause, so I scrambled to say, "Thank you," but I hoped my eyes conveyed the true depth of that gratitude.

She nodded in acknowledgement and smiled, a touch of pink coloring her cheeks, and I knew the full force of my meaning was understood. Having recovered she asked, "Do you wish to discuss it?"

I was staring off to the horizon thinking that the polite course of action would have been for me to say "No, that is very kind of you to offer, but no." That was exactly my intention, but then I looked at her and saw the earnest set of her features and the warmth shining from her eyes and I found myself relating all of the particulars of my discussion with Mr. Andrews without another thought. She listened intently and did not interrupt, allowing me to unburden myself in full. It was the first time, since I received the news of my father and brother's deaths, that I felt as if I had a partner and a lightness touched my soul. "What is your opinion?" I asked, rather anxious to hear her speak.

Rosalie did not answer immediately; it was clear that she was organizing her thoughts. I shifted nervously in my saddle as I waited for her reply. "You have every right to be angry with your father and brother. They did you, your family name, and every tenant on your land a great disservice with their reckless behavior." She paused, touching my arm, and my heart began to quicken. "But I believe that you do yourself an even greater disservice." I found myself puzzled and wished to understand fully and remained silent so that she knew to continue. "You say that you were not trained for this, nor have the knowledge that your father and brother had, putting you at a great disadvantage, but did it help them?" I remained silent. "From the little I've seen of you since you've returned, you care more about the people, the land, and your family honor than they ever had. It is *you* that visited your tenants and aided them when you did not have to. It is *you* who accepted the responsibility of being Sir Grayson Forsythe when it was thrust upon you. It was *you*, so many years ago, that left home to blaze a trail for yourself in this world, independent of your family's wealth. Grayson," she said, making sure I was looking her in the eye, "you are strong in spirit, are courageous, and kind. No one could be more fit to take charge of the Forsythe legacy than *you*."

Her words struck my mind, but more importantly, my heart. To hear of the man that she believed me to be and to see the truth of it etched in every beautiful inch of her face pierced my soul. There were no verses that could convey the depth of my gratitude for her fortifying words, so I simply placed my hand on top of hers and gently squeezed, hoping she would understand the profound affect she had had on me. Rosalie smiled and squeezed my arm in return. Then she moved her hand away and a sense of loss crept over me. The sun was beginning to set, casting her in a warm pink and yellow glow. It was as if I could see the beauty of her soul and I silently thanked Mother Nature for the vision before me. "It's getting late," she said, which stirred me from my thoughts.

"Yes, I'll escort you home."

"No, that's not necessary. I'm sure you need to be getting back." Did she not wish for my company? A silly thought, I know, but it came unbidden to my mind. I pushed it aside. "Nonsense. Nothing is more important than seeing you home safely."

"Very well," she said with a smile as she started her horse forward, "but I warn you, I'll make it there before you do," and she was off at a gallop. It was the levity that we both needed and I relished the game. But I had no incentive to outrun her on our journey back as I had a better vantage point from behind. I felt a mischievous smile take shape as the thought took hold, but our ride was over all too soon and I scrambled to think of anything that would delay our parting. Then it came to me. "Miss Winthrop, you mentioned earlier that you were coming to see me. Might I inquire as to the occasion?"

"Of course, but it seems silly now." She looked a little embarrassed.

Now I was curious indeed. "Please tell me," I said as we sat on our respective horses, side by side, in front of her uncle's estate.

"Very well. It was an invitation to a ball my uncle is holding at the end of the week. Will you come?" she asked, looking rather hopeful.

I looked her in the eye and took her hand in mine. As I raised it to my lips, I said, "I would not miss it for the world," and placed a gentle kiss upon it. I bowed and took my leave. As I was riding off, the image of her sparkling eyes stayed with me. Mr. Andrews's suggestion of taking a wife came to mind, but my reasons were quite different from his.

*****

The interim days passed and I threw myself into understanding the ledgers, inspecting the land, and talking with my tenants. Everything was in as dire a state as Mr. Andrews had said and capital was going to be the only way of mending the damage my father and brother had done. I began taking what little money there was left to finance repairs and replace equipment. I found myself helping in the fields, working side by side with my tenants. This was no time to put social standing above hard work. All of our livelihoods depended upon our success. The days blended together, but with moments of respite when I spotted Rosalie making her rounds to the cottages. She had told me that she had been doing so every year since before she had left for school and then, once finished, had resumed when her visits to her uncle also resumed. The estate felt like a second home having spent as much time here as a little girl as she did her uncle's. She felt a sense of obligation to care for the families since she knew Father and George had long since abandoned their duties. They had paid her ministrations no heed, both of them blind and foolish in almost every respect. Whereas Rosalie's beauty of person and character knew no bounds. I had decided to make my intentions known at the ball.

I took greater care in my appearance than usual and felt I might do Rosalie proud in my black jacket and perfectly tied cravat. Staring at my reflection in the mirror, it struck me how very much like my father I looked. His square jaw, full lips, and almond shaped eyes looked back at me and I found myself hoping that our resemblance ended there. Donning my hat, I left the estate and a tide of nerves threatened to engulf me as I rode to her uncle's, which only increased in intensity as I crossed the threshold and entered. The house was illuminated by hundreds of candles. The ballroom was filled with the aromas of lavender, rose, and other fragrances I could not name, which mixed with the scents of roast lamb and cakes. But there was only one item that I sought, and was grateful when a tray of glasses filled with punch came near. I took one, and made quick work of it to gain a semblance of control. My desperation for relief had brought me in close enough to overhear two young women, of whose identity I was unaware.

They were both very pretty, but their puerile chatter, of which I was the subject, rendered their appearance in a very different light. Apparently, I was the only one who was not aware of my family's appalling state of affairs. I could not get away fast enough, and began to look over the crowd to find the one person for whom I had intended to see. Every lady was well dressed in their finest frocks, ribbons in their hair, and their cheeks no doubt freshly pinched to bring a little extra bloom to their features. The men were no less presentable, each in their finest coats and donning the most fashionable knots in their cravats. At last, I found Rosalie in conference with a few other pretty ladies, but they were at a great disadvantage when compared to their friend.

As I approached, Rosalie turned around and our eyes locked. Hers sparkled in the soft candle light and suddenly my mouth went dry and I found myself wishing I had the forethought to have taken another glass of punch, but it was too late. Her friends were trying to hide their giggles as I attempted to find my voice and, at long last, managed to say, "Ladies," and bow my acknowledgements. Then, focusing my attention on Rosalie, I asked, "Miss Winthrop, would you do me the honor of your company for the next dance?" She nodded and eagerly took my hand as I led her to a place next to the other couples on the floor. The violins began to play and we all bowed and curtsied to our partners, but I didn't feel elated until I took her hands in mine. I drew her near as the dance required, and felt vexed as it forced us to part as we weaved our way down the line. Rosalie laughed and smiled every time we would meet. We danced three dances together, which was causing quite a stir, as my attentions were being remarked upon. It would have been more, but Rosalie had promised dances to others before I had arrived. The grimace on my face was undoubtedly visible to any who looked in my direction, but it didn't concern me. After tonight, we would, I hoped with every fiber of my being, be engaged.

I met Rosalie after her last partner walked her off the dance floor. She looked quite fatigued. "Would you like me to get you a refreshment?" I asked.

She was still a little breathless from her exertions, but said, "That would be lovely, thank you". Without delay, I set out to find two glasses of punch and when I had acquired them noticed Rosalie's uncle leading her out onto the terrace. I followed thinking that this may be my chance. I would be able to obtain his permission, since her father was not present, and her uncle could then inform him of my suit. But when I came near, the atmosphere was not a happy one. I should have left to allow them the privacy they required but I confess to being curious, so I stayed out of sight, but at a distance where I could over hear.

"Have you taken leave of your senses?" he asked her sternly.

"I have no idea as to what you're referring," she responded.

"I know you are too intelligent to not comprehend my meaning." He didn't sound as if he'd tolerate any deflections. "Your behavior with Forsythe is the talk of the ball."

"Sir Grayson," she said defiantly, and for the first time the title did not make me feel uncomfortable.

Her uncle groaned. "If you do not put some distance between you, nothing short of a proposal would make it respectable." I was confused, why would my attentions be so unwelcome?

"If he did, I would welcome his addresses. He is a superior man." I felt my chest expand with pride.

"Foolish child," he said sternly. "Baronet or not, an alliance with him would be a degrading connection for this family. The reputation of the Forsythe family is in tatters, his wealth spent. There would be nothing short of ruin and misery in your future if you were to accept him." My heart was beating fast. My happiness was slipping away and all I could think was that he was *right*. What kind of future could I offer her? Only one of uncertainty and hardship and Rosalie deserved better.

"I don't care," she protested. "He is the most honorable, feeling man I have ever met. No one present or future could ever be his equal." Each word hit me with great force. How could I give her up? She was a woman with conviction and indomitable spirit. My thoughts echoed hers. None could be her equal.

"Rosalie," he said in earnest, "he may be all that you say, but if he truly cares for you then he'll do what's in your best interest and let you go, allowing you to find a husband that can give you the stability you deserve."

How could I be so selfish? It was like my happiness of the past several days was ripped away from me in mere seconds and the hopes I had for my future lay shattered beneath my feet. I was about to leave when I heard her say, "If he asks me, I'll accept. I love him." She said it proudly. She loves me, I thought to myself. How could three words be the cause of both elation and anguish in equal measure? It felt as if my heart were cleaved in two.

"Then let us hope, my dear, that he does not." Her uncle walked right past me but turned and meaningfully caught my eye before moving on. It's almost as if he knew I was there the entire time and had wanted me to hear all. After he was out of sight I looked at Rosalie, who remained on the terrace looking out into the night. She was stunning; a thick lock of her chocolate brown hair cascaded down her back and her white dress with lace trimmings shimmered in the moonlight. A vision of our future unfolded before me - the estate well in hand, children enlivening up our lives, growing old together - but it was not to be. Her uncle was right, promising her such prosperity was not in my power. Even though I ached to close the distance between us and hold her in my arms, I tore myself away. My heart broke with each step that I put between us, my spirit broken as I rode away.

The next week, I immersed myself in my work trying to occupy every waking moment. Any time I was idle there was only one thought, Rosalie. Even though I could drive her out of my mind during the day, at night I dreamt of nothing but her and the life I imagined for us. My tenants and servants did not question my melancholy mood. No doubt the events of the ball were known throughout the village by now. The days passed in a fog and I did not see Rosalie until I was almost on top her as I was walking through the garden. It was like coming face to face with my dream, except she was even more beautiful in her green riding jacket and bonnet, which accentuated her large green eyes. The exercise of riding here lent additional vigor to her complexion. I cursed my mind for not being able to do her the justice she deserved.

"Where have you been?" she asked, upset.

"Here," I said gesturing around me.

"In your garden?" she asked with a slightly mischievous tone and I felt the corner of my mouth twitch in amusement.

How do you do that? I thought.

"Do what?" she asked and, to my embarrassment, I realized that I had said it aloud. There was no choice now but to answer. She would not accept anything less.

"Cut through the gloom of my spirit like the sun chasing away the morning mist." Emboldened by my confession, she drew closer to me and her nearness stirred the emotions that I had been trying so diligently to repress.

"Why did you leave the ball?" she asked. I could see the hurt in her eyes and hear the nervousness in her soft broken voice.

"It was the right decision," was all I could say without looking her in the eye.

"Says whom?"

"I do." She stepped back abruptly as if I had physically pushed her away.

"You don't mean that," she said with conviction, but the set of her shoulders spoke of her uncertainty.

"I do. I cannot offer you the future you deserve - stability, comfort, and a respectable family name." Each word tasted bitter.

"You sound just like my uncle." That's when I saw the realization flicker across her features. "You heard what my uncle said." The excitement in her voice was palpable as if she just solved a puzzle. "How could you let his words affect you so deeply? He means well, but he's short sighted to what is important in this world. Do you think that promise of fortune means stability and comfort? Look at your father and brother. They had both and squandered it away. It was fortunate that neither left behind a widow and small children to whom the burden would fall. Grayson," she said as she placed her hand on my face and forced me to look at her, "I would place my future in the hands of someone who would fight for what was important to them and constantly strive do what is right every time, over someone who is content to live off of the fortune handed to them and hope it will sustain their comforts and excesses. I could never be with a man such as that. I could never love a man such as that. It is *you* that I love."

Whatever reasons that had seemed just in keeping us apart melted away as the truth of what Rosalie said set my mind and feelings free. I gathered her in my arms and kissed her with a passion I could no longer contain. She set my world on fire and gave my life a higher purpose and there was nothing I would not do to secure her happiness. Our lips parted, leaving us both breathless. It took me a moment to regain my wits and say, "Miss Rosalie Winthrop, you are the other half of my soul and I would be the most fortunate man in this world if you would consent to be my wife."

"Yes," she said as she gathered my face in her hands and kissed me. Our arms wrapped around one another, pulling our bodies closer together - any space between us too much.

I wrote directly to Rosalie's father, all too aware of her uncle's feelings regarding our union, and I hoped that her father would look upon us more favorably. Sealing and addressing the letter, I sent it off to the post, though we knew we would marry regardless of his answer. Fortunately, several days later, his reply arrived giving us his blessing. Her uncle was not pleased, but could not argue. He too had received a letter from her father regarding our union and, apparently, Lord Nathaniel Winthrop had always hoped that we would marry, ever since we were children. He had no doubt that I could restore the Forsythe name to its former glory and, though Rosalie's dowry was small, Lord Winthrop had offered to give me a loan.

*****

Present Day
Today was hot, but I could feel the heat of midday begin to subside and I wiped the sweat from my brow. I had not foreseen my life ending up like this – me shoulder to shoulder

with my tenants, working on repairs to the cottages on my land. The loan we had received was a blessing, but I felt its weight as keenly as the hammer that I held in my hand. It was a debt that I could not let stand. My gaze, which had been locked in the direction of the estate, was drawn to my right and, instinctively, I knew the reason why. My attention was pulled to her as the tide to the moon and I watched as she gracefully walked to join me. She looked like a dream with her green muslin gown with white lace trimming. Her bonnet had come slightly undone due to the wind, allowing a lock of her hair to escape, and her intoxicating scent of orange blossom held me captive. I welcomed her to my side and held her hand in mine, thanking Providence for bringing us back together.

"Are you well?" she asked with concern.

Squeezing her hand reassuringly, I said, "Yes". I had not wanted to tell her that I felt burdened by her father's generosity, but she would not give way so easily.

"It is only...your expression before you saw me looked a bit dire."

"It's nothing of which you need concern yourself." I gave her a smile, but she was still not satisfied.

"The money Father lent you is troubling you, is it not?"

I looked at her dumbfounded. She had done it again. She was always able to cut through and see the root of a problem. Rosalie chuckled at my slack jaw and said, "I know such a debt weighs heavily on your shoulders, but..." she trailed off and made certain she had my complete attention by placing her hands on either side of my face and turning me toward her, "it is something that *we* will repay." Her emphasis on the word "we" resonated in me and I felt as if we existed in one blissful harmony. In her, I had found a match beyond my wildest imaginings – a true partner - and I found, for the first time, that I welcomed everything this life had to offer.

Out of the corner of my eye, I saw Mrs. Leighton approaching with a tray of lemonade. When she drew near enough she said, "I thought everyone might be in need of some refreshment." She had indeed brought enough for everyone, including the tenants.

"That is most kind of you," I said, stepping aside. I gestured for Mr. and Mrs. Pritchard to step forward along with Mr. and Mrs. Carter, a young couple that were my newest tenants, who had also come out to be of assistance today.

Then I passed a glass to Rosalie and took one for myself, when, to my surprise, the others raised their glasses and Mr. Pritchard said, "On behalf of all of us, thank 'e, Sir Grayson." I felt overcome and speechless, so made my response the only way I could and raised my glass to them in return and nodded my deepest appreciation. All of them looked at me with smiling faces that were true and honest. I had earned their respect and I felt a true sense of belonging.

Looking at Rosalie, I could see the admiration in her eyes and knew what I had to do. I took the glass from her daintily gloved clad hand and placed it back on the tray. She looked at me confused then flushed when I pulled her into my arms. As I bent down to kiss her, she put her hand on my chest to stop me and I was sure she could feel the racing of my heart.

"Wait, they'll see," she said, looking at the others, clearly embarrassed. I looked around to Mrs. Leighton, the Pritchards, the Carters, and then back to her, and losing my wits in the warmth of her embrace.

"Then, I'm afraid, my dearest Rosy, that they will have to become accustomed to our displays of affection, because we are going to be married for a *very* long time." Her look of shock melted into a smile that showcased her adorable dimples. As our lips met, the dark memories of the past were replaced by the bright light of our dreams for the future and I found myself, for the first time, thanking fate for its interference and forcing my return to Renwick Hall.

About Alanna J. Rubin

Writer, Whovian, Jane-ite, Trekkie, & Geek. She could go on, but you get the idea. Originally from Massachusetts, she never missed an opportunity to pick apples, carve pumpkins, or go to Salem for witches and haunted happenings. Now in Florida, not a day goes by when she doesn't miss the changing colors of leaves, but wouldn't give up not having to shovel snow. Often, she finds herself torn between watching a Jane Austen adaptation or hopping on the Tardis for an adventure in time and space.

Connect with Alanna online:
www.alannajrubin.com
twitter.com/AlannaRubin
facebook.com/AlannaRubin

Hearts of Monsters

By Lisa Barry

Prologue (6 months ago)

Kam stood near Ryan, who was front and center, until the elevator came to a stop. Ryan waved everyone down and following his own advice dropped to one knee. The elevator immediately became very crowded. Just before the door shooshed open, both Kam and Ryan's skin started to swirl into a kaleidoscope of gray hues, partially transforming in to a mix of stone and leather.

Verity stood at the back of the elevator. The sound of her heartbeat pounded loudly in Kam's ears. He could sense her chest tightening and the fear crawling through her skin. If it wasn't for her bravery, they wouldn't be here to rescue the monsters from the humans.

Verity had contacted them in a panic. As a trained nurse, she had been hired to help the psychiatrists of this institution, but had realized too late that the doctors work was not to help. She told the Guardians that unusual mind-altering drugs were pumped out like candy and the treatments barbaric. Before she could resign, she had been brought into a room and brain washed to care for the creatures held on Level C. Only, the brainwashing hadn't worked on her. She had been pretending for months, worried sick that if she was found out she would be toast.

It was when Noah, a captured Guardian, had shown up in one the cells on Level C that she finally found relief. With her help, his friends had come for him.

"It's clear." Liam's voice came from the hall outside the elevator. "Verity?"

Ryan and Kam's skin stopped whirling and they parted to allow Verity to exit the elevator.

"Where's Andy?" Verity asked just as Brick literally came through the back wall, Andy in toe, his arms hanging on to Brick for dear life. Andy's dark eyes were wide and distinct, his hair almost shaven. His mocha skin gleamed with a light sheen of sweat. Andy, in his late teens, was tall and lanky, and new to his ability. Brick was smiling.

"Damn, that's a rush," Brick said, his eyes shining. Brick was a huge, brute of a man with tree trunk legs, a thick muscled torso, and wide shoulders. His skin was a dark chocolate ebony, but his eyes were a vibrant green.

Many Guardians had their own special abilities, things that set them apart but also made them the best choice for a particular type of job. Andy, new to the Guardians, could go through solid matter and bring things or people with him, as long as he held on to them.

Liam looked at him and shook his head. "Noah's not here," he said.

"No," Verity whispered. She looked up at Liam. "He must be in solitary. I hope." The last was said quietly.

Liam turned to the others and gestured toward the rows of cells behind him. "Let's get everyone out of here, then we'll find Noah." Brick and Verity started down the hall while Kam, Ryan, and Danni, the resident witch, took up the rear.

Verity ran up to a cell, keys jangling from her hands. A glance inside told her what she needed to know - the young man who was covered in scales had not made it. She turned to Liam and shook her head. She ran past the next two cells, giving them barely a glance as they had always been empty. The next cell held the boy. He sat on the bed, his fine pale hair slicked down with water, and he smiled when he saw her. She unlocked the door and he jumped off the bed and straight into her arms.

"I knew you would come," he said. He saw Liam, Kam, and Ryan and positively beamed at them. They looked at each other knowingly and smiled back at the boy. Verity missed the point but was pleased that he held on to her tightly. He turned to her, smiled and gave her back a pat.

"You can put me down, there are others." He slid down and landed happily on his feet. It was a far cry from the diminished little boy she had met several weeks ago.

"Stay close, little one," Verity warned him as she quickly ran to the next cell. She stared through the bars down to the thing, a female, half submerged in a kiddie pool. Her eyes were slightly milky, her gills barely fluttering.

Verity sorted through the keys. As she unlocked the door she turned to Liam and said, "I don't know what to do for her but if she doesn't get help very soon, she won't make it either."

The door swung open and Verity moved out of the way.

"Shit," Kam voiced as he rubbed the long scar running from his left temple down to his chin. Verity scrutinized his face. He was frowning when he spoke softly. "How did they get a Siren?"

Liam knelt and gazed down at the Siren. She didn't move. He brought his gaze up to meet Kam's briefly before moving passed and settling on Ryan. "Think you can handle her?"

Ryan paused for a half second before pulling his shirt off and stuffing it into a black bag slung over his shoulder. His skin started to roil and turned a dull gray color. He looked exactly the same as always except with slick-looking, gray skin. He moved past Liam and Verity and leaned over the pool. Kam realized he was rubbing his scar and dropped his hand, backing away to give more room.

Moving very slowly, Ryan put a large hand over the back of the Siren's neck. The moment he gripped her, she flung her feet toward him but he was ready for it. Her feet hit him and bounced off like rubber. He raised her by the neck to meet his eyes. Her milky round eyes stared at him but that wasn't what scared Verity. The slit of a mouth opened exposing sharp, jagged teeth as she stretched her mouth wider than it should go. Ryan shoved his other hand under her jaw and pushed her mouth closed. He pulled her close to him.

"I don't know how much you understand, girl, but I am trying to help you. I'll bring you to the ocean."

Her eyes widened impossibly and she went limp in his arms. He pulled her out of the pool and turned to Andy.

"We've got to hurry." He and Andy rushed toward the wall where Andy and Brick had come through earlier. As they ran, wings sprouted from Ryan's back. Just before hitting the wall, Ryan slung the Siren over one arm and grabbed Andy's shoulder. Kam watched them vanish through the wall, his hand on his face once more.

Liam looked at him. "Get the boy and Verity out of here. We'll get Noah."

Kam nodded. He beckoned to Verity and she took the boys hand. They followed him to the back wall just as Andy came back through, looking a little pale. Verity left the boy with them and went to a cabinet in the corner. She pulled out a bottle of water and handed it to Andy. He nodded thanks and drank the whole thing. After a deep breath, he turned to the young boy.

"Hi," he said smiling. The boy smiled back.

"I'm ready, Verity." The boy turned to look at her and held out a hand that Verity took gently.

"We're going to have to get cozy," Andy commented to Verity. "Kam has to carry us all the way up. Hang on tight to the boy, I'll hold on to you and Kam will hold on to me. Don't let go. Ever."

Verity nodded at Andy stiffly. She glanced at Kam before picking up the boy and hugging him close. Andy hesitated only slightly before wrapping his arms around her waist. Kam wrapped his arms around them all. Andy's skin whirled and turned, enveloping them all in a foggy cloud. Kam's shirt ripped as his wings exploded from his back.

They entered the wall. The air was dense and it was hard to breath. The strange sounds of concrete rubbing together, tearing, and paper crinkles filled Kam's ears. He held on to everyone a little bit tighter and urged his wings to move faster.

Abruptly they were hovering above a grassy area near the institution. Kam landed gently and released them. Andy curled on the ground and sucked in the air. Verity fell to her knees clutching the boy so tightly he squeaked. Kam sat and watched her gulp in air as he pulled in a long clean breath of his own.

Verity glanced at him, his wings were tucked away and his shirt hung in shreds. He smiled to let her know he was okay.

A few moments later, Brick burst from the institution holding a limp, winged body.

"They'll be coming soon," he announced and lifted his chin toward a street. "We'll meet them later. Let's go."

Now

"Ambush!" Kam growled. The Guardians moved without hesitation.

Brick brought his sword down and over to cut down three Raks at one time. Kam stabbed with a dagger at one and swung his sword toward another bringing them both down with deadly efficiency. Ryan swung his cudgel down on head after head, hacking them into a bloody mess. Liam wielded his sword and knife like a ballet, slicing off arms, hands, and heads as they rushed him. The floor was slick with dark, oily blood.

And they kept coming.

The Guardians were pushed away from the ragged tunnels and further back into the room. There was no time to coordinate, only to act.

Kam wondered if they would need an apothecary after this mess. Ryan had not been practicing his combat as much recently and Kam's eyes wandered the room briefly to make sure his friend was okay. Kam had wondered where Ryan had been disappearing to, but hadn't taken the time to pry it out of him. Despite their friendship, some things could be left alone. Kam hoped Ryan might have found himself a girl. Kam growled as his daydream cost him the use of his arm.

Liam noticed and had a fraction of a second to see Kam's left arm drop to his side, a fillet hanging from his bicep before he started to fight his way over to him, only to be held away from Kam by the sheer numbers rushing him. As Liam's sword removed another knife wielding arm, he spared a glance and relief showed on his face when he saw Kam holding his own; one-handed with his sword, his wings now assault weapons.

The height of an average man, but stooped and covered with thick black fur, Raks looked smaller. Liam once commented to Kam he thought their faces looked like a cross between a wild cat and a pig. The foul creatures revered pain. A Rak considered both the delivery of pain, and the receipt of it, the ultimate in sensation. Luckily, there were not many clans left. They *usually* kept their torture and mayhem to animals in deeply forested, under-humanized areas.

Kam knew the others sliced, lunged, and stabbed as heartily as he, better even with the use of both arms. The weapons the Raks wielded seemed to slice right through the Guardian's armored skin. Earlier, Kam would have said it was impossible.

The Raks' attack on him lessened, maybe due to his injury. Kam saw Ryan moving so fast, he was blurring and yet the Raks were on him four deep. Kam watched Liam start his way toward Ryan, hacking through the muscled Raks, leaving a pile of bodies behind him.

Liam was only two yards away when Ryan went down. Ryan didn't make a sound, but Brick did. His roar echoed through the room. Throwing out his sword arms he changed, utilizing his special ability, whorls of gray taking him over as he become a deadly tornado. His outstretched hands became a deadly spin, knocking bodies helter-skelter while moving toward Ryan and Liam. Blood sprayed from the gray cloud and Liam knew Brick had been hit.

The Raks surged toward the others and Kam fell to a knee. He watched Liam move faster than ever, but still the Raks came. Liam faltered, and Kam lost sight of him.

The scream of spinning air and the war cries of Raks stung Kam's ears as Brick swept him into his arms and ran out of the cavern.

~~

Kam didn't cry, but that didn't mean his heart couldn't feel a deep grief festering in his chest. He had watched the casket as it slowly lowered into the hole at the Sangrine Metro Cemetery.

There had been so many people and none of them knew Ryan like he did. Like he *had*. Ryan had been his confidant, his jokester, his friend. And he missed him. Though Liam's body wasn't recovered yet, he would miss him, too. He was pulled back to the present by the oddest request.

"He said what?" Kam demanded, not bothering to hide his intensity. The lawyer, Mr. Sorents, cleared his throat and adjusted his glasses before from reading the will again.

"Kam, my brother, trust me on this. Go to the Sirens and tell them I'm gone, but that you'll continue in my stead."

"Continue what?" Kam's face was flush as he clenched his fists.

"I'm sorry, sir. That's all it says."

~~

Kam's wings held him steady as he floated over the Atlantic Ocean. He was dead center of the Bermuda triangle. After hunting down and speaking with creatures he'd never even heard of before, it had taken him two weeks to find out where the majority of the Sirens lived.

He was still on shaky ground, or air rather. He was looking for a floating island. He hadn't been able to get any more information than that and it drove his calculating mind crazy. Chess, Othello, war in the tranches, guns...anything but these nebulous directions.

The sun was just starting to peak over the horizon and he still hadn't found it. He would have to turn back again, the third day in a row. He cursed that he couldn't stay out in the open.

He took in a calming breath and turned south to head back to the Bahamas for the night when the first lightning struck. The crack on the water stung his sensitive ears and he pushed his wings faster. Three more zapped down. The ozone in the air was stifling. Kam swooped slightly while hardening his skin as much as possible while still staying light enough to keep to the air.

He watched the waves crash below as he flew and something caught his eye. The slowly rising sun cast a shadow, but it didn't make sense. Another bolt of lightning shook the air around him and he free fell for an exhilarating adrenalin rush before righting himself. The fall had brought him closer to the odd shape. If his eyes weren't deceiving him, he was looking at an island. The problem was not the island, that was normal in the Caribbean. The problem was that the island was *above* the ocean rather than on it. When he'd been told *floating island* he hadn't really believed it.

Kam tucked in his wings and steered toward the land mass. As the sun grew brighter, the island dropped. When Kam reached it, the bottom was just touching the ocean and it swelled gently under his feet. He closed his eyes and breathed in the salty air, enjoying the sun on his skin. He was close, he was sure of it.

A strange tongue spoke directly in front of him, a raspy hiss of sound. His eyes flew open. The Siren was beauty infused with beauty. Her smile made him happy. He wanted to do nothing but serve her. She whispered again. Everything went black.

~~

Kam opened his eyes and found himself in his human form, naked and alone on a cot inside a small bamboo hut with a palm frond roof. A plate of succulent fruit sat on bamboo table near the cot. Whatever magic she had used on him was long gone. He stood and pushed open the dried seaweed hanging in the open doorway, skin roiling into a protective leather. The sun was setting. He'd been out all day.

Not bashful, he stepped through the seaweed. The hut sat on a small grassy knoll overlooking an empty beach. There was no sound, no life, save the waves pulsing against the sand and a stray seagull standing on the grass near him.

Sighing in frustration Kam circled the hut. He could see more huts further inland, but not a soul in sight. He turned back toward the beach just as the seagull turned a powdery pink color and literally poofed out of existence, leaving the beautiful woman standing on the grass. She was easily six feet tall, as tall as Kam, with long blond hair that had vines or something similar entwined throughout it. He tried not to notice that she was naked too.

"I remember you," she stated huskily in accented English and looked him over. She ran a finger along her own face, following where the scar was on Kam's. "You're a warrior."

Kam nodded. He wasn't really sure of Siren etiquette but he knew he did not like magic, at least not used on him, so he decided to be as diplomatic as possible.

"Where is Ryan?" she asked and stood still, her eyes accusing.

"We lost him." Kam's heart pulled as he looked in her eyes, large pools of deep blue. She blinked and he saw her compassion and then her loss. She pressed her lips together. "I've come to replace him," Kam said, voice tight, "but I don't know what I'm replacing him for."

The gills on the sides of her neck flapped several times before she answered. "We are the last of our kind. There are not quite five score left of us."

Kam whistled. He never thought to hear that Sirens were an endangered species.

She continued. "Our magic is not as strong as it once was and the technology of the humans has kept them away from our music." She looked forlornly at the ocean. "I have lost my taste for the flesh since long ago, but it sustains our energies." She met Kam's eyes. "Ryan would feed us, bring us flesh from the land. It keeps us strong," she said and shrugged, "and keeps us from eating those we should not in this new age."

"But why stay here?" Kam asked. He wanted to reach out to her. "Why not merge with the humans and have everything you need?"

She looked passed him, apparently debating her answer. "We do not conform well and we cannot keep our magic when we sleep. We would be gone in a fortnight."

"I will help you," Kam vowed. He reached out to her. "What is your name?"

She looked at his hand and frowned before she blinked heavily at him and changed. Her eyes became a milky white, her teeth sharp and jagged like a shark. Her skin held a blue hue and her gills flapped lazily.

"I'm called Jaws," she claimed with a strange smile.

Kam smiled and slowly shifted into his gargoyle form, towering over her. He gave a low grumble before answering.

"Kam," he stated gruffly and held out his thick leathery hand once more. She turned her head to the side once before placing her small satin-soft hand in his. Kam changed back to human and then, smiling, brought her hand to his lips and kissed it gently.

Jaws blinked and then changed back to her magical façade. "My lack of glamour does not bother you?" she asked. Kam shook his head.

"I think you're beautiful either way."

They stood that way for a time before Jaws finally looked away and gestured toward the inner island. "Come meet my sisters, Kam."

Hand in hand, Kam walked beside his future.

The End, for now.

About Lisa Barry

Growing up in Florida was not a good enough reason for author, Lisa Barry, to avoid wearing black. A daily color choice, Lisa constantly pines for cool enough weather to wear boots.

Living with her supportive (and hot) husband and amazingly awesome kidlets, Lisa counts it a blessing that they still love her despite the deafening sound of her music muse throughout the house.

Writing and reading every minute she can, Lisa counts on the cats to keep her keyboard warm and on the countless gargoyles who listen carefully when she reads to them aloud.

Find more books by Lisa or just go and say hi:
www.lisa-barry.com
Email: authorlisabarry@gmail.com
twitter.com/authorlisabarry
facebook.com/authorlisabarry

Sarah and Molly's
High Sea Adventure

By Anne Cargile

Sarah ran for the ship, Molly clutching tightly to her shoulder, and her pack bouncing on her back. They would have been early, boarding at a relaxed pace, but the Queen had sent them on a last errand before they could leave and now they were definitely running late.

"We'll make it, Molly," Sarah said, panting. "They can't leave without us, we're to be the Navigators."

Molly nodded in agreement, but tapped Sarah on the shoulder to encourage her to move. Sarah often thought Molly had the better end of the deal, being small enough that she could always piggyback on Sarah's shoulder or in a sling bag.

The ship came into view and Sarah grinned. It was a thing of beauty, the *Butterfly*, all gleaming wood and bright sails. It had only recently been completed and this was to be its first voyage. Sarah and Molly had been picked to be the Navigators, which was an honor they were happy to accept. The *Butterfly* and its crew were to go out and discover what they could, and maybe even find treasure. Sarah had done a lot of research, with Molly's help, and had a general idea of which way they should go, but it would all be uncharted territory and anything could happen.

They finally reached the ramp to board the ship and Sarah hurried up. She stopped before stepping on to the deck and hollered, "Permission to come aboard!"

A red haired girl popped up from behind a stack of barrels and grinned. It was the Captain, Sam. "Glad you made it Navigator! Get on board, we're late!"

Sarah scrambled on board as she asked, "Is everyone else here?"

Sam nodded. "Yep, we're all set. Everyone is in position and waiting for you. Say hi to everyone then come up to the quarterdeck."

Sarah, with Molly in tow, quickly found the others and said hello. Ben and Frankie would take care of rowing when they needed it, and Mandy was the apothecary, in case anyone got sick, and was also in charge of food. Everyone was excited about the adventure and seemed happy to be there. Sarah was glad she was with such great friends on such a beautiful day. The rest of the crew Sarah didn't know very well, so she just smiled at them as she walked past and made her way up to the quarterdeck where Captain Sam had taken the wheel.

Sarah stood to the side while Sam called out orders to the rest of the crew.

"Ok everybody, let's get this show on the road. Anchors up! Start rowing us out to sea boys, and then we'll catch the afternoon winds."

Sarah felt the wind on her face as the ship pulled away from the dock and started turning toward the open ocean. "Here we go Molly. Are you excited?" she asked her friend.

Molly nodded and hugged Sarah's neck. Fairly quickly the *Butterfly* was pointed in the right direction and moving rapidly out to sea. A steady breeze filled the main sail, and land quickly disappeared behind them. The sun was bright, and puffy clouds floated above them. Sarah pulled out her maps from her bag and walked over to the Captain.

"Captain, I wanted to show you what I found. See these islands out here?" she said as she pointed to the map, "that's where everything I have ends. I think we try there first, see what we can find out."

"Sounds good!" Sam said as she turned the wheel hard to the right. Sarah felt the boat start to shift direction, heading toward the afternoon sun. Unable to contain her excitement anymore, she lifted her arms straight up and let out an excited shout. She heard answering whoops from the others and grinned. Captain Sam just grinned at her and winked.

The day was mild and for a while pretty boring, though at one point a school of dolphins swam alongside the ship. Sarah commented to Molly that their skin looked like satin, and wished she could have pet one. Ben and Frankie came up to the deck to sit with her, and after a bit Mandy came up and passed out sandwiches and succulent oranges.

Everyone was almost done eating when Molly pulled on Sarah's shirt and pointed behind them. Sarah looked back and saw dark clouds rolling toward them.

"Hey guys, check it out. I think we might have to get ready to take cover," Sarah said. She raised her chin in the direction of the approaching storm.

"Oh geez", said Ben, "did anyone bring any tarps?"

"I brought one," said Frankie.

"Captain Sam," Sarah called, "behind us! A storm is coming in!"

Captain Sam looked and her face paled. "Can someone grab me my rain slicker? It's in the hold down below. I can't leave the wheel or we'll blow way off course."

Mandy quickly ran below, while Sarah started cleaning up from their meal. It wouldn't do to have it all get wet. Within minutes Sam had her raincoat on, Ben and Frankie had the tarp tied up, and Mandy had all the food put away.

The crew huddled together under the tarp as the winds began to blow harder. Almost instantly the sky grew dark as night. Sarah curled over Molly. They were tucked well underneath the cover, but she could still feel the wind cut through her jacket with a winters' bite. The tarp started flapping in the wind, billowing up and then snapping down. She eyed the ropes that held the canopy in place and hoped they stayed put.

Then the skies open up and the rain poured down. In sheets so thick Sarah couldn't hardly see the Captain at the wheel, the intensity of the storm left her gasping. Mandy started sniffling and Sarah put an arm around her, just as frightened.

"I should have stayed home, Mandy moaned, her shoulders shaking.

"What would be the fun in that? This is just a bitty storm, no sweat!" said Frankie, grinning.

Just then a streak of lightening flashed across their vision, so bright and so close Sarah let out a little scream. They all screamed when the booming thunder followed almost immediately. The storm was right above them. Sarah looked out at the Captain again, fearlessly holding the wheel of the ship, rain slanting across, soaking her. Sarah thought the Captain was one of the bravest people she'd ever met. A loud ripping sound above their heads, and the crew watched as the main sail went flying off into the storm.

Sarah had no idea how long the five of them stayed under the canopy, it seemed like forever, with rain beating down on them and waves crashing over the sides, but eventually the wind calmed and the rain tapered off. As soon as the boat felt steady, Sarah scrambled up to the Captain.

"Did we stay on course?" she asked.

"I don't think so," said the Captain. "I did my best, but..." she trailed off, then continued, "we need to make landfall and do repairs. We can't continue with the sail gone, the boys can't row *that* much."

Sarah agreed and pulled out her maps. She'd kept them tucked under her shirt, and they had stayed pretty dry. She looked at the sun, and pulled out her compass. She made a note on the map and then plotted a course to a known island. It was small, and hadn't been explored much, but it would do. She showed the Captain, and the boat shifted as it was steered toward safe harbor.

"Can you see what else we might have lost in the storm?" the Captain asked,

Sarah nodded and went back down to the crew, and first let Molly and Mandy know the plan, then the boys, who had already gone below to row.

The journey was short and before they knew it, landfall was sighted. Everyone gave a huge sigh of relief. It had already been an exciting day, and now they had repairs to look forward to. Sarah had found out from Mandy that their fresh water had gone over in the storm. After they dropped anchor, the Captain decided to send a party on shore to find fresh water and resupply the barrels. The party would consist of Sarah, Molly, and Ben. Mandy and Frankie would stay and help put the ship to rights.

With that the search party set off in a small row boat to the shore. They were very happy when they got to the beach, and Ben even got down and kissed the dirt. Sarah laughed, and Molly just shook her head. She looked at Sarah as if to say, *boys - am I right?*

Sarah and Ben unloaded the water barrels and then Sarah set Molly atop the stack.

"OK Molly. We're going to leave you here to guard everything. We'll go in one direction for half an hour, then straight back, so we check in," Sarah said.

Molly nodded and executed a little salute at Sarah's orders, then blew her a kiss.

"Ready Ben?"

"Yep," he said, adjusting his pack. "I've even got chalk to mark our way so we don't get lost."

"Smart thinking! Let's go."

The two set off at a good pace, searching for signs of fresh water. They entered a fairly dense forest of pine and Sarah took a deep breath. She'd always loved that smell, it was so serene and reminded her of Christmas. The two didn't talk much as they struggled through the low lying brush. After a half hour of walking Ben gave the signal it was time to turn back. It was a good thing he'd used chalk on the dark trunks of the trees, or they might never have found their way back to the beach. When they got back to the barrels there was no sign of Molly. Sarah's heart nearly came up through her mouth in panic.

"Where is she, Ben? She wouldn't just leave," Sarah said, her voice trembling.

Ben was looking around at the sand, the footprints he and Sarah had left clear, and so were another set of prints.

"Look Sarah, someone's been here. Those prints are way too big for Molly," he said as he pointed.

Sarah ran over and examined the prints. They were of bare feet, not shoes and there was only one set of them. Sarah's eyes teared, someone had kidnapped her best friend.

"We have to go find her," she said, trying not to cry

"Don't worry Sarah, we'll find her." Ben's voice was firm and comforting. He gave her an awkward pat on the back as they started in a half walk-half jog to follow the mysterious prints.

To Sarah it felt like time slowed to a crawl as she tried to control her panic. She told herself they'd find Molly, but at the same time Sarah was angry with herself that she'd left her little friend all alone in a strange place. Sarah just hoped whoever took Molly was nice and didn't hurt her. She'd heard of islands where packs of mean beasts liked to stomp and destroy anything pretty.

The footprints eventually took them back into the forest. It became harder to find the footprints, but Ben was a good tracker and, taking the lead, he was able to see things Sarah would never have noticed. He was also still carefully marking the trees so they wouldn't get lost. Next to Molly, Ben was one of her favorite people.

Ben stopped, holding his hand up to signal a pause. He looked around, took a few steps one way, then the other, then turned in a circle, always looking at the ground. He looked at Sarah.

"The footprints stop here. I can't find anything after," he said with a puzzled expression. "It's like whoever it was just, disappeared."

From somewhere above them, they heard a giggle. Looking up in to the trees, they saw nothing at first, then a little face appeared. The hair was tangled and the face was extremely dirty.

"Hello," said Sarah. "Have you seen my friend? She's kind of small, and has red hair."

The person nodded and giggled again. It poked it's head out a little further and Sarah and Ben saw with a shock that it was a dryad. The girl's hair was all the colors of the forest, and her eyes were a bright leaf green.

More politely, because Sarah knew that a dryad could make your life miserable if they got annoyed, she asked, "Can you please tell me where she is? Molly is my best friend and I don't want her to get lost or hurt."

The dryad's face disappeared and Sarah almost cried. Ben patted her on the shoulder and handed her a handkerchief. Before Sarah could get too worked up the dryad popped up at the bottom of her tree, smiling. She waved her hand for Sarah and Ben to follow and took off, skipping lightly across the forest floor, her feet not even seeming to touch the ground. Ben and Sarah followed cautiously, not sure what the girl could be doing.

Soon they found themselves in a little clearing. In the middle was a small table with several chairs around it. In each chair sat a Companion, just like Molly. In fact, there she was! Sipping a cup of tea and sitting between a small bear eating honey on one side, and a rather fancy looking girl eating a cookie on the other.

"Molly!" Sarah yelled as she ran up to her friend. "Why did you leave the beach? I was so worried!"

Molly looked ashamed and hung her head, but then she looked up at Sarah and smiled. She pointed to her friends and shrugged.

The dryad spoke for the first time. "I saw her on the beach and invited her. I knew there was a gathering and thought she might want to come. I am sorry. We should have left a message."

Sarah took a deep breath. "It's OK. I'm just glad you're safe Molly." Sarah turned to the dryad. "Please, don't ever do that again. I nearly had a heart attack."

The dryad hung her head, tears falling from her eyes. "Is there anything I can do to make it up to you?"

Ben cleared his throat. "Um, actually, maybe you could help us. We need to restock our fresh water for the ship. Do you know where we can do that?"

"Oh good idea, Ben!" Sarah said.

The dryad immediately perked up at Ben's request and nodded vigorously. She cupped her hands around her mouth and gave a trilling little call. Before Ben and Sarah could blink, several dryads came out of the trees carrying barrels of water on their backs.

"My people will follow you to the beach and help you stock your boat. I'm so sorry about Molly."

"Wow. No, it's OK now. Thank you so much for this! The Captain will be very happy," Sarah said. "Come on Molly, we should get back, too." Molly came over and hopped up onto Sarah's shoulder, getting comfortable in her usual spot.

Ben thanked the dryad as well, and soon they were on their way back to the beach. It was an uneventful walk back to the beach, loading of the boat, and trip back to the ship. Once back on board the *Butterfly*, they found out the sail had been repaired and, with the fresh water, everything was ready to set out again. Sarah was feeling quite tired and wasn't up for much conversation.

"Sarah!" she heard her mom call. Sarah poked her head over the railing and saw her mom standing at the edge of the playground. She waved and smiled.

"I have to go guys. Will you be here tomorrow?" Sarah asked.

"I will," said Sam. "Me, too," from Ben.

Mandy and Frankie both said they were going away to visit family and would be gone for a while.

"OK. I'll see you tomorrow. And I'll remember to bring snacks, since Mandy won't be here," Sara said with a grin. She grabbed Molly and climbed down the ladder of the fort. When she got near the bottom, she jumped the rest of the way and then ran over to her mother.

"Hey honey, did you have fun?"

"Yep! We went on sea adventure!"

"Oh really? Well, tell me all about it while we walk home."

"Well, first I was almost late," Sarah began, clutching Molly tight. As she and her mother walked home for dinner, Sarah told her about the Butterfly and their exciting adventure at sea.

About Anne Cargile

After decades of trying to ignore the voices in her head and appear normal Anne Cargile finally sat down one day and let them take over. She habitually only shared her mental adventures with her garden plants, but they steadily worked to convince her to share with humans too. She finally gave in to their incessant nagging and has been working on writing and publishing her stories to "real" people. Anne currently resides in New Hampshire.

Connect with Anne online:
facebook.com/Anne-Cargile
Email: Anne.Cargile@gmail.com

The Last Man on Earth

By Dalia Lance

~ Meet Tasha ~

"You have to be frigging kidding me!" Tasha screamed as she threw the remains of her large, half-caf, soy milk, extra syrup, caramel, mocha latte across the room.

Sabastian, Tasha's fabulous assistant, watched as she became enraged when the remaining goo from the cup began to slide slowly down the wall.

Marcus, her manager, was sure that both of them were glad they didn't have to clean up after her.

She began screaming loudly and pacing around the room. It was hard to understand her.

"Bastion! Are you listening to me?" Tasha screamed, stamping her feet.

"Of course lover," Sabastian replied, tilting his head and smiling. Marcus was again, much to his surprise, impressed with the way that Sabastian maintained his apparent patience with Tasha. Very few people seemed to think these kinds of tirades were cute.

"They can't be serious! Do they know who I am? Do they know there is NO show without me? I could just quit. What the hell would they do then? Tell me...TELL ME!"

Marcus couldn't help but think, as he watched yet another emotional outrage, that she was one of the world's most, childish, spoiled, selfish people he had ever known.

Tasha hadn't been born to a rich or famous family. She wasn't royalty. She wasn't rich and famous for any skill or ability she possessed. She was famous for just being born.

You might be wondering what amazing physical or mental ability Tasha possessed to be famous for just being herself? It is nothing as glamorous as all of that.

~ History Lesson ~

To fully understand how someone like Tasha could become an instant celebrity at birth, a clearer understanding of why her gifts were considered amazing is needed.

In the year 1872 an important discovery was made by the research lab at the Institute of Human Evolution (IHE for short). Although the significance wasn't realized until a few years later, this discovery completely changed society was a whole.

Previously, everyone had been allowed to simply choose the person they wanted to

marry or have children with. This lead to an increase in the number of birth defects and degenerative hereditary diseases. Coupled with having multiple sexual partners, the spread of multiple debilitating diseases was also allowed.

In an effort to positively affect the health of the world, studies began at the IHE. It was found that most issues began on a genetic level, more specifically, the mingling of different genepools. As the study continued, it was found that most people were only genetically compatible with a very small number of others worldwide. Even the slightest incorrect combination of genes could lead to cataclysmic health disasters for a family tree generations later.

By the year 1902 a very controversial decision was made.

Every human was to submit to a gene test.

A massive undertaking, in the end the evidence was undeniable. If something didn't change, the health of the entire planet was in jeopardy.

Not only health, but the financial stability of economies forced to sustain the burden of an ever increasing population of people with avoidable illnesses was a heavy consideration of most governments.

When the program was first initiated, couples that wanted to marry submitted to gene testing in order to receive a marriage license. Everyone was denied.

The chance that a person would meet someone they were compatible with was about one in four million. Odds were never in their favor. Documentation indicated some people had tried with hundreds of potential spouses. This, of course, was not a workable solution.

In order to solve the problem, it was decided that every person would be tested at birth, the results tabulated, and there would be a system. The candidates with a genetic match would be introduced starting on the person's eighteenth birthday.

If one candidate was younger than the other, the older candidate would be informed they would have to wait, no more than two years, to meet their first candidate.

Each candidate after the first would be a little less genetically compatible than the previous one. Although still compatible, the first candidate was always the best and why most people chose their first match.

Matching was done on a genetic level. This meant that attraction was not the key factor a relationship and eventual pairing was determined by.

Since not all people had the same number of choices, and both had to decide, it changed the dynamics of most courtships.

Deciding on a mate could even be done by a lengthy interview process. Several companies had even designed a "Know Your Mate" kit with everything a person needed to know to ensure they were making the right choice.

Although some protest of this new method was muttered, it soon fizzled when divorce rates plummeted to less than 3% from over 35%. The general health of children of the new generation was found to be excellent, with almost no birth defects, and disease became almost unheard of. The movement was viewed more as a saving grace than control by the government.

Most people were born with two to five people to choose from, people they could choose to marry and/or have children with.

The highest number of matches that had been recorded had been six. This number was granted to a boy named Marcus Ashton Fletcher. He became a minor celebrity for this, but when he chose to stay with the first choice, the media quickly lost interest.

~ Born Famous ~

Back to little Natasha Tanner.

Tasha was the only person who had been born with eleven potential mates.

When her parents received the notification of their child's enormous number of potential mates, they sent a query to the Bureau of Human Sustainability (BHS), to ensure they were reading the information correctly.

That, and of course, posting the news on every social media outfit they could find.

At first they may have been genuinely excited about the amazing news. That, however, soon turned into a way to profit.

The news of such an extraordinary number went viral immediately. The moment BHS confirmed, little Natasha was suddenly a celebrity.

Her parents put her in ads for diapers, then clothing, then any product one could imagine. The public couldn't get enough of her.

Like most child stars, Natasha eventually fell into the trap of too much money and freedom, and not enough parenting. That was at age six.

That was also when Marcus was brought in to be her manager and guardian. At the time, he had been working with another celebrity that had a similar talent to little Natasha.

Christian had been born approximately three months after Natasha and had eight potential mates. This was big as well, although not as big as Natasha's. The BHS began to wonder if the two children meant a turn in general quantity that people could expect to be matched to going forward. This wasn't the case.

However, having a boy that was lucky afforded other companies to actually compete with those that snatched up Natasha. It created a sort of rivalry. Almost everyone knew who these two somewhat ordinary looking children were, and most had a favorite.

Marcus had worked with Christian and found it almost unbearable. He couldn't believe a child so young could be that rotten.

He chose to work with Natasha instead, assuming the sweet child he'd witnessed on talk show after talk show just needed someone to look out for her. He was wrong. Only because of the ever increasing paycheck and notoriety did he continue years of what amounted to a baby sitting gig.

Marcus now sat, looking at his client and knowing this ride would soon be over.

When Tasha had turned seventeen filming began on the first season of *Tasha's World,* a reality show that would follow her in the final year leading up to meeting the first of her matches.

Christian had his own reality show following a similar theme.

There had even been talk of potentially having the shows sometimes cross-over and blend both story lines together. There was one major flaw in that idea: Tasha and Christian hated each other.

It had started when they met as children. There was a time everyone had thought that they would be good friends. Marcus knew better. Since both children had been raised to be products instead of people, they didn't have much room for friends, especially with the competition.

~ The Princess Meets Her Prince ~

When Tasha finally turned eighteen it was a huge event. Record numbers of people tuned in to see who her first match would be. The network had made a very sizable donation to the BHS to reveal to them Tasha's first match in order to set up a meet on the show, on her birthday.

The party was huge and incredibly staged. Celebrities begged to be invited. The party was filled with people who wanted to have their face on camera during the highest rated broadcast of all time.

As the cameras rolled, Tasha, who was wearing a gown that made her look like a sweet princess, was placed in the middle of the dance floor with a single spotlight shining down on her as the rest of the room was black. As the gems on her gown, hair, and tiara sparkled she looked up to find a second spotlight form on a very strategically placed stairwell, and from a pinprick the spotlight opened to reveal a young man in a tuxedo, holding a white rose.

This was Parker, the first, unfortunately, of many matches. Parker stood a little over six-feet-tall, and he was strikingly handsome. He had short dark hair, a light complexion, and dark blue eyes.

At first the look on Tasha's face seemed like she was overjoyed as Parker slowly made his way to her on the dance floor. She took the rose as he handed to her and smelled it, then shyly looked down and away as he placed his hand on her chin, guiding her to turn her face to meet his gaze.

She smiled, she may have even blushed a little, as they began to dance to a slow song, with lyrics speaking to new and deep love. The song went on to be number one that week and remained on the charts for a couple months, simply because of that episode.

As they danced, the information about Parker was slashed across everyone's television screen. Parker was nineteen. He was a sophomore in college and was studying to be a lawyer. His family had a very prominent law firm in New York City.

On paper he looked perfect for Tasha. Then the story began to play out. It seemed for all the viewers like it was true love starting with that first night. After dancing, a romantic carriage ride, talking all night until they watched the sunrise, and then falling asleep in each other's arms. It seemed like a fantasy come to life.

The sweetness of it all was almost like a vicious sugary substance that stuck in the throat and choked if you tried to swallow. It made for amazing ratings. The wedding of the century was planned. Of course, the pair would spend some time getting to know each other. An entire television season in fact. Millions of viewers tuned in to watch the romance blossom.

Marcus, sitting on the sidelines of the charade, was saddened when he realized Parker believed it was real. He thought he was in love with the country's biggest celebrity. After all, she acted as if she was falling in love with him - until episode five. This is when the fights began.

The fights seemed innocent enough at first. Tasha was upset that Parker wasn't spending enough time with her due to his grueling school schedule. So, he of course cut back classes.

Meanwhile, Tasha was supposedly studying to be a fashion designer. Since a very young age, she had an established brand of clothes, shoes, jewelry, accessories, and cosmetics. She was going to learn to take over this empire and design everything herself.

Of course, those who knew Tasha, which only a few in her inner circle were truly allowed to do, knew that she didn't like to study or do work herself. Her main skill was unpredictably bossing people around, and choosing items presented to her to put her name on them and saying she created them.

What did this mean for Parker?

She dragged him around the world, with her film crew and of course, paparazzi, to fashion shows and release parties. Anywhere Tasha could be seen and treated like the event revolved around her, she was there with Parker in tow.

He became her arm candy for the parties. She wasn't interested in anything he had to say, his thoughts on matters, and if he mentioned doing something he wanted to do she rebuffed him saying, "It is cute how stupid you are." Unfortunately, this became a catch phrase on shirts, keychains, hats, stickers, and even the lyrics of an up-and-coming popstar.

Instead of this budding romance turning into the ever-after story Parker and so many of the viewers counted on, Tasha, and the producers, had other plans.

Parker, who had seemed to worship her at first, began to show he was not excited about what his blushing bride thought their future should hold. He began to refuse to go to the parties and special events. What had at first been fun and adventurous had turned into something exhausting and upsetting.

Although Parkers' family was initially excited about the match, they too began to lose interest in Tasha being the correct person for their son. Parker had three matches allocated to him from birth, maybe one of those would be better than Tasha they thought.

When he began to lose interest in month five, the producers had to act. Parker, his family, and any friends introduced on the show, were required to fulfill the entire season. That didn't mean that it had to be the perfect fairytale that the viewers wanted.

Making the situation worse, Christian met his first match. The ratings were not as high as for Tasha, however Christian knew how to play the game for the viewers, producer, and his potential mate; Christine.

The name thing made the whole thing even more adorable. Unlike Tasha's romance, which was taking a turn for the naughty in order to keep Parker interested, Christian behaved like a true prince charming. Marcus began to think he might have chosen the wrong horse to hook his wagon to.

Marcus decided to try to find out if Tasha had figured out what she actually wanted. He went over one night for dinner, cameras off, and no staff around with the exception of her normal household attendants.

When he arrived he found Tasha watching TV, her own show.

"What are you doing?" he asked, sounding a little more surprised than he intended. He made his way into the living room and sat on the couch opposite of the one she was in. She didn't look away from what she was watching.

"Natasha, can we talk?" he asked in his best calm but imploring tone.

"I told you not to call me that," she snapped back, still not looking over at him.

"Where is Parker?" he asked, changing the subject.

"That asshole is at his apartment," she said, turning to glare at him. "He said he will only be around during filming. He's...he...damn it," she said, throwing down the remote. Her tone was somewhere between rage and tears. "I don't know what the hell he is. He's stopped talking to me at all."

Marcus was a little surprised by this news. He knew it had gotten bad, he had hired assistants for Tasha to be his eyes and ears, but the last report was that Parker didn't seem happy, not that he was done with her.

"What happened?" he asked, trying to be careful. He knew that an explosive outbreak would make this evening completely unproductive.

Tasha looked over at him. "I don't know. He said I was a selfish bitch. He said he wished he could walk right off the show, but he didn't want to be in breach of contract. Whatever that means." She covered her face with her hands and began to sob.

Marcus was surprised that she seemed genuinely hurt. He knew she was capable of being upset, and even going into fits if things didn't go the way she wanted them to, but less than a handful of times in her life had she actually cried because she was hurt emotionally.

He got up off the couch he was sitting on and moved to sit next to her, putting his arm around her shoulder and letting her cry. Saying anything at all might make her stop, and he felt she probably needed to let it out. Even though this was his job, he did at times feel sorry for her.

She had not really grown up. She was raised to be a product, something people bought. She seemed to be guided by what she thought everyone wanted from her or what she wanted everyone to think of her.

It always surprised him that celebrities that appear confident on television or in the movies were the least confident people he met. Tasha was no exception. She used the art of tearing people down to make herself feel better.

After a few moments she looked up and wiped her eyes. She didn't say anything at first. She let out a deep breath letting her lips vibrate like the sound of a motorboat. She sounded tired.

"Did you like him?" Marcus asked as he let her go and turned to face her.

She shrugged. "I don't know. It doesn't matter. I have 10 more after all." In that moment Marcus watched any hope of Natasha deciding something based on what would make her happy disappear. She was now Tasha for good.

~ Crossing Them Off the List ~

The rest of the first season was a charade of Tasha fighting to win Parker back and then losing him again. They had epic public feuds and make-up moments, caught of course, by the press. Marcus was impressed at how quickly Parker adapted to his new role, even if he was heavily compensated. It's said that money can't buy happiness, but in the case of the Tasha Show it apparently did.

The last couple of episodes the producers made it seem like the two were heading to the alter. The show even set-up for the big day; the dress, the tux, the party. The two lovebirds, it seemed, realized they were meant to be together.

"He is my forever," Tasha was quoted saying right before the big day. The big day was to be broadcast live.

When the ceremony started and she was walked up to the alter, it was to the same song they danced to the first night they met. Parker took her hand and guided her to stand before the priest, lifting her veil to reveal...Tasha with tears streaming down her face. Huge, wet, turtle tears. Marcus would have been impressed at her acting ability had he not seen the make-up person spritz her with tear creating spray right before she emerged to begin walking towards this Oscar worthy moment.

"I can't do this..." she sobbed.

"But why? I don't understand," Parker asked, appearing confused and heartbroken.

"I...I..." (more sobbing) "I just don't love you," Tasha said pulling away from Parker, grabbing her dress and running towards the back of the church.

Parker stood confused, his gaze following her as she ran away from him. Camera panning across the people gathered. Shock and awe on everyone's face.

For the live feed it was amazing.

They cut the feed, which caused even more of a stir. The fans went crazy, social media blew up. The news channels had all been covering this one moment. This one, heart wrenching, ill fated, totally fake, moment. Marcus as her manager was impressed. As a person he was saddened. He knew this was just the beginning, and he was going to be along for the entire ride.

Christian's first season ended with a different twist. He found his soulmate Christina was hiding a terrible secret, she had already met and fallen in love with her second mate. His fans were heartbroken. How could anyone do that to the caring, sweet, loving Christian? He was devastated.

At least on camera.

With both of their first choices eliminated, the next matches were lined up to go. Each of the season's played out in a similar pattern: Tasha would seem like she had found the one, they would begin fighting, a new twist would be thrown in and the relationship would end. Sometimes there were more than one match per season.

~ When #2 is Boring ~

Season 2 introduced the public to the very plain, and very boring, Phillip. He was about Tasha's height at 5'7, was very thin, and had non-descript brown hair and eyes. Even with all the prepping the show did with make-up and clothes, he was completely average and just happy to be there. He added nothing to the mix, and in fact, when Tasha would react to something, Phillip would just agree. There was no confrontation.

Ratings plummeted. Since there seemed to be no drama that could be solicited out of Phillip, Tasha found another person who did react to her fits. Her assistant. When the ratings spiked, it was like throwing gasoline on a fire and culminated with Tasha firing her assistant on camera. She actually threw a drink in the poor girls face and then dropped the cup on her head. This was the highlight of the show and the unfortunate beginning of a pattern. The studio paid out and the ratings soared.

Phillip had to go, so she dismissed him as if he was the help. "I no longer require your services," she told him while sunbathing, after he brought her a drink she had required him to fetch. Tasha waived him away dismissively with her hand.

The new assistant, Samantha. Arrived. She seemed to run around in a perpetual panic. While it was entertaining to watch, along with her apparent inability to perform most of her assistant tasks, Samantha was one thing Tasha despised more than dumb - Samantha was stunningly beautiful. When potential mate number three arrived, his name was Emmett, the house became a constant cat-fight instigated by Tasha.

Marcus wasn't surprised that the producers introduced these types of dynamics, but he was surprised that they didn't want Tasha to know, at least at first. She could act, but not well for long periods of time. So instead, the producers set-up her world for her to genuinely react to it. It made for great TV.

Emmett was as attractive as Parker had been, tall, dark skin, hair he kept very short and caramel colored eyes, and he was a college basketball player headed for the pros. Tasha actually swooned over him a bit, but Marcus knew she wouldn't keep him. Keeping Emmett meant ending the show, but he knew a small part of her wanted to. Unfortunately, that part wasn't the one she put out in front.

The end of the season was Samantha fired and Tasha throwing things as she left. Then, Tasha upset, saught the consoling arms of Emmett only to find him leaving to go after Samantha. The whole thing was a farce, since Samantha and Emmett were not mated. It made for good TV and even started book deals about what it was like to work for, or try to woo, the amazing Tasha. Of course, the tell-all books were overseen by the show's producers so the scandals and views were what they wanted the readers to see.

~ A Pattern Emerges ~

With three of her potential matches down, season 4 became one of the most interesting of all of them. It started off with Tasha accidentally meeting her fourth match. His name was Blake. He was the president of one of Tasha's fan clubs in the Midwest.

Blake was twenty-two. He worked as a teller in a bank and had been a fan of Tasha's since she was younger. He'd always had a bit of a crush on her, and in high school he started a website and blog dedicated to posting the latest Tasha news from his perspective.

Tasha had begun a press tour around the country to meet her biggest fans and supporters. She was told it was because she needed to be closer to her fans. Viewership drove ratings, ratings drove the money, but most important, the more fans, the larger the masses worshipping her. Tasha was in.

She met Blake at the local diner where he ate lunch and posted on his site. When Tasha walked in, he stood up from the booth, his expression awestruck as she approached. He was slightly shorter than her, because she was, of course, wearing stiletto heels. She shook his hand and he waited for her to sit before he sat down again, his laptop posed in front of him.

As the cameras rolled she asked Blake questions about his favorite stories about her, and let him ask her the questions he had always wanted to. Most were tame like "What is your favorite ice cream" and "Who was her favorite celebrity that she met". Tasha easily handled them. When Blake asked her, "Do you and Christian really hate each other?" Tasha blurted out "Yes!"

Not picking up the hint that he was no longer on solid ground, Blake asked, "Are you intentionally not picking one of the mates to keep the show going?"

Tasha became visibly enraged and was about to go into one of her, now famous, explosions when someone off camera must have gestured to her. She closed her eyes and took a deep breath and said, "I don't think I have found my Prince Charming yet." She was smiling, but her eyes conveyed something quite different.

Blake didn't seem to notice that if she could have killed him with a look she might have attempted it at this point. He was so oblivious that he said, "I dreamed that I was one of your choices."

It was said with true adoration, and in true Tasha fashion she replied, "That's sweet," in a tone that was anything but.

As they finished Blake stood and helped her out of the booth. When she was standing, he hugged her. Tasha wasn't prepared and pulled back a little. The director had them re-take the scene so that it looked more genuine.

When Tasha headed out of the diner she muttered to her newest assistant, "It was like hugging a sweaty pig in a shirt."

Tasha got in the limo. Marcus was waiting. "How did it go?" he asked. He had watched the entire thing from the back of the diner.

"He was a stupid, fat, disgusting thing. I can't wait to get out of this waste of a town," Tasha said and gestured for her assistant to get her something from the mini-fridge for her.

"Well then, I have some bad news." Marcus was usually the one who had to deliver bad news to her, as he was the only person she couldn't fire.

Tasha turned, narrowing her eyes. "What? More fan club fatties need to drool over me?" she asked.

Marcus shook his head. "Blake is number four," he said, holding up four fingers.

It took a minute for Tasha to process this. When she finally did, she picked up her phone and started dialing. Marcus grabbed it out of her hand, shaking his head. "Not sure what you are about to do, but I wouldn't. We have dinner with the producers tonight. I would suggest," he said, pulling the phone back farther as she tried to grab it, "You contain the tantrum you are about to throw, and see what they have to say."

"Give me my frigging water," was all she said, taking out the swelling rage on her assistant. When the water was handed to her she took one sip and spit it back at her assistant, saying it was too cold.

That night the producers told her the pitch. A Midwest boy who ran her fan club and his shot at being her match. Tasha flat out refused.

It took many hours of negotiations before the producers got Tasha to be willing to let Blake down gently in a two-part episode. The episodes would focus on Blake getting himself ready to go on the first date with the amazing Tasha and Tasha preparing herself to meet the next of her mates. Tasha would know it was Blake of course, and would have to pull off some acting on her part to seem oblivious as to who it would be.

The meeting was set-up to be on the beach, at sunset, in Hawaii. It seemed more romantic than continuing to keep them in the Midwest. After all, Tasha was way too west coast for that, so the show flew Blake to Hawaii.

It was serene. A gazebo was set-up with twinkling lights. Tasha was wearing a clingy summer dress, her hair up in a perfect messy bun with little blonde tendrils caressing the side of her face. She was standing at the back railing looking out at the ocean as Blake walked in. The look of happiness on his face was heartbreaking for anyone who knew what was actually happening.

"Tasha?" his voice shaky.

Then she turned, first with an amazing smile that quickly faded. Zoom in for a close-up.

"Tasha. It's me Blake..." his voice begins to falter. He moves toward her and she holds her hand up to keep him at arm's length as she brings the other to cover her face

"Stop. Please," she says.

In a very dramatic moment she then turns as tears stream down her face. "I just...can't," she says as she runs out of the gazebo toward the shoreline.

Blake follows her. The cameras follow at a distance. Blake reaches her, she turns, they talk for a moment, then she falls against his shoulder. He puts his arms around her, rubbing her back. This was the cliffhanger they left everyone with until the next show.

The story was that Tasha viewed Blake like a brother. The producers decided that Blake should hang out with Tasha for the rest of the season. He was more than willing to be a part of her world, and on some level he believed she may change her mind when she got to know him.

~ From Boring, to Bad, to Worse ~

Mate number five didn't even last a full episode. He was from China, his name was Zhou, and he didn't speak English. Zhou worked with his family, had two brothers and one sister, and was a middle child. He was also trained in Kung Fu and aspired to compete around the world. This was all described in sub-titles. Since Tasha couldn't understand him and he was shorter than her, he was out.

Malcolm, mate six, actually lasted the remainder of the season. It turned out that Malcolm was also a celebrity. He had been a child actor, and had recently moved up to a more adult role on a weekly television show about vampires in a small town. He played one of the few werewolves in town, who was having a forbidden love affair with a vampire. Malcolm had recently turned eighteen, was six-feet tall, had bronzed skin, and movie perfect smile. The world had watched him grow from a small boy in to an incredible looking man.

The first meeting was arranged to be in conjunction with an episode of Harrison's, the name of Malcolm's character. There were several weeks of previews that led up to this episode.

Tasha was cast as Sally Rea, Harrison's childhood friend and the first girl he kissed before she mysteriously disappeared and was presumed dead because of a bloody shoe that was found.

Unfortunately, Christian, who was in fact a much better actor than Tasha, was also cast on the show and played Harrison's arch enemy. Christian's current potential mate was also on the show and played his current love interest on and off the show. This was his number five as well.

The three shows collided into one.

Tasha, aka Sally Rea, was to walk into the local diner where Malcolm, aka Harrison, and his buddies were hanging out. All Malcolm was told was that the girl playing Sally Rea would walk into the diner and walk past the table where he was sitting. He was to make eye contact, and after he looked away there would be a brief flashback where he would see himself and Sally Rea as children and some identifying feature she had, and he would know it was her.

Christian had spent the last week teasing Tasha and threatening to tell Malcolm what was happening. It had Tasha on edge on the set, so what little acting skill she had was put to the test when the set got quiet and the director called "Action".

The noise of the diner started and just as Tasha was starting to walk in Christian smacked her ass and whispered, "Go get-um tiger." This caused all of the nervousness she had held back to come flooding up, and when she walked into the diner she tripped on the first step. Instead of a grand entrance it was a disaster.

When she fell, Christian began laughing loudly and some of the cast members on the Vampire side of the camp joined in until a very unhappy director shouted "QUIET!" Everyone froze.

Malcolm walked over to help the mystery girl up only to see the very embarrassed, tear streaked face of Tasha. Malcolm asked her, "Are you ok?" Unable to respond, Tasha took off in the direction of her trailer.

At least two of the three shows got the reaction they were hoping for from Malcolm when he realized who she was. Then with a little guidance from Blake, realized why she was on the show and cast as his long lost love.

This was not how a fairytale romance starts in the storybooks, but it made for fun reality TV.

After about an hour worth of make-up retouches and convincing on the part of both Blake and her assistant, Tasha was ready to film. The scene went off this time without a hitch, and without Christian present.

Tasha made an appearance in a total of three episodes. It only took one to find out that Malcolm wasn't interested in Tasha. As a matter-of-fact, he wasn't interested in anyone of the opposite gender.

Although the system allowed a person to find mates that were compatible, it wasn't a guarantee that the person was your type. Christian found the entire thing amusing, and the cross-over of their two shows were highlighted regularly for the volatile fights that both of the stars were able to create almost instantly in each other.

To Tasha's credit, she didn't have to put that much effort in breaking up Christian and his latest match. Nicole, his latest squeeze, had already caught wind of the fact he was going to end it by the end of the season. With a little help Tasha showed her how she could make an even bigger impact.

Christian and Nicole were presenters at an award show, a live broadcast. They were to present the *Best Couple* award. They read the nominees from the teleprompter and then Nicole opened the envelope to read the winner. Instead she said, "Instead of the winners for best couple, I want to announce the award for worst couple. That would be us. Namely you, Christian. We're over." And she stormed off stage.

It led to a ton of press for Christian, and several days' worth of giggling on the part of Tasha. He even called when he found out the part she had played to start another fight. Both seasons ended with a bang, and both with their sixth potential mate being crossed off the list.

~ It's Like Watching a Car Go Off a Cliff ~

Season five turned out to be nothing short of a train-wreck. With five potentials left and with Tasha now only twenty-three years old, this season solidified for most viewers that Tasha was out of control.

The season opened to her sending her "brother" Blake on his way. She said that he had made their relationship creepy and weird. He had actually been her most loyal supporter and the backlash of how she had treated him began to take its toll on her supporters. They were starting to root for her failure in the world of relationships than to hope she got her happy ending.

Vegas had one of the largest pools in history for which number she would actually settle on. Most were betting on number ten or eleven.

When Marcus had taken some time again trying to find out if there was anything left of the person inside of the celebrity he was met with disappointment. He had tried to get her to see past the celebrity, past the show, and to the fact that she was slipping farther and farther away from the better genetic matches. This wasn't just emptying the suitor pool; it was literally emptying the gene pool.

To make matters worse, Tasha didn't seem to want to follow the advice from anyone on the show. Her first match of the season, Greg, was number seven, an undergrad studying marine biology and working at an aquarium teaching children about sea life. Tasha told him he was terribly boring, and when all of the activities he wanted to participate in were outside, like camping, she simply walked away from their first date.

Next was Mike, working as mechanic in his dad's garage. The show decided, after what was being referred to as the "Greg incident", they had to take a different approach introducing him to Tasha.

Mike got a make-over. He was ruggedly good looking, with light brown hair that had a slight curl to it. He had light blue eyes, and he was fairly muscular. Mike had been born and raised in Kentucky, so he also had a wonderful southern accent.

When the audience was introduced to Mike and watched him be prepared for his meeting with Tasha, the country fell in love with this boy-next-door.

However, on the show Tasha had fired yet another assistant, because she didn't like the way she looked. Tasha was cementing her new title of being a world-class bitch.

Marcus was asked to assist with getting his client under control. He had to admit he wasn't sure it was possible. It was hard to threaten the only person the show needed, with the only other show in the same ratings band as hers being Christian's. She made them money and she knew it.

Enter in Sabastian.

At first he had been brought on to the show as an assistant to one of the make-up artists, but there was an instant chemistry that even Marcus couldn't deny. When the idea was proposed to take on the role of her assistant, Sabastian made sure of only one thing - that Marcus was the only person that could terminate his employment.

The show agreed.

Marcus was charged with introducing Tasha to her new assistant. In the past, Tasha had been allowed to perform interviews and pick a person from the selection that had been given to her. In this case, she didn't have a choice.

There was a feeling that she wouldn't receive this news at all well. Marcus didn't lead up to it, or even try to sugar coat it. He walked into her dressing room with Sabastian in tow. "Tasha, this is your new assistant. No, you do not have a choice. No, you cannot fire him. No, I am not interested in what you think about it. His name is Sabastian. I believe you have met." Marcus then walked out the door with Tasha's mouth hanging open.

He stood outside the door anticipating the tantrum, and there was silence. He was tempted to open the door, but thought better of it.

The next week's show was the introduction. Mike was to meet Tasha to go to a private viewing of a movie. Tasha walked into the theater to see him holding a tub of popcorn. Tasha was...nice. Since the show wasn't scripted anything could happen.

She walked up smiling. "You must be Mike," she said.

He smiled back and said, "Nice to meet you," with that wonderful accent and it seemed to make Tasha smile more. When she looped her arm through his to walk into the theater the curious looks on the faces of the crew couldn't be counted.

The night seemed to go smoothly. The movie was funny and the cameras caught both Mike and Tasha laughing. Tasha even fed him a few pieces of popcorn.

After the movie the two went for ice cream and Mike told her about his family and asked her a bunch of questions. All of which she answered honestly and kindly. The night ended with a chaste kiss between the two and a promise of another date the next night.

The world was collectively stunned.

This continued with Mike, and no one understood why. This sudden change was very un-characteristic of Tasha. The speculation of the change and pulling apart every detail made for amazing media coverage.

When Christian started a band on his show, it didn't compare to wondering why Tasha had appeared to be falling in love.

Even Marcus was shocked behind the scenes. Tasha appeared calm, cool, and collected with everyone. She seemed nice.

"Are you on drugs?" Marcus asked as she sat in the make-up chair getting ready for the next shoot.

"What? No. Well, not right now," She replied.

Marcus opened his mouth to ask more, but decided the better route would be to walk away and, like so many others, watch the spectacle playing out in front of him.

On top of the other weirdnesses, Tasha treated Sebastian, or "Bastian" as she called him, with respect and actually seemed to want to have him around.

One afternoon during the taping of the last episode of the season, Sabastian was standing watching the crew set-up and Marcus walked up to stand beside him.

"Hey," Sabastian said, nodding his head in Marcus's direction.

The last episode was to center around Mike asking Tasha to marry him. It was again staged as a romantic day together that ended up at a candle lit picnic under the stars.

Then, as the crew set up the heart shaped pillows for the happy couple to lay on, Sabastian made a sound that sounded somewhere between a snort and a laugh.

Marcus looked at him and then facing forward again he asked, "What the hell is going on?"

Sabastian turned and looked at him with a little bit of a smirk on his face. "Good television of course."

During the picnic the real Tasha resurfaced the moment Mike popped the question. The first line of her rant was, "I would never marry a pathetic insect like yourself." It went downhill from that point and ended with a stunned Mike being left with all the heart-shaped pillows.

Marcus's phone immediately blew-up with calls from the producers wondering what had happened and how come they didn't know about it. They were not really upset because, as Sabastian had said, it was good television, but they didn't like surprises.

When the dust had settled a little Marcus made sure both Tasha and Sabastian understood that keeping him in the loop was not just a good idea, but required. Tasha rolled her eyes, but Sabastian understood. After all, Marcus was the one that could fire him.

~ The Beginning of the End ~

With three remaining matches the planning meetings began. The producers begged Tasha to make each potential mate last the entire season. She, of course, would attempt to promise something and then not be able to hold up her end of the bargain.

Case in point was number nine: Vince.

He was from New Jersey. He was Italian, had a thick accent, and was also very overweight. He wore mainly sweatpants and T-shirts that were not only several sizes too small, but were also usually stained.

Even when the show cleaned him up, they knew, there was no way Tasha would be part of it. As they filmed the pre-meeting episode, Vince showed the crew the tattoos he had on his chest and back. They were all of the cartoon character Popeye, the Sailor Man.

Sabastian had to leave the set because he couldn't get his laughter under control.

Plan B became making as much of a spectacle out of the event as possible. First, they blindfolded Tasha and made sure she couldn't see or touch Vince during the first episode when they met.

Then, for the second episode, they played a guessing style dating show. Tasha ended up asking three Jersey boys, Vince included, a series of questions to decide who her match could be.

The questions were ridiculous. They made for a lot of laughter and inappropriate commentary, but in the end, she didn't pick Vince.

They couldn't keep her away forever so by episode four the unveiling took place. In less than two minutes Tasha walked away.

Not only did they not have an entire season, there was a slightly larger problem that the producers had to figure out a way to present at the end of the season.

A new plan was formed.

Tasha would spend the rest of the season doing a sort of "Where are they now?" and revisit all of her past mates to see how they were doing.

This had its own various adventures. Most were now happily with their mates. The hardest episode, which they saved for last, was Parker.

Tasha had a hard time walking into the room to meet with Parker. She broke down. Sabastian rushed to her side as she crumpled to the floor and held her as she sobbed.

Watching it unfold, Marcus could see the heartbreak. For everything Tasha had become in her life, during this journey she had lost something that could never be replaced. She had lost love. Possibly, her true love.

When she was able to walk into the room, there were two couches set-up and Parker stood up from one. In his hands he held a single white rose.

Tasha froze.

The camera zoomed in on the tears that streamed down her face. She closed her eyes and the world watched as she took a few deep breaths. In a minute that seemed to stop time, the Tasha that Marcus hoped she was stood there. If he looked close he could see her shaking. Marcus looked over at Sabastian and could tell that he was thinking the same thing. They wanted to rush out to her, to give her the support that she most desperately needed. They couldn't, what was happening was TV gold.

Tasha finally let out one final deep breath, looked up at Parker, who also had tears falling from his eyes, turned and walked slowly out of the room. This time Marcus didn't hold back and he and Sabastian surrounded her and walked her back to her trailer.

Sabastian had to make a statement the next day to the press. It read that Tasha was not prepared for the emotional toll this season had taken on her, being reunited with all of those who had fallen in love with her before. She was going to take a little time for herself and reflect on those important in her life.

The final episode turned what could have been emotional to bizarre. The tenth match was named Steven, who went by his chosen name, Moon Caller. He owned a small novelty shop called The Apothecary in Miami, Florida.

He was a fortune teller, healer, and warlock. He was fairly tall, very slim, and had pale skin. His hair was dreadlocked with shades of blue, purple, and black.

Tasha was not introduced to Moon Caller in person. Instead, she was played clips that were recorded during his intro episode. He said he had been visited by his Moon Guardian who had told him that he needed to stay clear of the woman about to arrive in his life, as she was toxic and would be his undoing.

Moon Caller, it turned out, always listened to his Guardian.

He did have one bit of fortune telling for Tasha: "Sometimes Karma is a mean bitch." When he was asked what that meant, he simply said she would soon find out.

~ The End of the List ~

Marcus had hoped that this day would not arrive. As he watched the various promos play that he had been sent to review, he couldn't help but realize that he had wanted her to have found someone and been happy.

She may have lost some of her fame doing that, but what he knew, that she didn't, was that fame is not a comfort, or strength. It is cold, and a burden.

The farther from the first match she got meant the less compatible, on at least a cellular level, her mate would be. If Vince and Moon Caller hadn't been a direct indication of this, he didn't know what would be.

As he got to the last promo he picked up the phone to call the marketing department to give his thumbs up when it began to ring. It was the head of the Network.

Marcus answered and was told that a car would be arriving to pick him up in ten minutes and to be ready. He hung up and could only think *this wasn't good*.

When he arrived at the Network offices an assistant was outside waiting. He was rushed into a conference room where he was greeted by the Network Head, all of the show's producers, and six people he had never met before.

He was asked to sit and then the bomb was dropped.

They had gotten the news of Tasha's final match.

It was Christian.

He had just ended with his second to last match who had left him standing at the alter in his last episode.

Marcus wanted to ask if they were sure. Of course they were sure. As a joke, this would have been amazing, but the looks on the faces of everyone in the room said they had never dreamed this to be a possibility.

Many discussions took place about what to do, the direction of the show, and how would they handle Tasha. The six additional people in the room were from Christian's show. Collectively, they had no idea how to approach this either.

After several hours, several arguments, and a lot of questions, both camps agreed there was only one thing they could do. They had to tell them before the filming started.

Marcus volunteered to tell Tasha. He didn't want to, but knew that he and Sabastian would be the best shot at getting this to an outcome that at least didn't involve too much violence.

Marcus asked Tasha and Sabastian to stop over at a hotel when they were done shopping for the day.

Tasha walked in, fresh coffee in hand and dropped the many bags she was carrying.

Sabastian put down the bags he was carrying and tidied up the ones Tasha dropped.

"I have news," Marcus started, "You are going to want to sit down," he finished, gesturing to the couches and chairs.

"What now?" Tasha blurted out.

"Well...We know who your final match is." Marcus kept his tone as calm as possible. He knew this was bad, but seeing her sitting in front of him, ever the product of the celebrity she had created herself to be, he found a little irony in the situation, and with that, a little humor as well.

It didn't take more than a second from when Marcus said the name for Tasha to launch herself off the couch.

"You have to be frigging kidding me!" Tasha screamed as she threw the remains of her large, half-caf, soy milk, extra syrup, caramel, mocha, latte across the room.

Sabastian, Tasha's fabulous assistant, watched as she became enraged when the remaining goo from the cup began to slide slowly down the wall. Marcus was sure that both of them were glad they didn't have to clean up after her.

She began screaming loudly and pacing around the room. It was hard to understand her.

"Bastion! Are you listening to me?" Tasha screamed, stamping her feet.

"Of course lover," Sabastian replied, tilting his head and smiling. Marcus was again, much to his surprise, impressed with the way that Sabastian maintained his apparent patience with Tasha. Very few people seemed to think these tirades were cute.

"They can't be serious! Do they know who I am? Do they know there is NO show without me? I could just quit. What the hell would they do then? Tell me...TELL ME!"

Marcus smiled now.

Tasha looked at him and screeched, "This isn't funny!"

Sabastian went back to trying to calm her as Marcus walked to the window and looked out. The screaming and cursing eventually degraded into crying and sobbing.

There was a point when she seemed to go numb and simply stared at nothing for over an hour. Then suddenly she said, "I want to see him."

"Him who?" Sabastian asked.

"Christian. I want to see him. Does he know?" She looked at Marcus, who only nodded.

Marcus pulled out his phone and made the call.

When the final season of each of the shows began filming there was an agreement with the networks. They would run the first episode at the exact same time. The stars were prepped, and filming began.

The outbursts, teasing, and fighting from both of them were exactly what the fans wanted. Finding out that they were each other's final partners created more fan reaction than any other rivalry.

When Tasha was interviewed and asked what she thought of Christian and the fact he was her final match, she could only shrug and say, "I guess this is what happens when you are stuck with the last man on Earth. You get the bottom of the genepool."

About Dalia Lance

So here is something about little ole me; I have had a very interesting upbringing starting with growing up in Hollywood, CA. Never shy, I learned that if you are not willing to try something new, you may let life simply pass you by. I love meeting people from all walks of life and these experiences inspire me on a daily basis. As a true friend once pointed out "You are never a complete waste, you can always be used as a bad example". So what's the worst that can happen?

Connect with Dalia:
www.DaliaLance.com
Facebook.com/authordalialance
Twitter.com/dalialance
Tumblr: WhoreTips

Dead of Night

By Rhiannon Matlock

Chapter One

I woke with a start. Not like in the movies where the person jumps three feet in the air, or fidgets like they are having a seizure. Instead, I jerked once as my eyes drifted open. A sense of lingering anxiety knotted my body like a bowtie and my throat was raw, as if I'd been gagging. It was a familiar feeling, though it took me a few moments to realize why. The dream hit me then, particularly the last part, and with a groan I pushed myself into a sitting position.

After rubbing clear the cobwebs, I discovered that I was still on my couch. The plush peach cushions stared at me with an imprint of my face and a little spot of drool coloring the satin. I hadn't even made it to my bedroom.

Pushing myself up all the way to my feet, I suppressed a whimper as my head pulsed with pain. Pain. What a funny, funny thing pain was. It hurt, yet in some situations it was better than feeling other things.

A strange cooing sound drew my attention to a nearby window. The glass pane was tall and double glazed, but there was a hint of moisture in the corner. It didn't surprise me. The building was old and not everything fit together as perfectly as it once did. As a result, sounds and air passed through with better ease than they should've. I was going to have to replace it at some point I supposed. It'd been a while since I was bothered by such things.

I spotted a black bird hopping along the sill, fighting bravely against the winds that whipped through the buildings of New York City with a fierceness that would put the most ruthless politician to shame. Nature had nothing on maternal instinct as the black bird forced its way toward its nest of offspring.

A sad sort of smile settled on my lips. How well I knew the power of that instinct. I shook my head and started to the kitchen. The carpet was plush and soft under my feet, but I barely recognized it over the chill that was creeping through my apartment.

Stopping by the thermostat to adjust the heat before I got to the fridge, I wondered how I'd slept through such cold. It was of little consequence, but it gave me a numb sort of feeling to think of how unaffected I was.

A moment later I was standing in front of my fridge. There was precious little occupying the giant, metallic box and I sighed. I didn't know the last time that I went grocery shopping, but I was beginning to wonder what it mattered. Grabbing the last of the milk and some cereal I went to my dining room table and started to eat. There were no sounds beyond the little whistle of wind created in the nooks of the windows, and unfortunately the lack of stimulation allowed my mind to wander. Without conscious thought it drifted back to my dream and made me clench my jaw

The image of Rose was almost tangible. Such a beautiful child. Thinking of her made me sadder than I'd been in a long time. She'd been destroyed by a singular event, one that wasn't of her own causation, and wasn't something she could ever do anything about. I wondered if that was what drove her over the edge. Having had a similar experience of my own I know that's what drove me so hard at the time. I could still recall the last day I'd seen her and her brother. It seemed like it had happened yesterday, not three years ago. Even now I felt that familiar spin in my universe, as if I'd tilted off axis that day and had never really found center again.

In an attempt to shake off the thought I forced myself to look away from the abyss of my cereal and toward the window. The outside world existed beyond those panes and I thought if I could concentrate on that, it might help.

It was a poor attempt at distraction. Thinking of the people beyond my walls only reminded me what time of year it was. As if to reinforce the thought, I caught sight of the twinkling lights of a Christmas tree in the window across from me. Though

I tried to be home as little as possible, in the past several years I'd spied the family that lived in that apartment. Husband, wife and two kids. I'd never met them, but occasionally I fantasized what it would be like to live that life. It had been so long since I'd had a family my thoughts were more like vague notions than real scenarios.

I sighed and looked back to my bowl. This wasn't helping. I wasn't sure if it was the time of year or what, but I couldn't control it any more, this feeling of helplessness and being unanchored. I was adrift in a sea of uselessness and it was getting harder and harder to fight.

I got up abruptly and started to pace. I had to do something. Something that would take my mind off of things. But what? There were parties I'd been invited to and work acquaintances that I could call for a night out, not to mention a few dates I'd failed to call back. But none of it appealed. It meant I had to interact with people and I just didn't feel up for it.

No, I needed something else. Something I could do here. Alone. I had alcohol, and before I knew it I was pouring myself a shot. The dark liquid slid past my throat and buzzed along my nerve endings, but it didn't quiet my thoughts. I took another. It helped but the feelings didn't abate entirely. I needed something else. I thought of the only room I hadn't entered in years, a studio of sorts. Certainly there were things to do there, but the memories within were painful and definitely not something I could confront at the moment. Nope, something else.

For reasons I couldn't explain I thought of my gun tucked away in my closet. The feel of the cold steel was almost real in my hands. I froze, unable to reason out why I thought of it. I forced a reason. I could clean it. It'd been a long time.

Scared, but desperate for something to latch onto, I moved to the hall closet and retrieved the small safe that held my gun. My hands trembled as I returned to the table and all but dropped the box onto it. It made a loud clang, making me jump a little. What was I doing?

Without understanding, I reached toward the solid metal enclosure and then stopped just as I touched the lid. It was cold and unforgiving. Much like the promise of what it could bring. Of their own accord my fingers steadied as an image of what else I could do with the gun popped into my head.

Snatching back my hand as if I'd been burned, I realized just how serious I was. The real trouble was I that could do it. It wouldn't take much from me to end things. Right here. Right now. It was a daunting thought, but one thing stilled me and then made me tremble once more. My mom. She would never forgive me if I went through with it.

A new urgency dawned within me and it had nothing to do with finding a distraction. I had to get out of there. Now. I turned and, without bothering to brush my teeth or check my schedule, I grabbed the overnight bag from the opened hall closet and all but ran out the door.

Chapter Two

Tall pine trees, painted in black, thrust up from the ground straight into the sky on either side, lining the tiny two lane road like a gauntlet. Ahead of me, the high beams of my head lights shot straight into the night like a laser beam, chiseling through the inkiness and highlighting only a fraction of my surroundings. There were no street lights, no clattering of civilization, hell, there weren't even any signs to indicate where I was. An eerie and discouraging thought.

Everything was so quiet. Outside the purr of my car as it glided along, I could hear almost nothing. To break up the monotony, I'd rolled the windows down, letting the sound and chill of the air as it whipped by be the cadence that kept me awake. When my lids started to close despite the icicles forming in my eyes and nose, I decided it wasn't worth getting hypothermia for nothing and rolled the windows up again.

That almost instantly made it worse. I looked to my console for relief. A series of screens and fancy knobs peaked up at me but gave me no succor. I wanted to turn on the music and blast the heat, but I couldn't. Those were sure routes to sleep for me. What I really wanted was a bed. But not yet. I had to get there first. If I ever got there, I muttered silently to myself as I thought about what had gotten me into this situation.

Nothing worth thinking about, I told myself as I pulled my mind to the present and looked around again. Thinking was what got me into this mess in the first place. I sighed. I was lost, and just to add insult to injury, I had no cell reception and no NavMap. If anything happened, I could neither call anyone nor tell them where I was.

Creepy images danced behind my eyes, each one more gruesome than the last. Horror movies notwithstanding, I had more reason than some to fear the darkness, knowing only too well the possibilities of what could happen behind its veil. I shook my head and worked to brush the nagging feeling in the pit of my stomach away. It was harder than it should've been.

Aside from the lack of sound, there was a stillness that sat heavy upon the shoulders of the night, as if the universe was aware something was amiss and was holding its collective breath. Stop being such a baby, I told myself as I readjusted myself in the seat. God, I was so tired. Of their own accord, my eyelids started to droop once more. I needed rest. Not more than a few years ago I'd been conditioned to take the beating of little sleep, but not anymore.

I couldn't believe how much of a wimp I'd become. In another life, I relished the hours of darkness like a vampire might. Late nights, getting hauled out of bed at random hours, pushing myself to the limit, and beyond. But not anymore. Now, I was a chump who grumbled when she had to give up even some of her beauty sleep.

I pinched myself to ward off the sleepiness, but it did little to lift the fogginess that was starting to settle in permanently despite my best efforts. My vision blurred a bit as I felt myself drifting off. I couldn't discern if what little I was looking at was real or not. Despite the spookiness of where I was, I had to get off the road soon before I wound up injured, or dead. A chill that had nothing to do with the air outside swept over me. I was about to turn off toward the shoulder when a sound racketed through the quiet like a cannon. It was the unmistakable resonance of a gun.

Chapter Three

My hand clamped involuntarily to the wheel in response. I straightened and let my eyes scatter over the horizon, searching for what had caused such a god awful noise. Out in the backwoods, without the din of the city to muffle it, it sounded like a bomb.

It could be a game enthusiast I thought, then dismissed it. That was no rifle that had gone off, it had sounded like a 9mm, and there was little out in these woods that you'd hunt with so small a gun.

Jangled nerves pooled in my belly as I tried in vain to locate the source of the sound, but the engulfing blackness that surrounded everything outside the harsh beam of my headlights yielded nothing. Seconds ticked into minutes and nothing appeared. I was about to chalk it up as an odd circumstance when movement caught the corner of my eye. I didn't have to turn my head because before I knew it, the dark mass that had emerged from the woods stumbled straight out into the road in front of me.

Oh shit!

I had no time to think as I yanked the wheel hard and fast to the left. The car jerked, throwing me in the process, as I barely managed to avoid the stumbling figure. The icy road was unforgiving that night as my wheels lost traction and I began to slide out of control. Throwing the car in neutral, I wrenched up the e-brake and started pumping the floor brakes as I held on tight. My beast of a vehicle fish tailed and skidded over a few more feet of slippery asphalt. Automatically, hundreds of tiny spikes released from the wheels, catching the road just before I plowed head first into a recently formed snowbank. The sudden stop catapulted my body forward before the seat belt snapped taut and smashed me back to my seat, cranium first.

I gulped for air, my body vibrating with adrenaline, a dull sort of ache radiating out of my head as I sat forward and tried to take a look around. That proved to be a difficult as the windows were completely fogged up. I realized I was panting like a racehorse and, forcing myself to inhale and exhale slowly, I turned the defroster on and reached to assuage my throbbing neck. I thought about what I'd seen and for a second I thought it was just a figment of my imagination. No, someone was out there. Why they hadn't come up to my car yet, I didn't know, and the not knowing troubled me.

The windows cleared up a little but not enough, so I rubbed out a little hole in the mist and took a peak outside. I could see nothing. I felt like one of those idiot females in those old scary movies, the ones that go out into the woods with a known monster about with nothing but a flashlight and a stick for protection. Yet here I was, sitting in the car, contemplating going out into the darkness. *Come on, Rach, you're not new to this sort of thing. Just be a big girl, go out there and see what it is.* I always was the worst kind of hypocrite.

I held my breath and stepped out of the car so quickly I didn't have time to change my mind. There was nary a whisper and I could hear own my breath as it traversed up my lungs and exited in a frosty curl from my lips. Involuntarily, my tongue flicked out and licked my mouth. The simple motion bathed my withered lips, giving temporary solace before the bitter winter air sapped them dry once again, leaving them even more tortured than before. I started to lick them again when I realized what I was doing and stopped. I was behaving like a scared little girl and I needed to knock it off.

"Hello?" I called out, my voice sounding squeaky even to my own ears.

No sound was returned. I considered getting back into my car and driving away but as much as I wanted to, my feet would not take me. I cleared my throat.

"Hello," I said again, this time with more confidence, even if I didn't feel it.

Still no response. My gaze shifted, searching vainly for the man I'd seen but I saw nothing but black. I needed a light but the one on my wrist band was too weak. I remembered I had a good old fashion flashlight in my trunk. Yep, definitely one of those idiot females.

I wasted no time admiring the sleek lines or wide, tough body of the car I loved like a child as I tucked my hands under my armpits and made my way toward the back of the vehicle. A burst of wind cut through the trees as I started to move and my teeth started chattering almost instantly. The thick wool sweater I wore had been enough inside the comfort of my car but outside, the corroding cold was starting to cut into my bones. I glanced at my wrist band. Green lights from its screen broke up the obscurity of the night. December 22nd, 2058, 1:15 am, nuclear car battery at 37%, temperature 13 degrees. I stopped reading there and shivered as I reached the end of my black beast. Holding up my wrist, I touched the inlaid screen of the thick leather band and a series of holographic images appeared. I pushed the icon that was my car, and navigating the options a little more, I quickly found the button for the trunk and tapped it. It opened with a slight pop and I dove in, foraging into the jungle that was my luggage compartment. After a few well-articulated curses, I found my little light and checked it for charge. It worked. Yay.

I shut the trunk, the sound reverberating off the dead silence that enclosed me like a tomb. I pointed the contraption in the direction of the mass I'd seen earlier and started slowly toward it. The soft glow from the light bravely bore through the interminable inkiness, while my heart beat like a big brass band inside my chest. It was so loud that I was sure some feral animal somewhere could hear it and was licking its lips in wait.

As I continued forward, the thick aroma of pine needles and sweet sap glided through the crisp air, filling my nose and sidetracking my overactive imagination. That particular fragrance always reminded me of Christmas and the very reason I was out there in the first place. *Not now Rach, you need to focus.*

My foot landed on a soft patch of snow just then, crunching so suddenly and loudly that it made me jump. With unreasonable fear, I swished the light this way, then that, to see if anything was running for me. There was nothing. No animal, critter or creature had stirred. It made me realize just how alone I really was. Well, not quite. I continued forward as if a puppet on marionette strings until finally the light caught the edge of something. I should've fled instead. The unnatural placidness was a sure sign something was wrong. I told my poor dad once, god rest his soul, that I would rather be dead than afraid. If he hadn't been scathingly mad at me before I said that, he certainly was afterwards. Step by step the vague lines became sharper and sharper until the image was clear. It was a man! And he wasn't moving.

Chapter Four

I wasn't sure what I'd been hoping to find, but as I stood there like a dumbstruck child, two schools of thought roared within me. The first was to get the hell out of there and never look back. I had no idea who this man was, and considering that he'd followed the sound of a gunshot, it didn't seem like such a good idea to stick around. Then the second thought reared its ugly head. I couldn't just leave him like that.

Even while the debate warred inside my head, I inspected him as best I could from where I stood. He was on his side, his face was nearly plastered to the pavement. It was fairly obvious he was hurt. I mentally sighed. With my training, to leave him would be tantamount to murder. I wasn't going anywhere. My father's warning that a man would be my downfall rang through my head. I didn't think this was what he had in mind when he said it though.

"Sir," I called out softly.

When I got nothing, I tried again, this time in a higher voice.

"Sir, are you okay?"

Still nothing. I sucked in a deep breath. I didn't have time to second guess myself any more. Every moment I stalled was another second he could possibly not have. Pushing the fear aside, though not my vigilance, I closed the distance between us watching for even the slightest sign that he was in fact awake and luring me in, but there was no movement from him as I knelt down at his side.

"Sir, can you hear me?" I said as I shook him lightly.

There was no response.

"Are you even still alive?" I murmured as I started to inspect him.

Fresh perspiration pasted his hair to his forehead but he didn't appear to be breathing. I touched his neck. He was cool to the touch and despite shifting positions on his neck, I felt nothing. No, please, don't be dead. I reached for his wrist and shivered again. A nasty scar slashed down from the top of his wrist to the base of his palm. The skin was jagged but smooth, meaning recently formed but it was healed, so not my concern at the moment. No, the biggest problem was the lack of pulse.

Leaning back, I shined the light on him and nearly blanched at what I found. Red, thick and splattered, coated his white pajama shirt, and his bottoms were in tatters. Whatever had happened it'd, been bloody and violent. He looked like he'd checked out upon falling to the ground. I pressed a finger against his wrist again.

I was about to write him off when I saw the faint rise and fall of his chest. Then, at last, I felt the soft thump of blood as it coursed through his veins and massaged my forefinger. My body slumped with relief. He was alive.

My solace was short lived as I recognized that while he had a pulse, his heart beat was weak and thready.

That wasn't a good sign, and usually meant a loss of blood somewhere. Considering his clothes, it was likely he had a gaping wound somewhere, most likely a bullet wound.

I bit my lip. I was nervous about continuing. He was a complete stranger, covered in blood out in the middle of the woods, and I had no back up. For a moment I hesitated, but intrigue won over caution as my eyes caught sight of his shirt again.

The pattern was all wrong and with the amount of sweat coating him, his heart should be beating like a racehorse, not moving like a turtle. Curiouser and curiouser.

I placed his hand at his side and leaned back to look, shining my light across the full length of him. No obvious signs of injury were evident but I needed to inspect him further. I also needed to not be so damn exposed on the street I concluded.

Taking a chance that there weren't going to be any motorists for the next few minutes, I retrieved my car, parked it lengthwise across the highway near him and turned on my emergency blinkers. Next I shoved open the passenger door to bath the area in more light and give any would be drivers a heads up before I returned and scooted closer to get a better look. Opening one of his eyes, I shined my light on it. His blue iris was barely visible, the pupil heavily dilated, but the white part was regular, not red and splotchy. That was a good sign.

Popping the light in my mouth, I felt around the parts of his head and shoulders I could reach for any lesions, abrasions or contusions, but all I found was that his skin was loose, almost like it had lost its elasticity or something. I found nothing that would explain his sudden collapse or the blood. Tucking away the data, I nibbled at my bottom lip. I needed to shift him to finish my assessment but to do that I needed him secure. I needed a neck brace. As the thought skipped through my mind, I remembered some of the things in my trunk and groaned. It wasn't a great idea but I had no better.

I retrieved a pillow, an old medical kit, and a roll of duct tape I'd thrown in my trunk ages ago. Returning, I pared the pillow down to the right size and tucked it into the crook of his neck before I moved to his middle. Next I settled one hand on his hip while the other gently cupped the back of his head. With a quick prayer, I gave a tiny push and inch by slow inch, I rolled him to his back. My arms floated up from the released strain and I smiled in triumph, but it was short lived. I wasn't done yet.

After fastening the brace, I went about patting down his legs and arms and lifting away his coat as best I could to check for breakage or protruding bones. Nothing revealed itself. I placed my knees on either side of his hips to keep from jostling him and glided his sweater up with a gentle, but deft stroke. Grabbing the flashlight, I shone it on him and sucked in a small breath.

Open cuts crisscrossed his chest, almost as if he'd been using himself as a cutting board. *What were you doing? Running in the woods with scissors?* The thought was frozen in my mind but there was no obvious answer. I leaned forward, placing one hand to the ground to steady myself as I inspected closer.

The cuts were shallow and were already starting to clot, so they were not the cause of his low pulse. Dammit, what was wrong with him? A scent drifted up my nostrils. It wasn't a repugnant smell but very...different. Pine was the strongest aroma, but it was interlaced with a musk and a underlying fragrance that I couldn't quite place. The smell was strong, and it struck me that it was coming from him. I wanted to pull away but I couldn't, I was utterly absorbed by the mystery of him.

It wasn't until I felt the splash of his hot breath against my cheek that I realized just how close I'd gotten. Pulling back, I ignored the slight buzz across my body and climbed off. Whatever was afflicting him was beyond my training and that was my cue for the inspection to be over.

Chapter Five

It had taken some monkey-looking theatrics to get him into my car and strapped in but seeing that the man in question had at least fifty pounds on me, I considered myself heroic for the deed. Once I'd gotten behind the wheel though, all my enthusiasm had gone straight out the window. I still had no idea where in God's name I was. It was then I remembered seeing an atlas in my trunk, and popping out of the car once more, I retrieved it, feeling like a jack in the box.

Flipping to the right page, it didn't take long for me to locate where we were and where the nearest town was. My dad taught me to read maps when I was a kid. It wasn't a usual skill to teach anymore, but dear old pop had taken the scout motto of 'be prepared' to heart and had passed the gift on to me.

Incidentally, I also found the best route back to my intended destination. I closed the map and started the car, hoping that this little adventure was almost over, as I still had no idea who or what the man beside me was. Based on the fact I couldn't find any real injury on him, I concluded the blood on him wasn't his. This was both good and bad news. He would live, most likely, but it also inevitably meant the blood was someone else's. It was possible it belonged to an animal, but the gnawing sense of dread in my gut told me that it probably belonged to another human being. A dead one perhaps. Just please don't kill me, I thought to myself over and over as I drove. The only thing that placated me was the fact he was still unconscious.

Fifteen minutes later, I arrived to the outskirts of the town and found a recharge station. So pleased to see the innocuous platform way out there, I found myself smiling despite everything as I pulled into one of the slots. Civilization, I thought with satisfaction, meant people and people meant safety. At least of a sort.

The "slot" was nothing more than a space marked off in rectangular fashion by what looked like spray paint. The slab was made of a gelatin that slid out of the way, when instructed, to reveal a nuclear generator underneath. It was tricky when you were first learning to drive because if you parked in the wrong spot, the hose that came up from the generator and plugged into your battery would latch onto the wrong place and your car was wrecked. I, however, was not a neophyte.

"Engine off," I instructed my vehicle and I looked over at my passenger. He was so still that he looked dead. After a moment's hesitation, I put a finger under his nose to see if he was still alive. It took a second but the soft breeze of his breathing finally hit me. It wasn't strong, but at least I hadn't killed him in transit. That was always hard to explain to the authorities.

Leaning back, I looked at him, really, for the first time. In the brighter light provided by the station, I felt protected enough to indulge. He had a strong face despite the dark circles under his eyes and hollowed cheeks. If anything, the lean look accentuated his solid jaw line and his tanned skin mostly hid the strain housed in those circles. His mouth was almost succulent. Everything considered, he was quite attractive. I frowned.

Bundy, Steigler, and others were deemed handsome and look how they turned out. Sadly, my thoughts nearly always turned pessimistic. I hadn't started out that way, but the nature of my previous professions had influenced me. Looking at him I couldn't help but wonder, what events had led to him stumbling out of the woods like that? What was his story? Was it heartbreak, failure, or something more sinister that led a man to cold isolation in the middle of winter, covered in blood?

For the first time in a long time I felt not just fear, but the stirrings of a mystery. My heart sped up a little but the sound of the gunshot that had heralded the man next to me filled my ears. I frowned and shook my head. What was I thinking? It was time to call in the cavalry. The police and paramedics could take it from here.

I looked at the window, noted the utter lack of reception, and cursed the boondocks silently. With a sigh and the faintest tendril of regret, I reached for the door handle to let me out when an unexpected sound stopped me in my tracks.

A groan escaped from nearby and my body reacted instantly. I bucked as if shot and then stiffened. For several seconds I just sat like a proverbial frozen deer waiting for the car to come smashing into me. Even my breath was trapped inside my lungs, scared to move least the noise trigger something else. I had to move. I had to move.

"Wait," came a raspy, desperate male voice. "Please."

It was like a cannon in my head. A rush of adrenaline surged through me and I realized with some satisfaction that I was willing and ready to fight. Still, I couldn't stop the mad beating of my heart and the deathly fear that was coursing through me. When nothing happened, I slowly loosened my iron grip on the door handle and looked over at the man. For the second time in as many seconds, I flinched. I wanted to scream, but my tongue halted in my mouth, glued rigidly in place.

Violet colored eyes, rimmed with a soft blue hue, looked at me. They were brilliant, exotic, and scary as hell as they bore straight into me. Somewhere in the back of my mind, I was shouting at myself to look away, but I found I couldn't.

"Hello," he said weakly, breaking the spell that seemed to be holding me.

I exhaled a pent breath.

"Hi," I replied, not quite sure what else to say.

We were quiet as we stared, kind of like circling dogs, looking for chinks in armor or ways to proceed without getting bitten. When he failed to speak, I took the initiative.

"Who...uh, who are you?" I asked.

"Just a traveler," he replied with effort.

"Right. Just a traveler. Who's running around with a gun?" I asked, though it was more of a statement.

Something in his eyes shifted and he looked troubled.

"I have no gun," he said.

"Doesn't mean you didn't," I said. "I heard a shot."

He tried to sit up but whatever words he was going to say were lost as he dissolved into a hacking fit that racked his entire body. I put a hand on his shoulder in automatic response and slowly his coughing subsided.

"Thank you," he said with a wheezy breath.

"Well, at least you're polite," I muttered.

He tried to shift but ended up just grimacing.

"Are you okay?" I asked.

He gave a brief nod. "Been better, been worse."

"Tough guy, huh?"

He gave me a genuine smile then and it transformed his entire look in a flash. I felt myself relax. Slightly.

"What were you doing out on that road?" I queried.

"Walking," he replied hoarsely.

Smart ass. He gave a weak smile that almost looked like a smirk.

"I was," he insisted, but then started coughing again.

"Well, either way, I don't think it's a good idea for you to be talking much right now," I said quietly.

He gave a brief shrug and I realized I was still touching him so I pulled away.

"Listen, I'm going to be back in a second. I'm just going to call the paramedics..." I started to explain, then stopped.

He was shaking his head somewhat fervently and the cough came again. I reached for him again but he sat forward.

"You don't need to call anyone," he said, and paused to catch his breath. "I'm fine and my recovery will be swift."

"Fine? We must have different definitions because you can barely say five words without nearly losing a lung."

Besides, I thought to myself, what about the other guy? He shook his head again, more quietly this time.

"I see. So does this mean that you don't want hospitals, or you don't want cops?" I asked, hoping against hope he was just trying to be macho.

He fidgeted and my stomach dropped.

"Sure, uh, word of advice. Don't tell a stranger you don't want the cops around. Especially when you're covered with blood. Doesn't really give the right impression."

He looked at me for a long moment. His violet colored eyes appraising me, making me feel like squirming.

"You're not afraid of me," he finally said.

"You're wrong," I said lightly, "I'm terrified of you, but you can barely hold yourself upright so I'm managing."

He gave a faint smile. "I'm not a criminal."

"You're something," I mumbled.

"Please," he entreated quietly, "just drop me somewhere, forget about me."

I gave him a dubious look and he shook his head again.

"It's not safe," he said.

"What do you mean by that?" I asked.

Instead of answering, his eyes searched mine, as if willing me to comprehend. I studied him. Cops can be overbearing, arrogant assholes but over the years there was one thing that I learned the hard way. Just about anyone can plead their innocence with absolute conviction, but it doesn't make what they are saying true or right. The only people that ran from cops were people with something to hide.

"It's not that," he said softly, as if reading my thoughts. "It's just not that simple."

For the briefest of moments, I considered his request.

"Okay," I said softly, lest he hear the lie in my voice.

His face softened and another, brief, smile lit his face as his head fell back against the seat.

"Thanks."

The last part was said so softly I was almost sure I imagined it. Not more than a couple seconds later, I heard rough but even breathing. He was fading quickly.

"Hey, wait a second," I said, trying to keep him from going unconscious on me. "What's your name?"

He didn't answer, so I shook him a little. He stirred slightly.

"What's your name?" I asked again.

"John," he said softly.

"John what?" I asked.

When he didn't respond I shook him again and he groaned.

"What's your last name?" I asked.

"Doe," he said in little more than a mumble.

John Doe?! You're freaking kidding me. I was about to reach for him again, but his breathing had deepened and I knew he was really out of it now. Dammit.

My mind whirled. I wanted more information but I forced myself to pull back. Not your job, Rachel. Leave it to the authorities.

Still, I had no idea who this man was or whether he could end up hurting me. So I pulled up a camera app on my band and snapped a photo of him, just in case I was gone and the cops need someone to look for.

With that thought, I stepped out of the car and looked around. A pay phone sat at the far end of the establishment. I almost smiled. It was probably the last one still in existence, but considering the terrible reception, I was grateful for it. I made my way over and dialed 911.

The officer was dubious as he took my statement, but I didn't care. They'd have to come. After I hung up, I ambled toward the convenience store and just as I was about to reach the sliding doors, I saw the reflection of my vehicle in the glass. I came to a weary stop, processing what I'd seen far too slowly. With jaw slightly agape, I turned to see the passenger door of my car slung wide open and the only thing still sitting in it was the brace. The stranger had up and vanished.

A terrible anxiety gripped me as I looked around the station. There was not a sound, not of man nor beast. My eyes drifted back to the car. I'd swear on my life he'd been out cold, but the yawning passenger door and the lack of him in my seat was evidence to the contrary. Had he heard me make the call? Did he know who it was? I'd told him that I wouldn't report him and then seconds later I did just that. If he was going to attack, now would be the time. A gust of wind battered its ghostly hands on the glass behind me, shaking it in its tracks and making me jump. God, I was such a wuss I thought, as I held my hand to my chest.

When I finally turned back to the sliding doors of the store, I saw the clerk leaned over the counter, staring at me with no small measure of confusion. I must look like the village idiot. I thought about going back to my car, but I didn't feel safe. If the man who called himself John had just up and walked away, then he was in good enough condition to come after me.

Stepping inside, it was as though I was suddenly protected against an oncoming tidal wave. The girl behind the counter leaned back, but I could feel her eyes on me as I wandered the store. I wasn't really interested in anything, but I touched nearly every packet of food there was. Eventually, the clerk found me in one of the isles.

"Is there something I can help you find?" she asked.

Her thick drawl was polite enough, but I was fairly certain she was under the impression I was trying to steal something.

"Not really. Just trying to pass time," I replied.

"Oh," she said, though still looked a bit wary.

I didn't blame her.

"Actually I think I'll just pay for a charge up," I said.

"Okay, well come to the counter and I'll ring you up."

I followed after her, glancing out the window as I did to see if John was there, but he wasn't.

When I got to the counter she told me how much my purchase would cost. Without a word I lifted a hand, pulled my coat away from my wrist and held the band up to the reader. Some people had chips embedded that did the same thing, but this was safer according to my dad. It was also slower when the network was weak or overloaded, and way out here it was taking a bit for it to be processed. With a mental sigh, I started tapping on the counter to break the silence as time slowly marched forward. It wasn't long before I felt my body giving into the tiredness once again. It was worse than before. Whatever adrenaline had been propping me up was leaking out of my body like a tipped tea pot. Before I knew it my eyes started to droop.

"You okay?" the cashier asked me suddenly.

The unexpected sound and interest took me by surprise. In the City, everyone was so busy they barely gave you the time of the day, but this was the country and people here actually looked at you. I gave her a weak smile.

"Yeah, just a little tired," I replied.

"Well, there's a motel jus up the road on yur left, if ya wan."

The thought of a bed lifted my heavy eyes considerably.

"Is it clean?" I asked.

She shrugged. "It's the only one around for miles."

Not encouraging, but before I could ask anything else the cash register beeped, letting me know my purchase was approved.

"Thanks for the tip," I said, and gave her a little wave as I exited.

Stopping before I stepped down from the store platform, I looked around once more. I was still on alert, but I felt better knowing the cashier was there and was a potential witness. Reaching my car, first I shut the passenger door, then I climbed into the driver seat and called for the computer to turn on. The windshield lit up in front of me and a faint, familiar hum ensued. Touching the glass, I scrolled through the options till I found the recharge app and hit the "go" button. As I waited for the battery to recharge, I looked at the vacant seat once again. Where in the hell was he? How was it possible for him to just up and disappear like that?

My head was swimming. The harder I tried to think, the worse my fatigue got. I thought about getting up to call the cops back to let them know there was no need to come, but it wouldn't matter because they had to respond. Besides, I was too damn tired to move.

Slowly the exhaustion wore through any remaining resistance I had and I found my head resting against the dashboard. I just couldn't keep my eyes open any longer. As darkness crowded in on me, images and memories started to swirl. In moments, I was down for the count.

Chapter Six

A loud knock ricocheted inside my car, startling me awake. Shaking off the sleep induced grogginess, I rubbed my eyes and glared up at whoever or whatever made that terrible racket. My gaze landed on the tall uniformed frame of a police officer standing just a couple of feet from me. Traveling up his thin structure, my eyes landed on a cherubic looking face with absolutely no hair on it, and dark black eyes that looked at me sheepishly. He couldn't be much older than twenty and by the nervous twitch of his fingers, I was guessing he'd probably seen as much action on the job as a goat in the city. Great. This was going to be interesting.

"Ms. Davenport?" he asked.

"That's me," I said with a yawn.

"Are you the one who called in a few minutes ago?" the young officer asked hesitantly.

Like there was more than one Rachel Davenport in this tiny patch of nowheresville, I thought as I stood up and suppressed a moan at the pain that erupted from my head. I had a hell of a headache. I wondered if there was an apothecary nearby so I could get something for it, but quickly dismissed the idea. I'd just have to suck it up.

"Yes, I'm the one who called in," I said, rubbing my neck.

"Okay then. Well, uh-" he stopped and looked at me with a quizzical quirk of his brows.

From nearby, someone cleared their throat.

"What Officer Torres means to be saying is, where is the body?" another man said with a thick Virginian accent.

I looked over to see another uniformed Officer, only this one was still sitting in his car. He was a big bellied man, with a scruffy gray beard and a toothpick sticking out of his mouth. If it wasn't for a pair of sharp eyes watching me from under his patrol hat, I'd almost have said he was your typical redneck. He had a knowing look on his face though, that meant he'd already summed up and categorized the call. He was the worst kind of cop. I turned back to Torres.

"If you're asking if he's dead, then the answer is no. I never called in a homicide."

"No one is saying that," Torres returned quickly, "We just don't see anyone here."

"So we want to know where the body is," the big cop chimed in.

"We'd like to know what happened," Torres corrected immediately.

I looked back to the Officer sitting in his car and found the gold name stenciled into his black shirt.

"Did you know, Officer Gill," I said, "that the penalty for not taking proper notes at a 911 call is up to 6-week suspension, without pay? Regulation 22.94 I believe. Not to mention bad form."

One glance at his empty hands was enough to wipe the smirk off his face, as well as stir him from his seat. I didn't wait for him to get prepared to take my statement as I returned my attention to Torres.

"I was driving down the road when a man came out of the woods," I said, starting to explain.

Torres frowned but held up a finger, indicating for me to pause. He touched his band and after a few moments he found the record option and turned it on.

"Can you repeat what you just said, ma'am?" he asked.

I did so.

"What road?" he queried.

I pointed in the direction I'd come from.

"For the record, Ms. Davenport is pointing towards Route 223 South," Torres said, and then looked back at me. "Where did this man come out of the woods at?"

"I have no idea," I replied. "There weren't exactly posted signs."

He blinked as if he didn't understand what I meant by that. I nearly rolled my eyes.

"It was approximately two miles if that helps," I added.

"It does, thanks," he said seriously. "So can you tell me what happened next? Did he attack you?"

He sounded so eager. I couldn't help but wonder if this was his first call ever.

"No" I said, "he didn't attack me. He just stumbled out of the woods and then collapsed."

"Oh," he replied and was clearly confused.

"What?"

"In your call you stated that he was in your car."

"He was. I loaded him up and brought him here before I called you guys," I said, feeling like I was explaining things to a child.

"It's not that I'm not impressed by that but..."

"What's the issue, officer?"

"So uh, just to make sure I'm understanding this, you found a man you didn't know in the middle of the road, in the middle of the night, and you put him into your car?" he asked.

I almost cringed at that.

"Well, when you put it like that, I feel like an idiot," I replied with a faint smile.

Torres glanced at Gill as if to get permission for something and when the big bellied cop shrugged, it was all he needed.

"You uh, you've seen the alert right?" he said a little anxiously.

"I have no idea what you're talking about."

"There was a Federal alert issued a few days ago and there's been a lot of chatter that any unknown persons that you run into should be reported."

I blinked. "You can't be serious."

He nodded.

"Well, by that decree I should report you, Officer Torres, because I definitely don't know who you are."

Torres had nothing to say to that as his cheeks flared pink. For all of his floundering, he did sound sincere so I took pity on him.

"The Feds issue alerts all the time," I explained, "I don't really pay any attention to them. Besides I don't think they sent that one to the City."

"Oh, uh, okay," he stuttered, and then seemed to recover as his shoulders straightened and he caught my eye. "So uh, this man, can you tell us where he is now?"

My jaw clenched. I suddenly felt all kinds of stupid and the words that came out next were like glass. This was the very thing I wished that I could avoid. I cleared my throat.

"I don't know."

Torres's eyes went round and I heard Gill snort. Just great.

"I'm not sure I understand, ma'am," Torres said carefully.

I sighed. I didn't either.

"When I found him I checked him out before I moved him."

"What do you mean by that?" Torres asked, butting in.

"I inspected him against the NPG," I said, then saw his confusion and clarified, "the National Paramedic Guidelines. Anyway I checked to see if he was alive and tried to assess what kind of condition he was in."

"Oh," he said again. I was starting to wonder if he had been raised by a family of owls.

"And to answer your next question, no, I didn't find anything wrong with him."

"I see," he said, though it was obvious he didn't. I couldn't exactly blame him on that count. I was confused too. "So what happened after that?"

"I came here and called you guys."

There was silence and I looked from one to the other. They looked about as convinced as a pair of pigeons.

"Is that all, Ms. Davenport?" Gill asked, speaking up for the first time in a while.

I looked at him and gave him a cool expression. "Yup."

"So you mean to tell me," Gill said, "that you just happened to be moseying along back here in our woods, and you just happened upon this man?"

The gleam in Gill's eyes was one of disbelief and his tone, of condescension. I wanted to snap at him, but instead I gritted my teeth and nodded.

"Right," he said. "Well, assuming all that is true, you'd have us believe that you got him here and then after you called us, he just up and disappeared?"

"I believe that's what I just finished saying," I replied.

"Well shit," Gill exclaimed, slapping his thigh, "I ought to just get in my car here and start whistling down the road. Maybe then he'll just come out of hiding."

"Maybe he will," I flipped back, very annoyed by this time.

"What's his name, huh?" Gill prodded.

"I have no idea," I said through clenched teeth.

"So you gonna get around to the part of just how exactly you found him?" Gill asked. "Were ya just traveling around, looking for a stranger or something?"

"I heard a gunshot and-"

"Oh, so now there's a gunshot? Why didn't you open with that?"

I bit my tongue. I was so tempted to mouth off, but engaging a dull cop was not the smartest of moves. I looked back to Torres.

"The man I found was covered in blood and his clothes were ripped, like he'd been in some kind of fight. If I were you, I'd check to make sure there wasn't a dead body somewhere."

Torres made sure everything was recorded and then looked up.

"So...are we done then?" I asked.

"Well, there isn't much to go on, but if you could come down to the station and give us a description that'd be great," he said.

I was tired and judging by the bored look on Gill's face, he had no intention of following up on the case. It made my decision to not show them the photo I'd taken all that much easier to justify. Let 'em work for it. Still, this little run in wouldn't be worth it if I didn't give them something so I ducked into my car and carefully retrieved the pillow I'd sacrificed earlier.

"I used this as a neck brace," I said, "it'll have his DNA."

"That yur pillow?" Gill asked, while Torres took it and sealed it in an evidence bag.

"Yup, but I'm sure your tech guys will have the equipment to sort out what's what and my DNA is on file."

"I'm sure it is," Gill replied, his smirk back.

I ignored his comment.

"So if that's it, I'd like to be on my way now."

Torres snuck a quick glance at his partner, silently communicating something. Gill sighed as he looked back at me.

"What were you doing out at this time of night?" Gill asked.

"Why?"

"Just curious," he said with a shrug.

"No, you're not. You're looking for an excuse to not follow up."

It came out a little snappier than I intended and I could almost see the gleam return to Gill's eyes.

"You've got some anger issues don't you?" he prodded.

"That's not your concern," I bit out.

"What are you doing out here?" he asked again.

"I'm visiting a friend," I replied, not rising to his bait.

"That friend have a name?"

"They sure do, but I'm pretty positive you don't need it."

Gill gave me a long look before he glanced over at Torres and gave a tiny shake of his head.

"Don't much matter," the big cop said over his shoulder as he turned and made toward the driver's seat of his cruiser. "I'm sure I can find you again if I need to, especially with your prints being on file and all."

The sentence was punctuated with the slam of a car door. Gill was apparently done with the whole thing.

"Sorry about all that," the young cop said with a sheepish smile, "I'll make sure everything is taken care of from here though, okay?"

I nodded, but knew nothing was going to happen. It didn't matter. Whatever they did was their business. At least now my part was over.

Chapter Seven

After the cops left I tucked myself back into my car and took off. I debated if I should stop or not. It wasn't that much farther to the Oliver's, and I really wanted to see them, but as I started driving again the bone deep tiredness set in once more and I decided I really didn't want to see those damn cops again if I crashed.

When I saw a rickety sign for the motel, I turned in. It was a small, low lying, brick complex that looked old, but quaint. There was a plaque on its front pillar that said that it had been established in 1990, and I couldn't help but be impressed. Somehow this simple structure had survived the brutality of the Oil Crisis in 2025. A period of history fraught with both the worst of humanity and the best of it. A time that fascinated me in some ways because despite our propensity as a race for self-destruction, we managed to come together in the eleventh hour and pull ourselves up by the bootstraps. I wondered briefly, as I stepped through the sliding glass doors, if we weren't again headed in the same direction.

The lobby was tiny, with little more than a couch and coffee maker on one side, and a green, faux marble check-in counter on the other. There was no one at the counter, but there was a little sign and an arrow indicating a screen to tap to call the clerk. I reached over and hit the screen, dinging the bell.

A few seconds later the door behind the counter creaked as it lumbered open. I almost expected a hatchet-bearing zombie to appear from behind the wooden frame and grin at me evilly. No such thing happened however. Instead, a portly man with a neatly trimmed white beard stepped out from behind the door labeled "Staff Only". He spotted me and his soft brown eyes crinkled as he smiled.

"Good mornin'," he said in a thick Southern accent. "How can I help ya?"

He was pleasant and friendly and I took to him immediately.

"I'd like a room if you don't mind," I replied with a subtle drawl, sliding back into old habits without even thinking about it.

He gave me a surprised look.

"Your accent is good," he said. "Georgia?"

I smiled and nodded.

"Nearly seven years," I answered with a little nod in acknowledgement of a fellow southerner.

His smile widened as he tipped his balding head back at me.

"Well then, for you darlin', you can have whatever you like."

"In that case honey, give me the deluxe suite. I won't settle for anything less than a Jacuzzi tub and a king size bed."

My air of society was brief but amusing to both of us as he gave me a mock salute and went into the inlaid computer in his desk to set up my room.

"So, why you'd move from the last of God's country?" he asked as he started typing.

Old resentments twisted inside me and I found any good left in my mood evaporating. He must've caught my sour look because the next thing he said was, "I'm sorry, that's really none of my business."

I gave him a weak attempt at a smile, though I said nothing. I really didn't want to talk and he seemed to understand because I was left alone with my thoughts. They travelled straight to the stranger from the road. I wanted to not be curious, but I just couldn't help myself. I couldn't figure out how he'd gotten out of my car in the condition he was in. If this was the only place around for miles, then it was logical he could end up here. I bit my lower lip. You really shouldn't Rachel. It's not your job.

"Hey," the old man's gentle voice broke through my thoughts, "you alrigh?"

I looked up to see him staring at me, his dark eyes filled with concern. For some reason it made me feel bolder. I knew I shouldn't, but I found the prospect of digging in just a little too appealing. I bit my lip and mentally shook myself to get in the right frame of mind.

"I know this is going to sound strange," I said, letting my face fall and making my voice go smaller. "Have you, uh, I mean have there been any guys who sorta stumbled in here in the last half hour or so?"

"Would any fella' do?" he asked, giving me a curious look. "Cause around here ma'am, that might not be specific enough."

I smiled and pulled up the photo I'd taken. Tapping on it, it sprung up from my band into the air. I touched the button on the bottom of the image to flip it around.

"This is the one I'm interested in," I said, with just a touch of hope added in at the end.

"Oh. Is he yur boyfriend or something?"

"Well, no but-" I cut myself off.

The expression on the clerk's face was coloring toward suspicion and I knew this was going south fast. Oh, boy here we go. I didn't have to of course, but in for a penny, in for a pound.

"Well," I said with syrupy sweetness and a faint blush creeping up my neck, "he's my fiancé, but we just had a fight and I kicked him out of the car, so I'm not sure where we stand. I...I just really need to talk to him."

The man raised his brows and looked at me uncertainly, deciding if he should believe me or not. My blush grew stronger and I looked to my feet as if embarrassed.

"I thought he was cheating on me," I said, "so I hired a PI to check into him, and well, we came up here for a little alone time, but somehow he found out about it and he wasn't too happy."

It came out in a rush, as though I was trying to defend and explain myself all over again. I hesitantly looked up at the man from behind lowered lashes. His face had fallen and I could tell he bought it, hook, line, and sinker. If only Grams could see me now. She had been a real starlet in her day and, as the only female child in the last couple generations, she'd tried her best to bestow her gift on me. She'd taught me well, but that line of work wasn't for me. I liked the grisly and gruesome more than fame and fortune. Go figure.

The old clerk took another look at the picture.

"You guys into mud wrestling or something?" he asked at last.

I was confused for a second and then looked at the image. The man was a mess. I gave a sheepish smile as I clicked the photo closed.

"Yeah, something like that," I replied.

He chuckled, then said in a sympathetic voice, "I haven't seen yur fella but ya want me to send him to yur room when he shows?"

"If he shows," I mumbled miserably.

"Well, unless he wants ta walk all the way home, he'll show."

I leaned in conspiratorially and the old man did as well, obviously lapping up my story.

"This might sound bad," I said softly, "but would ya mind calling me first? I don't know what kind of mood he'll be in when he gets here."

"Of course," he said with a wink.

For the briefest moment I felt guilty for playing him, but when he handed me a scanner, I tossed the remorse aside. Pressing my thumb against the small, metal plate that would read my fingerprint and give me access to my room, I waited patiently for the computer to beep.

"Room's ready to go," he said after a moment. "Hope everything works out."

"I'm sure it will, and thank you," I replied, the lie falling easily from my lips as I headed back outside.

A soft glow from the stray light posts in the parking lot lit up my car. I started toward it but something slowed me. A sensation, like that of being watched. The hair on the back of my neck prickled and my muscles tensed. I wasn't a superstitious person, but something felt amiss.

My eyes struggled to penetrate the stark threshold of black just beyond the parking lot, but I couldn't see anything beyond the few cars in the lot and the faint outline of trees. Still, I could feel something out there, something concealed under the shadows gifted by the light. A shiver ran up me as the wind kicked up, tossing my hair about. Errantly, I brushed back the long strands just as a loud, screeching squawk rent the silence of the night.

I nearly jumped out of my skin. Taking a second to calm down, I laughed at myself. I was being ridiculous. Jumping at the sounds of a bird for christ's sake. Even with that, I didn't move. My bag was in the car and there was a change of clothes in it I could use, but I didn't feel like getting it. Stop it, I scolded myself, there's nothing there but the wildlife.

I sighed, shaking my head at my foolishness as I retrieved my bag and walked to my room. Without succumbing to any more of my overtired imagination, I drew the curtains closed and flopped onto the bed, practically bouncing off the flat, unforgiving surface. The joys of travel, I mused as I discarded my coat and bra, then burrowed between the scratchy sheets and laid my head on the threadbare pillow. As I started to drift off, I thought of the stranger again. The mystery of him gnawed at me but I just couldn't concentrate any more. Whatever his story was, it was none of my business and I really should keep it that way.

Chapter Eight

The darkness was a gift that he used to the fullest. Traveling during the day was taxing, but at night, especially in this part of their world, it was liberating. No lights to reflect off of him, and no people to interfere with his work.

At last, the woman he'd been trailing had gone to sleep. The creature he was tracking was here somewhere. Of that he was certain, and he was of the mind that he would show himself soon.

Jah'ls pale eyes penetrated the darkness to suss out whatever clues he could find. His hearing extended, but the wind was rampant, rustling the branches nearby and creating a sort of chanty, like a hum in the background. A few birds flittered about nearby, every movement causing him to jerk his glance this way, then that.

Aside from those small critters that dared to be out at this hour, there was no other movement, and no other heat signatures aside from the ones inside the rooms. Despite the plethora of reasons why he should move on, he stayed where he was. The one he sought was here, hiding amongst the living. It was his modus operandi, but even with that knowledge, Jah'l was having trouble locating him.

Closing his eyes, he sniffed the air once more. The scent had been stronger back at that station where the woman had stopped, but still it lingered here, on her. Logically, it was enduring on the woman as a result of her contact with the creature, but Jah'l was more experienced than that. There was too much freshness in the smell. A faint sound, like that of a throat clearing, sounded in his head and he opened his eyes.

"Hello, Jule."

The voice was clear and clean, and female. A tendril of annoyance flicked through him at the continued mispronunciation of his name, but he said nothing.

"Where are you now?" she asked softly.

"On the trail," he replied, his silver eyes flashing with displeasure.

There was a little shock that came through their connection but it was quickly tamped down. She said nothing, but the irritation in him flared. Not because he was being contacted or even that tabs were being kept on him. That was par for the course when it came to his boss, and she was one of few he allowed such control. No, his exasperation came from the one he was tracking. Twice the mongrel had slipped through his fingers, and that was not usual. At all.

"You were close," she stated at last.

"Yes."

"The camp?"

"It was covered."

"By him?" she queried.

Truthfully, she needn't have asked as she could've viewed the scene if she wanted to, but it helped him to dispel his frustration and she knew it.

"Yes," he replied again.

"Well, at least he's getting better at covering his tracks."

Jah'l snorted. The man was a rank amateur as far as he was concerned, not even worth the effort to track, yet somehow he'd been tasked and now, he was being eluded. For days. Not tackling that subject, the woman moved on.

"The one who found him," she said, "the woman, were they in contact long?"

"No."

There was a sense of relief through the line that he didn't quite understand. Why did she care? Another casualty at the man's hands at this point shouldn't bother her.

"Did the woman say anything to anyone?" she asked.

This time she looked and saw the structure with generators and bright lights in his mind. He didn't know what they were called, so didn't try, but he'd arrived just as another vehicle with swishing red and blue lights, pulled up. The scene of them questioning her and her responses ticked through his head. He heard his boss laugh softly.

"She's amusing," she said.

Jah'l said nothing to that. There was another pause, this one lengthier.

"There's something unusual about her," she stated finally, but her voice was distant.

He didn't ask how she knew that, because she would never give a satisfactory explanation. Instead he waited. She was most likely rifling through his images and by the short intake of breath, she'd landed on the last scene, when the woman in question had stopped and turned directly toward him.

"She sensed you," she said, clearly surprised.

That wasn't something that happened often. There was a stretch of silence and he tensed.

"Is he with her?" she asked.

Jah'l understood the question in all its multiple meanings.

"Nearby," he said.

"You're certain?"

"Yes."

"Watch her," was all she said.

"What about him?"

"He will follow," she stated simply.

"And if I find him?" Jah'l asked.

"Do not engage."

With that, their connection was severed. Something was afoot. He could feel it. His boss had faltered, just for a second, which could only mean that something had triggered. His gaze refocused back on his surroundings. Life for the woman in the motel was about to get a whole lot more interesting.

About Rhiannon Matlock

Born in 1981 before YouTube, Twitter or Twilight, Rhiannon Matlock remembers when you played your songs on Walkmans and actually had to tell your mother where you were going before you went out to play.

Now a well-seasoned traveler who still considers herself a child at heart Rhiannon enjoys such diverse activities as bungee jumping, white water rafting and volunteering in third world countries, but dislikes slow drivers and people who malign their friends.

Rhiannon doesn't like to talk about herself much, insisting that everyone else has a much more interesting story to tell. She especially likes to spin a good yarn, particularly ones where the white hat wins.

Connect with Rhiannon online:
facebook.com/rhiannonmatlock

Jacob

By Erika Lance

Part One: The Policy Change

It was one of the worst days in months at the ward. Brynn was at her wits end nearing the end of a fourth 12-hour shift. Out of instinct she had just ducked a flying bed pan. She looked up to see who her assailant was and found that it was Margaret. Brynn sighed and moved around the desk.

"Are you ok Margaret?" Brynn didn't know why she was asking. Working in the mental ward of one of the largest regional hospitals St. Michaels, she knew anyone who had been checked into her floor was less then ok.

Actually, that had been true until about two weeks ago. Hospital management had changed the strict admission policy that used to govern this portion of the hospital. In the past, in order to be admitted to the Psych Unit a patient had to, at least at the time of admission, show signs they had a condition that needed treatment.

A doctor would evaluate before admission paperwork even began and decide to admit the patient or not. Although Brynn had seen many flaws with that system, it *had* kept those who really didn't need treatment out of her area of the hospital, and her out of having to do paperwork for every one of them. Because the hospital had changed its policy to no empty beds, life was now a nightmare for all of the staff in Brynn's unit, doctors included.

The policy change, made by upper management, was an attempt to up the profits of the hospital. This didn't take into account patient care, and Brynn had found that in the business of healthcare, the bottom-line was more important than the people they were caring for.

As the Lead Charge Nurse, Brynn was responsible for all of the other nurses and charts in her unit. While most people had the misconception that nurses are run by the doctors, nurses are almost an independent unit, with the exception of those functions that a nurse cannot do, such as write prescriptions or perform surgery. Everything else, keeping track of the patient's status, meds, and overall information, sat squarely with the nurses.

Because Brynn's unit had followed the policy of only admitting those who needed care, they had empty beds. These beds were routinely filled with the hospitals cast outs from other departments, not because the patient didn't legitimately have a problem, but usually because they were a difficult case to manage.

The change in policy applied to the entire hospital, but Psych felt it the most. Always under staffed, attempting to take care of patients that didn't have any issues regularly got in the way of taking care of patients that did. Such as Margaret, who had suffered a breakdown after the death of her husband, had been admitted after she began to fly into violent rages.

Margaret had been picked up and brought in after an incident at a grocery store that involved the destruction of several end cap displays. Looking at the frail and still visibly sad woman in front of her, Brynn couldn't fault her for being mad about her current lot in life. She could ensure she wasn't on the receiving end of the rage however.

Brynn walked up to Margaret and asked, "What is wrong?" Brynn was prepared for anything, including being punched in the face by this grandmother, so it was heartbreaking when tears started streaming down the woman's face.

Wrapping her arm around the sobbing woman, Brynn turned her and walked her toward her room. Knowing there wasn't a pill or shot in the world to take away the pain of losing a husband of over forty years, she motioned to the med nurse for some Valium to help Margaret sleep.

Part Two: Filling a Bed

Just as Brynn got Margaret settled she heard the one page she hoped not to receive in the less than fifteen minutes before she was supposed to head out, a patient being brought up for admission. With no doctors currently on the unit, admission was required until he or she could be evaluated in the morning.

When Brynn got to the desk there was a young man, wearing scrubs, sitting in one of the wheelchairs that the emergency room used to bring up intakes. He was accompanied by one of the interns relegated to the task of moving patients from unit to unit.

As she neared the two, the young man looked up and directly at her. His eyes were a piecing cobalt blue, and he looked at her face as if expecting something.

The intern cleared his throat, which made Brynn realize she was staring. The intern, she thought his name was Chris, but they never were at the hospital long enough for it to matter or for her to care, handed her a folder and the clipboard gesturing where she needed to sign saying, "Turkey and Bed," and nodding in the direction of the wheelchair.

"Turkey and Bed" was code that usually meant a homeless person looking for a meal, a shower, and a warm/safe place to sleep. The name 'Turkey' was because turkey sandwiches were usually on the menu in the cafeteria. Because the young man was wearing scrubs and holding a bag on his lap, she could almost confirm this to be the case.

She signed the receipt of the patient and handed the clipboard back to Chris, or whatever his name was, who quickly left. Most interns didn't like hanging around in Psych, and those that did were usually a little bit off in the head themselves.

Brynn opened the chart. The young man's name was Jacob Morrison, and this was not the first, fifth, or even tenth time Mr. Morrison had been seen by the doctors at St. Michaels. She reviewed the latest chart. He said he was seeing things that weren't there. This was a typical excuse used by the homeless to get them in for their brief stay. Because they had no form of payment, they would they would stop seeing things pretty quickly, and be released back into the world.

She looked up at him. "Do you know where you are, Mr. Morrison?"

"Jacob," he replied.

"What?" Brynn asked.

"Jacob. You can call me by my first name." He smiled.

He had a warm smile for someone who had obviously been living on the streets for some time.

Brynn smiled back. "Ok then...do you know where you are, Jacob?"

He held the smile and said, "I am in the Psych Unit of St. Michaels on the 8th floor. It is Thursday, the fourth of October, at about 10pm would be my guess."

Brynn nodded.

"Do you know why you are here?" she asked.

This was part of a series of questions to find out how lucid a patient was. Especially for those being admitted at night, it was important to determine if they would need any form of sedation before they saw the doctor in the morning.

He looked down then, pursed his lips together and then spoke. "Yes. I am seeing things that aren't there. It has been happening the last couple of days." This was rehearsed. She had heard it hundreds of times.

"Can you walk?" she asked.

"Yes," he said nodding.

"Ok then, let's get you a shower. I assume you remember the rules?" she asked.

Again he nodded, then stood up from the chair. He was carrying a backpack, along with what she assumed were the clothes he had come in wearing. They make the patients take them off in the ER for fear of bedbugs or lice.

"I need you to give me your backpack, which I will lock-up till you check out, and I will make sure your clothes are washed tomorrow," she said as she reached out her hand.

"Can I keep my book?" Jacob asked, handing over the bag of clothes first.

"Sure," she replied, and he reached into the bag and pulled out a very worn copy of *Cabal* by Clive Barker, and then handed her the backpack.

She looked at him a little puzzled. "Are you sure that book is a good idea given the reason you're here?"

"It keeps me grounded," Jacob said, and headed in the direction of the showers.

Brynn stored his backpack, which had symbols all over it, written in different pens and markers she saw. She also tagged his laundry and put it in the bin, then had a tray of food brought in. When she was done she saw Jacob emerge from the showering area.

"Are you hungry?" she asked, holding out the tray near the common room and indicating there was a table there he could sit at.

He smiled again. "Yes. Thank you."

He took the tray and went to eat.

Brynn placed him in a bed and turned over all the paperwork to her replacement, Sarah, for the night. She checked in on him one more time before she left, and made sure she introduced him to Sarah.

He smiled, studied her face for a moment, then nodded and went back to eating.

Part Three: Is This a Health Issue?

Brynn managed to get a full six hours of sleep. She felt like it was a new record, considering how the week had gone. She almost felt refreshed when she put on her scrubs, made a protein smoothie to take to work, and ate her oatmeal.

As she drove in, Brynn got a text from the overnight charge nurse. "B – Marco on your floor today. Wanted to warn before you got here."

Marco was the last person she needed assigned to her unit this week. He had been assigned to the psych floor unit for over four years, three-and-a-half more than Brynn and most of the other nurses and techs believed he should have been.

Unfortunately for all involved, Marco was under the delusion that he was the most amazing thing to exist on the floor, and in the hospital in general. He regularly refused to listen to her as the lead, and when it came to doing intake paperwork he would suddenly need to be somewhere else. He had once angered the med nurse so badly, she had charged immediately into HR to file a formal complaint. Since Marco had been caught on camera everyone believed that would be the end of his reign on the floor. Apparently, that wish was just not intended to come true.

As the elevator doors opened she heard the sounds of a struggle and screaming, and she saw Marco and the med nurse, Chris, trying to restrain Jacob.

Jacob's eyes were locked on Marco and he was screaming, begging to be let go. Brynn dropped her stuff on the desk and headed to the med cart. As she typed in her code she asked, "What set him off?" She ended up repeating it twice, each time louder than the last.

"I went to check on him and he just started freaking out," Marco said, while Jacob struggled to get out of Marco's hold.

Brynn approached and yelled, "Jacob!" For a brief moment it seemed to snap Jacob out of the panic he was in. He was pale and sweating. Brynn could tell he was having a true attack.

He met her gaze and said, "Please help me...Please!"

Before Brynn could say anything to sooth him, Marco said, "I will help you...right back into your bed for the day." He turned to look at Brynn and nodded while saying, "Do it!" Brynn hated sedating patients unless she had no other choice, but this wasn't one of those situations.

"Jacob! Look at me!" Brynn knew she had only moments to retain any hope of controlling this situation. Jacob began to turn his head toward her when Marco let go with one arm and grabbed the syringe from Brynn's hand, removed the cap with his teeth and jabbed it into Jacobs arm.

The look on Jacob's face was a terror that Brynn had rarely seen. It was the look a child had when their abusive parent walked into the room.

The drug was fast acting and Jacob began to slump in their arms. "What the hell was that?" Brynn asked Marco. "That was me handling the situation, which you seem incapable of doing." She rarely wanted to hurt another person, but this was one of those moments. Brynn narrowed her eyes.

Chris said, "Let's get him cleaned up and into bed." Brynn looked down and saw that Jacob had soiled himself. Brynn looked from Marcos to Chris, and she could tell from the look Chris gave her she needed to do what he said.

They brought Jacob into his room and Marco let him flop onto his bed, then walked out. Brynn waited until she thought he was out of earshot to ask Chris, "What the hell happened?" She began to peel off Jacob's clothes and clean him up.

"I don't know, B. Marcos arrived about an hour ago. We began to hand out the breakfast trays, and when Jacob came up to get his tray he took one look at Marco and...it was like he knew him or something," Chris said as she continued to remove the dirty clothes and wipe Jacob down.

"Just looked at him and freaked out?" Brynn asked. She saw they had returned Jacob's clothes. She grabbed the bag and began to dress him.

Chris nodded. "Yes. Jacob backed away, but Marco followed him and eventually cornered him in the common room. When I got there the screaming had already started, and Jacob was trying to away from him. He kept saying something about monsters. He said Marco was a Reaper, or something like that."

"Monsters?" Brynn asked, looking down at Jacob's tear streaked face. "Has the doctor seen him yet?" she followed up, before Chris answered the first question.

"No. Not yet."

Brynn stood up. "Monsters," she whispered.

"What?" Chris asked.

"Nothing, just wondering if this is medical," she said as she gathered the laundry and
headed out of the room.

"Are you thinking delusional?" Chris asked.

"It would explain the freak-out. The doctor would have to decide for sure," was her reply.

When Brynn got to the desk she put her stuff away and grabbed Jacob's file. She would hopefully have time later to review it. She grabbed the other charts and began the work that Marco should have been doing, but she was thankful that he wasn't sitting next to her as she could feel her rage begin to boil again over what had happened.

When Dr. Hillman arrived a little after ten Brynn had, much to her surprise, all of the charts ready for review. She handed them to him one at a time as he reviewed them. Most he just signed off on. When there was a proposed discharge, or an intake, there was more work, but mostly the nurses made recommendations and the Doctors signed off. When Dr. Hillman got to Jacob's file, he paused. He flipped through some of the last charts within the file and then looked at Brynn. "Drug case?"

Brynn shrugged and said, "I don't know. He seemed coherent last night. If it's spice though, there would be no way to know."

The doctor nodded, made a note and then said, "Order a CBC and a tox screen," and handled the folder back.

Asking Dr. Hillman if he was interested in seeing the patient first, before ordering any tests, was ridiculous. Most of the time doctors treated the patients by the doctor's opinion of what he thought was wrong with the person. Unfortunately, most mental conditions are a combination of symptoms. Instead of being able to test for what a patient was suffering from, they had to test for all the other things it could be and eliminate them. For instance, when someone is schizophrenic they would test for syphilis. If the patient didn't have that, then they might have a mental disorder.

If a doctor was unwilling to take the time to figure out if the person was on drugs, had a medical condition, or was just suffering from a chemical or hormone imbalance, then the patient ended up in an endless cycle, not being treated for what was actually wrong with them.

Brynn took the folder and smiled the practiced smile of a nurse. "I will let you know as soon as the results are in."

Taking blood from Jacob was easy. He was still out and therefore could not consent. Not that they needed his consent, but having the veil of patient rights was sometimes worth the work.

The results were negative. When Brynn relayed the news to Dr. Hillman, she had to remind him who Jacob was and the reason for the tests. Jacob was labeled delusional and prescribed injections of Haldol, Ativan, and Benadryl. The injection needles were huge and painful. He would be knocked out for hours. It also meant that he was staying. It was considered harmful to society to have someone who wasn't on proper medication roaming the streets. So, until his illness was under control he was now a resident.

Part Four: No Real Choice

When Jacob woke up that night he was given a late dinner. As he was finishing the second pudding Brynn had made sure he had, she walked in to check on him one more time before she left for the night.

When she came in the room, he didn't look toward her before he said, "When can I leave?" His voice held a hint of anger.

Brynn walked closer to him. "I am not sure, Jacob..." She waited to see if he would turn around. "We just want to make sure you are ok. That's why you came here, isn't it?"

His head fell a little before he said, "I came here for food and a fucking shower. We both know that." He raised his head and looked at her. "I want to leave. You can't keep me here."

This was one of the parts she hated most about her job, where she took away the patient's right to choose. Called the Baker Act, the hospital could hold a person for 72 hours without their permission. Then, if the doctor proved they needed that extended, there was an attorney appointed to the case and it went before a judge.

"Jacob, you had a pretty bad incident today. Dr. Hillman feels it would be best..." She was cut off.

"Dr. Hillman didn't even talk to me. Dr. Hillman is keeping me drugged to the point of coma. Dr. Hillman isn't here." Jacob was getting worked up. His face had become flush and he stood up as he shouted, "LET ME GO!"

Brynn began to move toward him using the most calming voice she could. "Jacob it is just for..." He picked up his tray and threw it at her before stumbling.

"You," he said, looking her in the eyes again, the drugs still in his system, "can't stop me," and he headed for the door. Chris, the med nurse, came around the corner and Brynn could tell he had more meds on him.

When Jacob saw Chris in the doorway he paused, then he began running. He pushed right past Chris, and Brynn moved to hit the alert button.

As Jacob took off down the hall Brynn called for a Code Grey, the psych unit had a runner. Within moments Jacob was restrained and getting another dose of his drug cocktail.

Sarah, the nurse taking over for Brynn, offered to do the report. It was about an hour of paperwork, and Brynn was on her eleventh hour of being on the clock. Her nerves were frayed, and she knew she needed to get something to eat and take a break. Brynn thanked Sarah, grabbed Jacob's file and headed out.

Part Five: Monsters Are Real

Brynn called for take-out on her way home. It kept her from eating junk food and she didn't have to cook. When she got home she took a long, hot shower, then poured herself a glass of wine and ate her dinner while watching some mindless sitcom. It was her nightly ritual to unwind.

She cleared away the to-go boxes, poured herself another glass of wine, and pulled Jacob's file out from her bag.

She went back to the beginning, which started when Jacob was eighteen. It appeared he had records from before he turned eighteen, but as a child those records were sealed. There was a notice that the records would have to be requested from the State, which meant he had been in the foster system. Most children with a mental disorder in the foster system stayed there.

His records indicated that he came in to St. Michaels every couple of months. He was usually only in for the night and then released. She could tell that Jacob was one of those people who could work the system, always claiming something easily treatable that needed a prescription, which Brynn was sure he would fill and sell on the streets.

As she flipped through chart after chart it all began to blend together, until an incident about six months before. He came into the ER, again complaining he was depressed. There was a new intern on staff that night, Nathan Montgomery. Brynn remembered him because he always made her uncomfortable when he brought someone up to the unit.

The file indicated that Jacob had a reaction when Nathan entered the room to do the initial exam. Jacob wouldn't respond to questions, and when Nathan called for help, Jacob pushed his way out of the room and ran out of the ER. He had not returned until this most recent visit.

Brynn knew there had to be something more to this. A person wasn't usually as sane and stable as Jacob appeared to be and then suddenly have a violent reaction to a particular person. Jacob had a problem with Marco and Nathan, specifically, but they didn't look anything like each other.

Brynn sighed and put the file down. Polishing off the last of her wine, she wished she was heading to a huge bed covered in fluffy pillows and satin sheets where she could sleep for as long as she wanted. Instead, it was a full size bed with cotton sheets she hadn't had a chance to wash in weeks, and she had to be up again in six hours. Not the life she had dreamed of.

As she was falling asleep she remembered something Chris had mentioned. Jacob had said just before he had been sedated that Marco was a Reaper. It was a very specific statement.

Her phone went off and she thought it was her alarm. After trying to turn the alarm off and realizing it wasn't going *off*, she answered the phone, catching it on the last ring. "Hello?"

"Brynn, it's Chris." His voice sounded strained. "I need you to come in...now!"

"What's happening?" There was a pause. "Chris?" Brynn asked, feeling some panic. Chris finally continued, but his voice was almost a whisper and he was speaking fast.

"Marco is here and is waking up the patient. Said he needs to talk with him before the doctor gets in. Get here...now!" He hung up.

Brynn looked at the time, 2am. She sighed, got out of bed, dressed, grabbed her bag and keys, and headed out the door. Chris hadn't told her which patient, but she already knew.

When she exited the elevator there was a huge commotion around the room Jacob was staying in, with security pounding on the door. As she approached, Chris came up and filled her in. "Marco decided to speak to him alone. He went in and locked the door. That was fifteen minutes ago. I heard laughter and then yelling, more like screaming, and then silence."

Brynn looked at the officers. "Break it down," she said. One of the guards nodded to the other and readied to do her request when the door opened.

Marco walked out with his arms covered in scratches, and there was blood. Brynn pushed past the guards and went into the room "What the hell do you think you are doing?" she directed at Marco.

When she got into the room, Jacob was on the floor. He had bruises and scratches, and a wound on his head. She knelt down and took his pulse. His pulse weak but he was still alive. "Chris!" she hollered and began looking at his wounds.

Chris helped get Jacob onto the bed, and had brought a kit with him. "I got this. Go deal with that," he said, gesturing to the door. Brynn looked down at Jacob one last time and then nodded to Chris and went out.

Security was still waiting, and she pointed at Marco standing at the nurses desk and said, "Have him escorted to ER to check his injuries, and then I want a report filed."

Marco looked back over at her and a smile crept across his face. Brynn swore that she saw something in his eyes. A darkness that sent chills down her spine.

The security guards approached him and he put his hands up. "I'll go willingly." He turned to look at Brynn, and in a voice that attempted to sound sultry, "This isn't over," and winked.

When he was through the double doors she went back to check on Jacob.

Chris had him mostly bandaged. "I think Marco injected him with insulin."

Brynn sighed. "What was Marco doing here? What are you doing here?"

Chris shook his head and started putting the kit away. "I got a call from Trina. She told me her and Mike, the med nurse, both got sick and had to leave. They started to call around and got a hold of me and Marco." Chris stood up. "It was really crazy and I dunno, Marco is a dick, but I have never seen anything like that. He just lost it."

Brynn helped finish the clean-up of the room and checked on Jacob. He seemed stable, but would need some further tests when the doctor got in, to make sure.

She took a little time to ensure the rest of the floor was ok. Chris took on the duties of the charge nurse, and she did the meds and helped with charting. She saved Jacob's for last and as she updated the information she flipped through to see if Marco was anywhere in his records. He wasn't.

It was four in the morning. Chris had gone to get some coffee and a snack for both of them, promising that it would be something that had arrived at the hospital pre-wrapped and wasn't made in the cafeteria.

Staring at Jacob's file, Brynn decided to do something that was not normally a great idea. She went to the patient lockers and pulled out the backpack Jacob had come in with.

Brynn pulled out a shirt that said, *Succulent Apothecary*, which Brynn assumed was a band or a head shop somewhere. He had ripped jeans, socks, sneakers, and a hoodie that had symbols drawn all over it in different inks.

She looked at the backpack with the matching symbols. She checked to see if there was anyone around. She knew she would hear Chris when he opened the doors at the end of the hall.

In the backpack she found more clothes. They were dirty so she pulled them out and put them in another laundry bag to be cleaned. She found soap in a bag, a toothbrush and toothpaste, a comb, an old cell phone, a wallet that only held an expired ID, a folded up photo of a family, and two books that looked like journals.

Brynn pulled out the first journal and found more of the symbols when she heard the sound of a door being opened. She put the book aside, loaded the backpack into the locker, closed it and grabbed the bag of clothes and book, and headed back out.

She dropped the bag in the laundry pick up after filling out the slip and Chris looked at her, questioning. "Found it sitting out in the other room. They must have forgotten to wrap it up."

She didn't know why she was lying. Chris she could trust, he wouldn't care, but for some reason, she cared.

They sat drinking the coffee and eating the powdered doughnuts and mini chocolate chip cookies Chris had found. This would not be her choice normally, but the warm coffee and sugar provided a kind of comfort.

Chris got up to make a round to check on everyone. It would take a few minutes, so Brynn pulled out the book. It was a diary of sorts. It had some dates and notes, but also a lot of sketches of horrible creatures. As she flipped through the pages, she noticed the notes were descriptions of when and where Jacob had seen these monsters.

There was more detail then Brynn would have imagined. Some of the creatures had names, others had the description of how they smelled, or how Jacob felt when he saw them. It also listed how many times Jacob had seen them.

Brynn pulled out his chart and looked for the date of the emergency room visit where he had run out. She found it and compared it to the journal. She was shocked at what she read. The creature didn't have a name, but it had a large bulbous head with an elongated jaw. He had drawn at least three rows of teeth, and spittle dripping down the front of the almost skeletal frame. Long claws protruded from its three fingers, and it had what looked like eyestalks in its shoulders. Even though it was only a sketch, the image was so real. If she closed her eyes she could imagine this thing was there, looking at her as if she was a succulent morsel it wanted to rip apart and then eat. Brynn shivered. She closed the book and knew that for Jacob, the monsters were real.

Part Six: The Reaper

Brynn was scheduled on the morning shift with another two nurses, and did the morning rounds on autopilot. When the breakfast arrived, she was giving out the Styrofoam trays and spoons, and was surprised when Jacob got in line.

She was reaching for the next tray when his red-rimmed eyes met hers. Jacob's eyes were a darker blue then she remembered, and he had dark circles underneath.

As he reached for the tray there was a sorrow in his gaze, the kind of look she saw sometimes in patients that decided they were trapped, like animals in a cage when all the fight has gone out of them.

Brynn had thought she was numb to it, that look, but suddenly felt the same sadness as the first time she had seen that look on patient's face when she had started, years ago. Whatever wall she had erected, shattered.

She handed Jacob the tray and he let his lips form a small smile. "Thank you".

All she could do was nod. Brynn pursed her lips. She knew she was tired, but somehow this was too much and she felt tears stinging her eyes. She finished handing out the trays to the remaining people in line and then rushed to a bathroom in an empty patient room.

She placed her hands on the sink and let her head hang for a moment and just breathed. *What in the hell was wrong with her?* She had grown fond of some of her patients before. Most of them were good people and she had empathy. Most had a very traumatic life or life event that brought them here.

She turned on the water and splashed her face. The cool feeling let her calm a little. She splashed it one more time and turned off the water, grabbed a couple of paper towels and used them to dry her face.

She threw them in the trash bin and turned to make sure she didn't look terrible. The moment her eyes hit the mirror she saw Marco, or what she thought was Marco. His eyes were completely black and he had spiked ridges down his forehead. He opened his mouth and a forked tongue snaked out toward her. Brynn jumped and spun to defend herself, only to find no one behind her.

When she looked into the mirror again hers was the only face she saw. She looked around and back to her reflection and moved out of the bathroom quickly, shutting off the light.

Her first thought was that she losing it. A person in her position would say she was going crazy. She was seeing things that weren't there, and those things were the stuff of nightmares. Knowing she lacked sleep, she could chalk it up to that. Some part of her hoped that was the case, that she was simply nearing the end of her rope stress-wise. A couple days off to rest would fix it. Seemed simple enough.

As she walked back to the desk she thought of the journal and grabbed it, flipping through the pages until she found what she was looking for: The Reaper.

Her eyes were glued to the page. The monster's eyes were black, the head had ridges all over it that matched the ones she had seen on Marco in the bathroom, and the tongue was long and forked. How could she have imagined exactly what was drawn here? Had she seen the page earlier and some part of her subconscious recreated it? The rational part of her started trying to explain it. She *had* to explain it.

Just then Dr. Hillman walked up. "Whatcha reading?" he asked.

Brynn jumped, so wrapped up in her own thoughts that his voice startled her. She looked up at him, and then grabbed a pencil to mark the page and put the book down. "Just an old journal," she said, faking a smile. "Anything juicy in there?" he asked with a little laugh in his tone. She knew he was just trying to make her smile, but he had picked the wrong morning. "Only if you were a thirteen-year-old girl," she replied, again faking a smile and a little laugh.

Dr. Hillman went through all the files and chose four he said he wanted to meet with, Jacob was one of them. He also made sure to order a couple more blood and urine tests for Jacob based on the incident that happened.

When he handed her the order for the tests he said, "Heard about Marco. Was it as crazy as they say?"

Brynn didn't know how to answer. What Marco had done was wrong. If they found he had given Jacob anything that the doctor hadn't prescribed, his career was over. What she couldn't understand was why Marco would risk it. There was no way this young man was worth that to him, or was he? Brynn looked at the doctor. "It was very weird. Not sure if Marco just needs a break."

Dr. Hillman nodded, grabbed his coffee and headed to the treatment office where he could meet with the patients one-on-

one. Brynn thought then to call down to find out what had happened with Marco.

Part Seven: You Are Never Alone

Brynn called the Emergency Room and was placed on hold for what seemed like hours. It was most likely fifteen minutes, but lack of sleep, the craziness that happened last night, and seeing monsters herself had caused an almost collapse of whatever shreds of consciousness she had left.

"Hello?" said a voice on the other end of the phone. "Who are you holding for?" They sounded slightly annoyed.

"I was waiting to hear the status of a nurse brought into the ER by security last night, Marco Ramirez." Brynn had no hope of holding back the annoyance of asking the same thing the fourth time this call.

She heard shuffling papers and then, "Says here he never finished the intake paperwork." Brynn said, "What?" knowing the answer was the same. "Didn't finish paperwork. Listen we are slammed down here, so if there is nothing else?" Brynn shook her head and realized the person couldn't see her. "No...thank you," and hung up the phone.

The next call she made was to security. The guard who answered the phone told her Marco went to the bathroom and never came back. Since there were no bathrooms in the ER rooms they let him go to a general one. After thirty minutes of him not coming out, they went in and he was gone. The guard continued to talk but the receiver fell into Brynn's lap and her hands went to her face. It was only when Dr. Hillman tapped her on the shoulder did she notice the phone.

"You ok?" he asked, there was genuine concern in his voice.

Brynn hung up the phone. "Yes, I am fine. Just tired." She looked up and applied the fake smile, or as close as she could come to it. Dr. Hillman narrowed his eyes. "Do you need something?" He was intimating that he would write a prescription. It seemed like a nice gesture, but it always bothered Brynn how easy it was for some doctors to "be nice" until they needed something in return.

"No. Thank you. Just need an actual night's sleep."

He laughed a little at that. Brynn debated telling him about Marco and how he had run. She didn't know that Dr. Hillman would do anything but comment on the issue and try to comfort her. She didn't need comforting.

She reached for the folders he was holding. "Anything I need to note?" Back in job mode. "No. All good." He smiled.

Normally she would have taken the comment and just put the paperwork away, but she didn't understand. "Do I need to file anything on the situation with Marco?"

Dr. Hillman shook his head. "Mr. Morrison doesn't remember anything from last night. My guess is whatever caused the issue was a reaction to the drugs he was on."

It took every bit of strength Brynn had left to not lunge over the workstation and punch Dr. Clueless in the face. Instead she smiled and said, "That must be it." Confirming that he would in fact be no help with Marco.

Dr. Hillman grabbed his coffee again and headed for the doctor's lounge and Brynn set to work on the charts, saving Jacob's for last. She didn't understand. Did he really not remember the attack?

She read through the very sparse notes that the doctor had made. Nothing.

Brynn grabbed the journal and slid it into her bag, then let the charge nurse on duty know she was heading out. She was going to be useless if she continued to stay. She walked past the common room and saw Jacob sitting reading his book. With what he saw, she could not imagine how that book was calming.

When Brynn got home, she took a long hot shower. She needed to calm the thoughts racing through her mind. She normally used a towel to wipe the steam away when she got out of the shower. Tonight she left it there. She told herself she just didn't care but deep down she knew she was scared of what, or more specifically who, she would see.

Part Eight: No Truth

Brynn had been lying in bed for about an hour when she decided she could no longer deny that she couldn't fall asleep.

Normally with a day like she'd had sleep came easy, but not tonight. She got up and made herself some chamomile tea and as she waited for the water to boil she noticed Jacob's journal poking out of the top of her bag.

Part of her knew opening it was a bad idea. As a trained as a nurse, she had heard patients describe their delusions before. She used to love to listen and watch them in their own worlds. She didn't want to be in Jacob's world.

She started with the first page. Jacob described the reason for the journal:

I know that I am different now. I haven't met anyone else that sees them, the monsters. The first one I saw was when I was ten. It was a substitute math teacher. Looking back now and knowing what I know, I did everything wrong. It knew I could see it and it followed me home. My parents...I would say they protected me. They did it by dying. I was saved by running.

After that I never let a family like me. This way I wouldn't stay. Only long enough to be fed, get a change of clothes. If I saw one I knew I had to leave, fast. I started carrying everything I needed with me. I could never lead them to people again.

I found the symbols in the days I spent in libraries. They mean protection in different languages and cultures. I have never found anything about the monsters themselves.

I sometimes see creatures in video games and comics that look similar. I think they are from a dark part of our pasts that have been buried, and no one wants to dig them up.

I am now eighteen. I am free of the system, for now at least. The only thing I can do is make sure I can never get trapped. The last one almost ended my life. If you are reading this, I might be dead. I hope I am dead, and not trapped by one. I would rather die quickly.

As she thumbed through the pages, they described each encounter. Where, when, and every detail Jacob could remember.

He wrote that every time he encountered one of them he would attempt to get at least twenty miles away. He thought that seemed to be the distance where they, the creatures, could no longer find him.

He described in detail the how he almost lost his life in the beginning because he didn't know the creatures could track, and would follow once discovered.

Jacob had researched everywhere he could think of, but he didn't know how the creatures knew he could see them for what they really were. He also didn't know what he looked like to them.

She came across the page with the Reaper again. It was one of the creatures that Jacob had almost lost his life to. Chills ran down Brynn's spine when she remembered the mirror and the look in Marco's eyes when he walked away from her.

Then it suddenly occurred to her. Marco knew she could see him.

Part Nine: Trapped

Brynn threw on a pair of jeans, shirt, hoodie, and sneakers. She grabbed the journal and her bag and raced back to the hospital. The entire drive her mind was fighting itself. A large part, the rational part, knew this couldn't possibly be real, that she was having some kind of breakdown and this was a result. There had been cases of shared delusions, and although rare, it would explain everything.

All of her training, everything she knew, told her this was the case. But a small part of her, the part that crept in right as you were falling asleep, the part that made you hold out hope that those things you can imagine are real, told her that what she and Jacob were seeing *was* real.

She quickly parked her car, grabbed her bag and badges, and ran up the stairs to the unit. She got through the door and saw Chris behind the desk.

"I thought you were off tonight?" he said, looking a little startled to see her. She must look almost frantic, she thought. Then it occurred to her she didn't know what to say, or how to say it. Why would she need to talk to a patient, let alone in the middle of the night?

"Are you ok?" Chris asked. She could tell he had already assumed she wasn't. "I..umm...I" She was fumbling. "I am...I forgot...something." She walked into the storage room and got Jacob's back pack and his clothes. She took a breath and tried to come up with what she was going to say. She walked out and started with, "Chris, I know this is going to sound..." She couldn't even finish the sentence before she felt a chill go up her spine and she turned in time to see Marco enter in from the hallway doors.

When she turned, Brynn didn't see the Marco she knew, she saw the Reaper in all of it's gory details. She was paralyzed. The claws were dripping, it's barbed tail moving from side to side, it's maw grinning as if a cat playing with it's prey. Brynn couldn't even breathe; she had never been this terrified in her life.

"Marco you can't be here. I am calling security," Chris said loudly. It broke her trance and Brynn used the moment to turn and run towards Jacob's room. She didn't look back for fear she would not be able to move again. There was a commotion behind her and as she opened the door to Jacob's room, she dared to glance back to see the Reaper swinging at Chris.

She closed the door and moved over to Jacob's bed with only a little light from under the door to guide her. "Jacob?" she whispered. "Jacob. Wake up...Please." She knew she sounded desperate, but she knew she didn't have a lot of time. Even though Chris was larger in stature than Marco, Chris didn't know what he was actually fighting.

"What?" she heard Jacob say.

Brynn felt a little sigh of relief as some tension that he might already be dead released. "Jacob, it's Brynn. Your nurse. We have to go. Marco, I mean the Reaper, is back." She grabbed his clothes and handed them in his direction. When his hand touched hers there was a warm tingle. She tried to remember if she had actually touched him before, but couldn't remember.

She stood up and went to listen at the door. As she looked away to give Jacob some privacy to change, she tried to strain to hear what was going on with the altercation. She didn't hear anything. She slowly opened the door to look.

She had to put her hand over her mouth to not scream at the vision in front of her. The Reaper was standing on top of the limp and bloodied body of Chris, pulling out entrails from his abdominal cavity and eating them.

She was about to turn when she felt the same warm tingle against her back and Jacob's voice whispering in her ear, "We have to go...Now!"

He grabbed her hand and slowly opened the door, gesturing for her to be quiet. He started to look to see what direction they should head. Brynn knew that the only way out without raising alarm was past the creature. She pointed down the other hall. It would set off an alarm and a lock down, but she would figure out how to get past all of that once they had a head start.

She pulled his hand and began to move. They got almost to the end of the hall when she heard a growl and a roar. It had seen them. She swiped her badge and pushed on the door.

Once she cleared the door she began to run down the stairs. The alarm was sounding and there were seven floors and fourteen flights, and she knew they had to stop on the second or third because security would be waiting on the first.

She trusted Jacob was behind her and kept moving.

They were down about four flights when something crashed into the door above. She didn't trust herself to look up and kept moving.

At seven flights down the door above busted open. She heard the roar again, sounding more aggressive. It was moving, and fast. When she got to the next landing she pushed the door open and again hoped Jacob was following.

She looked around trying to get her bearings as to what floor she was on. *Pediatrics? Shit!* she thought and took off in a random direction. She hoped it didn't hurt the kids here.

Most of the floors were laid out the same and she just needed to head in the direction of another stairwell. Just as they reached it there was a scream behind them. Brynn turned to see that the creature had a woman, a nurse, by the throat and was holding her up.

Jacob grabbed her arm. "We have to go," he said as he pulled her through the door. Without letting go, he flew down the stairs, pulling Brynn along. When they got to the second floor

Brynn stopped. "We have to exit here." Jacob pulled open the door and moved her to go through first. He removed his hospital bracelets and dropped them inside the stairs. They heard a familiar crashing from above. It was in the stair well.

The second floor was the main floor of the hospital. It held radiology, pharmacy, and most of the administrative offices. Most were closed. Brynn moved quickly towards a staff only area that had an exit to the parking garage. The alarms were still going off and they had to jump back once when a couple of security guards were heading down another hallway, doing their sweeps.

After that slight delay, they wound through several corridors to the door they needed and exited to the garage. Brynn ran to her car, unlocked it for both of them, and told Jacob to get in the back seat. Her windows were fairly well tinted and she didn't think anyone would see Jacob back there.

As she drove out of the garage she was stopped, but only for a second as she showed her ID and was let to pass. *They are really too trusting,* she thought as she sped away.

She kept checking her rear view mirror, thinking at any moment it would be behind her. After she had driven several blocks Jacob said, "It is not that fast." Startled, she had been so wrapped up in making sure she didn't drive off the road and trying to calm her burning lungs, she had all but forgotten he was back there.

"What?" she asked, her throat dry from running.

Jacob sat up and met her her gaze in the rearview mirror. "They are not that fast. It will chase us, but it will take some time to catch up." She almost didn't hear the words he was saying. His eyes, his face, his lips they had all changed. There was a glow to them.

All of a sudden she heard a horn and realized she had drifted out of her lane. She righted the car and decided to keep her eyes on the road. "I live about fifteen minutes from here. We can go there."

She assumed Jacob nodded because he didn't say anything else and they drove in silence for the rest of the ride.

Part Ten: Choices

When Brynn pulled up to her house she got out of the car and walked up to the door. She heard the other car door and as she turned the key she felt Jacob behind her as they went into the house. She went to the kitchen first and threw her bag on the counter, then opened a cabinet to get some glasses and started filling them at the fridge.

When she turned to hand Jacob a glass she saw he was looking at his journal that had spilled out of her bag.

"Did you read this?" he asked without turning to face her.

"Yes," she replied.

He opened it and seemed to be looking randomly at the pages before turning to meet her gaze.

Brynn looked at him in awe. Jacob took the glass from her outstretched hands. "What do you see?"

She blinked, and then swallowed another sip of water. Licking her lips, she said, "You are glowing."

Jacob's furrowed his eyebrows. "Glowing?" he asked. His voice had an intensity that was causing a reaction Brynn wasn't sure she could explain.

She nodded and continued, "Your skin has a light glow beneath the surface, like when you see a light under ice."

Jacob smiled. "What else?" he said, urging her on.

"Your eyes have a crystalline quality. They are blue, but sapphire blue, and they look like a gemstone." She paused for a moment then continued, "Your features are more angular then they were before and there are tiny lines that criss-cross your skin. I didn't see them at first, but in this light as you move, they are there."

Jacob turned and picked up his journal, then grabbed a pen from her bag and began to draw something. It only took him a few moments and then he turned to show her what was on the pages. "Like this?" he asked.

The sketch, although using black ink, had captured what she described. She smiled. "You are pretty good at that."

He smiled back. "Thanks. It has been a useful skill."

Brynn didn't know what else to say standing in the kitchen with a perfect stranger. A very alluring perfect stranger.

She closed her eyes and took a long deep breath and opened them again.

"Are we far enough?" she asked.

Jacob looked around as if trying to sense something. "I think so. Does he know where you live?" he asked.

"No." She shook her head. "He shouldn't." Jacob didn't seem convinced.

"We should go somewhere else," he finally said. She nodded, put the glass down and went to her bedroom to grab a couple things. Then to the bathroom for a toothbrush. As she did these trivial tasks she decided to focus only on what needed to happen next.

Too many thoughts pulling at her would cause her to waiver, and even though this was her house she wasn't safe. When she had gathered everything she thought she needed she found Jacob waiting at the door with his backpack in hand.

"We don't have to go together. It is dangerous...you know...I'm dangerous." He wasn't meeting her gaze.

He was right. He was dangerous. It took only a moment for her to grab his hand and say, "I know."

Nothing else needed to be said. They got in the car and drove for another few hours until they decided to stop at a motel that was just off the highway. Brynn checked in for them. She paid in cash, but they asked for ID so they had her real name. She figured it was pretty safe because Marco, or whatever Marco was, would have to call every motel for miles and miles to find them.

The room had two queen beds and Brynn went to the bathroom. They had been on the road a while and she needed a moment alone. She was exhausted. She had a million questions she needed to ask him, but knew it could wait. She finished up, washed her hands, and shut off the light.

When she entered the room Jacob stood up from the edge of the bed and walked up to her. Before she knew it, he had wrapped his arms around her and she was in the most comforting and stimulating hug she had ever had. She closed her eyes and just breathed him in.

For the first time in days she felt at peace.

After a couple minutes Jacob whispered, "Thank you."

Her instinct almost took over and she was going to ask ,"for what?" But she knew. She had saved his life tonight. Then she felt a stabbing pain as she remembered Chris and the other nurse. She had no idea who else had died tonight because of this. They had just been in *Its* way to get to Jacob. He pulled back and looked down at her, his thumb wiping the tears streaming down her face. She wanted him to say something, anything, that would make what happened ok. He wouldn't...couldn't. Because nothing could make a loss like this ok. Jacob had lost his parents to one of these things. He knew the cost, and the pain it brought.

He pulled her close again for a moment and then whispered, "You should sleep." He backed up toward one of the beds and pulled the covers aside. She sat down on the now exposed sheets and he knelt down and began unlacing her sneakers, pulling each one off and setting it aside. He helped remove her hoodie and she laid back in the bed as he covered her with the blankets.

He looked down at her and smiled slightly, then bent further and kissed her forehead. "I will be right here," he said. She smiled back and rolled to the side, letting herself fall into darkness.

Part Eleven: Endings

Jacob watched her fall asleep knowing the burden she now had. When she had described how he looked to her, he hadn't known if he should explain that he saw the same thing in her face. His drawing was based on how she appeared to him, not just the words she said.

He worried this would be too much for her. He didn't know what she was, or himself now, this was all new to him. Jacob had been alone for a long time. He'd had friends from time to time, but none of them really knew, until Brynn.

He watched her sleep for a while and then used the restroom and got into the other bed. He wanted to be next to her, to feel what he felt only when he touched her, but he needed to give her time. She had just unknowingly given up her whole life. She couldn't go back.

Jacob would tell her in the morning about the Reapers, that they didn't forget, and never stopped hunting. He would tell her how far they needed to go to truly be safe. He had never seen one that powerful before. He looked at Brynn who looked so small under the blanket. She didn't realize how strong she proved to be tonight.

He didn't know when he had drifted off to sleep, but he woke up to a very cold breeze across his skin. He rubbed his eyes and reached to pull the blanket up. He looked over to Brynn's sleeping form, but the bed was empty.

He jumped up and scanned the room. Her shoes, bag, and stuff was still there. He looked in the bathroom and it was empty. He came back into the room and saw the drapes were moving. He pulled them open and found the window wedged open with something. He pulled on it and found it was the book he had left at the hospital. His heart started racing. There was something sticking out of the middle of it. He opened it, and pulled out a lock of Brynn's hair. In some kind of black substance on the pages, it read "Mine now."

About Erika Lance

I would say I was fortunate, some would say otherwise, to have a chance to live across the US. Originally from Minneapolis, MN I spent most of my formative years in Hollywood, CA, then NM, CO, GA, WI and FL. Moving around a lot meant I got to see so many interesting parts of our country and the cultures that are all around us. All through my life I was lucky to have many artists; writers, actors, painters, poets and musicians. It made for a very wild upbringing. I grew up as an elusive female nerd. My head was either buried in a book or playing RPGs (if your cool you know what that means), it made for an imaginative existence. My love of writing started at a young age and although I wrote a lot for myself, it took hitting that certain moment in my life to decide I wanted to share my universe with the world. With that said, it will most likely be an amazing ride so old on tight.

Connect with Erika:
www.erikalance.com
Email: erikalance@gmail.com
Facebook.com/Erika-Lance
Twitter.com/AuthorELance
Instagram.com/AuthorELance

PART II

Mini-Shorts

At every ISG meeting we do an exercise where three members each pick one word. Members then have five minutes to compose a story with the chosen words. (There are times when we choose four words and take eight minutes to write.) As with any creative outlet, members take each other into new worlds the way only writers can.

For our 5th year anniversary, we decided to have a little fun and share some of our writing exercises. In the following pages are just a few exercises from each author featured in this book.

Enjoy!

Lisa Barry

Lime ~ Attitude ~ Board

Plank stared at the ship with one eyebrow raised. How was he supposed to take *this* to the Samana Islands. This, this...abomination of boards should be sunk not sailed. His first mate stopped next to him.

"It's the best we could find, sir."

"The best?" Plank sneared.

"I think your attitude will improve when you see what is has to offer," Manny said in low voice followed by a cough. Before he could say anything more, a woman climbed onto the deck.

"Ahoy!" she hollered, "Please, come aboard. We've been waiting for you Captain."

One look at her legs, another look at her chest and Plank swung up and onto the deck.

"Master," she said bowing her blond head, "my name is Lime. My crew and my ship are hereby yours. We are at your disposal."

Both of Planks eyebrows flew up this time as he glanced at his first mate.

Parallel ~ Feather ~ Bubbles

The feathers were still falling from the sky in soft clouds. It would have been so beautiful if they weren't splattered with blood. It wasn't until Bubbles showed up that I even had an inkling of what had made the Angels explode. The chagrined look on her face told the story and it was gruesome.

"Please tell me only some of them are dead," I said my heart thumping heavily in my chest.

Her lips twitched and a tear ran down her face.

"Bubbles," I whispered. She was the happy one. The one that never let anything get her down, the parallel of joy.

The poor thing had awoken one day thrilled that her power had finally come in. A power so horrible and so devastating that even those of us who would be more inclined to use such a weapon were afraid of it.

"All of them everywhere?" I asked.

She shook her head, more tears fell. I sighed with relief.

"Ok so on Earth then." She nodded. "Ok," I whispered to myself, "only the angels on Earth are destroyed." I wondered how long it would take the ones from Heaven to notice.

Squid ~ Blue ~ Box

Jen ran a manicured nail over the box. "You say this holds the key to your heart?" she purred.

Donel nodded and then frowned at her. Probably not in the way you were thinking though," he said and picked up the box to slip it into his jacket pocket.

She stopped him and took it, inspecting the intricate lock on the side. It seemed to be some kind of puzzle. A squid was engraved on the top.

"Why a squid?" she asked handing it back to him and he tucked it away in relief.

"It's a long family story," he commented and started to rummage in the pantry for more dried fruits and beef for his trip. A blue flower in between two storage baskets caught his attention. He was too late. The smell of the potent weed hit his senses and numbed his nerves almost instantly.

Donel thumped rather than slid to the ground. Jen jumped up and down clapping like a child and dug the box from his jacket. She giggled.

"Don't worry," she murmured, "I'll take good care of this key."

~~*~~

Anne Cargile

Sunglasses ~ Whine ~ Rude

The whine of the engine was not pleasing Ken's ears. His darling was in trouble and unfortunately there wasn't anything Ken could do about it driving through the desert. He patted the dash and murmured, "Next sign of life hon, I promise to stop and see what's wrong."

Ken pushed his sunglasses up his nose and squinted ahead on the horizon. He wasn't sure, but it looked like some sort of civilization was coming up. The landscape created some weird optical illusions though and it could be anything from 5 to 50 miles away. He wouldn't have even been in this situation if his client hadn't been so rude on the phone. Ken sighed. He knew taking over managing a burlesque troupe out of Des Moines, Iowa had been a bad idea, but it had seemed like such a great opportunity. Of course, he'd been a little drunk at the time.

Nail ~ Tweezers ~ Shower

The call that had set Ken in motion across the desert to Des Moines had been a little confusing, and rather scary. Rudy, the lead singer had gotten caught up with a new beau, according to Ed, the one who had called Ken in desperation. About all Ken could make out was something about a shower, haunted tweezers and nail polish that wouldn't stay on. Ed had been more than a little hysterical and Ken had done his best to calm him down. With promises to get in his car immediately and drive straight through, instructions for Ed to stop whining and splash his face with water and to keep an eye on Rudy, Ken had thrown his go-bag in Wanda's backseat and torn off. The Utah desert might be gorgeous, but it sure was freakin' desolate Ken thought. He needed a gas station, pronto. Wanda was getting too hot and he didn't have any water in the trunk.

Absent-minded ~ Glare ~ Brushing

Ken pulled up to Pet Wussy and heaved a sigh of relief. He'd finally found a gas station, just in the nick of time, and Wanda had gotten a new water pump. He'd been on his way in just a couple of hours, and thanks be to energy drinks and a few pep pills, he'd driven straight through.

He hauled himself out of the car and stretched mightily before walking up to the front door. The guard, Nellie Ken thought was his name, was absent-mindedly brushing his? her? hair while watching Oprah on a little TV.

"Hi there. Is Ed around?" Ken asked politely.

The death glare he got in response was enough to fry what little was left of his temper. He pushed his sunglasses up onto his head and glared right back.

"She's inside," Nellie said and waved his? her? hand toward the front door.

"Not much of a guard, are you?" Ken asked.

"Honeychild, I'm only out here, 'cause I don't wanna deal with the crazy sheet in there!" Nellie said, then promptly proceeded to ignore him.

Shell ~ Address ~ Soap

Ken knocked on Rudy's dressing room door. After a minute, and no sound or answer, he opened it. The room was a disaster. Feathers, sequins, it looked like a Pride Day parade float had exploded. He nearly screamed when something grabbed his arm and turning to see what it was he saw Ed. But this Ed was a mere shell of his former glory. Mascara and eyeliner were streaked down his face in ribbons of black and his once gorgeous hair – Ken groaned.

"Ed, what the hell happened?" Ken asked, trying to address the situation calmly.

"Thank god you're here," Ed sobbed and collapsed into Ken's arms. "I swear it was the damn tweezers! The man at the pawn shop said they'd been blessed and would unerringly find every stray hair to pluck! I bought them as a gift for Rudy along with some special soap."

Ed wailed a little more and Ken patted him on the back, trying to be patient.

"Go on Ed, where's Rudy?"

"He'd DEeeaaad!" Ed cried.

"What?! How?"

"The tweezers did it! He took them in the shower, and, and, and – he couldn't stop plucking!"

Alanna J. Rubin

Avulsion ~ Mug ~ Eternity

Alric was walking down the sandy alleyway, entranced by the silhouettes of the three great pyramids in the distance. He was too enthralled by the scene before him to notice that he was being followed and taken by surprise when these men shoved him to the ground and mugged him. They were covered in black tattoos that honored the destructive god of Set and with no explanation, they tore his heart from his chest with their bare hands, as if through avulsion. Alric lived just long enough to see his still heart in the hand of his murderer.

He thought that was going to be the end, until he found himself at the silver scale ready to weigh his soul to see if he was worthy to enter the afterlife, where he'd live out his eternity. Alric, didn't think it was possible to feel this nervous when he was dead, but the white feather on the left side of the scale suddenly looked very heavy.

Absent-Minded ~ Glare ~ Brushing

The young man, wearing a tweed suit and spectacles, was absent-mindedly brushing the spines of the dusty books as he walked down the path between the bookcases. He was deep in thought, but a glare coming from his left pierced through the flurry of activity in his mind. Annoyed at the interruption, the young man came to an abrupt stop and turned to see the source of the problem. As soon as he did, he stood there transfixed. A fragile looking black leather bound book, entitled "Your Story", which he'd never seen before, was glowing. Entranced, he picked it up causing the glow to become brighter. He opened the book, and the pages began to flutter in a sudden wind that grew to encompass him. He was gone, the book now occupying the spot on the floor where the young man was moments before.

Mechanical ~ Steam ~ Buttons

There was someone in the dark room with me and its body moved unnaturally. I could hear the release of steam right before its next footstep hit the ground with a loud thump and the thumps were getting closer. Frantically, I felt around the smooth cool walls looking for a way to escape, but my sense of touch revealed no windows or doors. I couldn't even find a crack. Panic began to set in as I felt the heat of the steam upon my skin. I was now backed up against one of the unforgiving walls, my hands pressed behind me. I was going to die here. That's when I suddenly felt a button beneath my hand and with desperation and no idea what would happen, I pressed it.

~~*~~

Nicole DragonBeck

Zombie ~ Shell ~ Haunted ~ Exit

The Zombie stumbled awkwardly towards her, its rotten face twitching. She was haunted by the memory of the last time she ran into one of the pitiful, undead creatures and the terrible message it relayed to her from the other side.

It stopped in front of her, and she tried hard not to gag at the smell. Its eyes were wide and white and filled with a terrible knowledge, the kind only death can bring. She waited anxiously for it to speak, but it did not. It lifted one emaciated arm and handed her something. It was a necklace. A gilded shell swung gently. She had to pry one of its fingers off it before she could examine it.

"What is it?" she asked.

When it answered its voice was made raspy from lack of use. "Listen to it," it told her. "It will lead you to the exit."

Her arms tingled. This was what she was waiting for, this was what she needed. She was terrified. She thought she could see pity in the dead eyes of the messenger, and that was the most terrifying thing of all.

Hostage ~ Tattoo ~ Return

Holding the faerie hostage proved to be more challenging than she had originally anticipated. For one thing, it bit. For another, it glowed brightly when she was trying to get some sleep, and only smiled annoyingly when she asked it to stop. She chained it to her desk, not trusting it to be too close. Its wild face was covered in tattoos, strange glyphs that made her eyes ache if she looked at it for too long. As she was doing now.

"You know, you can return as soon as you tell me how to get a message through."

"You are very stupid," the faerie said in its squeaky little growl.

That was about as much as she'd been able to get out of it for the month it had been here. It wouldn't even tell her what it ate, and as a result was thinning down alarmingly.

"I don't know how many times I have to explain this to you," she said through gritted teeth.

"But my friend is in your world, and I need to get him back."

The faerie crossed her bony arms and glared.

"Why won't you talk to me?" she pleaded.

"You really are stupid. You have me in chains, you haven't fed me for a moon, and you wonder why I won't talk to you."

"I tried that," she said, pleased with the forward progress. "But last time, you killed my cat, blew up my bathroom and tried to strangle me."

Lips ~ Reprobate ~ Crossword ~ Propeller

One had to admire her spunk. She was a lone sprite, and everyone knows that sprites only get their power in numbers. She was also chained to a wall, hand and foot. Her pretty lips were pulled back in a snarl of frustration as she tugged at her bonds, but they were dwarven-forged; they wouldn't come free in a million years. She sank down, not yet defeated, but sorely in need of a rest. And some water would be lovely.

Her head jerked up as her pointed ears picked up the heavy tread of metal boots. She focused her glare on the door, and was rewarded with the sight of the Demon overlord. He did not flinch or cower as she had hoped, but perhaps that was because he was a little short on brain power. The Demon stood twice her height all ebony and fire. His cruel eyes took in every wound, cut and bruise on her pale flesh.

"You are a reprobate," she told him loftily.

He still did not flinch, but he stopped and blinked rapidity. She decided he looked like a large cow.

"I'll use that in the next crossword I compose," he told her gruffly.

She snorted. "You don't even know what it means."

"No matter. I'll make something up." He grinned evilly, the firelight making his pointed teeth flicker and seem more sinister than they really were. "Now, are you going to give up your little secret, or are we going to have another day in the playground?"

She couldn't help but wince as her body forced her mind to remember the playground. A series of demonical contraptions, with barbed wire, spinning propellers, dull knives, temperamental cannons and then just when you began to get really bored, there were the starved crows and the maimed wolves. Every fiber of her body begged her not to put it through the Demon torture chamber again. But she could not divulge the secret the Demon wished her to. She didn't actually know what he thought she did.

And that was when inspiration struck. If the Demon, who could make a boulder look intelligent, could make something up for a crossword, then surely she could to.

"Okay," she sighed. "I'll tell you."

The Demon started to drool.

~~*~~

Dalia Lance

Honey ~ Threat ~ Mischief

"Wow this is sticky" he said pulling his hand from her thigh.

She wanted to say something witty back to him but she was still clinging to the hope the mood wouldn't be completely destroyed by this horrible use of honey.

"I thought you liked it sticky and sweet" she purred.

He got a mischievous smile and then placed his hand right back where it was. She began to move his hand up her thigh but it wouldn't budge. He was now actually stuck. With every motion of trying to free himself there was a threat of him actually tearing her skin off.

She tried to remain calm but finally yelped when he pulled too hard.

"I am so sorry" he said. This wasn't his fault, it was hers. She thought using spun honey seemed like a sexy idea, but it was either too cold or too warm or whatever that caused a caustic plastering effect.

"Don't worry... Umm... Want to try a shower? She asked hopefully. He nodded, however she wasn't sure how they would actually get there.

Trip ~ Blink ~ Coffee

How many cups of coffee had she consumed this morning?

Was it morning? Not enough coffee she thought.

Wait... She tried to blink. Her eyes were terribly dry and she realized she was lifting her head trying to open them back up again.

Her foot hit something and she started to trip reflexively reaching out for something to catch her fall. She felt fabric and something hard, no wait, soft and hard. Oh crap she thought. This is bad.

She shouldn't have been walking. She debated falling and making it appear as if she was fainting and then realized she had debated it long enough, and held onto whatever she was holding long enough that the faint wouldn't be believable.

Finally prying open her left eye she looked up to see that she was teetering and only being held in place by her handhold on Mr. Baxter's... Oh crap...

She sighed, shaking her head.

"Ms. Kelly" his voice cutting any thoughts she was having. "Would you kindly let go?" he asked.

Oh my god she thought. She hadn't let go...

Strap ~ Shower ~ Burn

Sean wondered if the eye hook he saw in the ceiling above the shower meant what he thought it had. He had come in to use the restroom while Sarah continued making dinner.

He tried to take his attention off of it long enough to finish up what he was in there for. When he did, he washed his hands and unable to see a towel in sight, opened the small door to the right of the sink. The logical place to put something like a towel.

Instead he found a strap. As he pulled on it, he discovered it wasn't one strap but a set of them. Actually, it was one of those sex swings. He glanced back up above the shower and fully realized what he was looking at.

His mind began to explore the possibilities when a knock on the door startled him and he heard Sarah's voice through the door "Everything ok in there?"

"Yes. Sorry. Yes." He stuttered. What the hell was he sorry for he thought.

"Hurry up before I burn dinner and force you to take me out." she said playfully.

Best date ever! He thought putting the straps back in place.

~~*~~

Erika Lance

Puff ~ Rubble ~ Flat

Ouch, actually ouch a lot he thought to himself as he was lying flat on his back. There were little jagged points digging into his back as well. He lifted his head, which for the record felt as if it weighed ten pounds and realized he could only hear ringing.

This was bad.

He remembered two things, hitting the red button and the small puff of smoke that glided out of the machine.

He sat up and shook his head as if this would help clear the sound in his ears. Big mistake he thought as he almost fell back against the skin piercing rubble beneath him.

He looked himself over taking inventory, two feet, two legs, two hands with arms intact and they all seemed to begrudgingly move. So far so good he smiled to himself, until Jimmy raised his gaze and saw a few dozen soldiers with guns trained on him and a swimming pool size hole in the hull of the ship.

(this was Erika's first story ever :))

Slow ~ Forget ~ Fantasy

Being in a police station was the last place she thought she would end up tonight. Actually, she hadn't really pondered where she would be. So, she couldn't say this was the last place. But, when asked, should most likely would have answered differently.

"Is this some kind of sick fantasy?" that was the voice of the detective they had brought in to interrogate her. He wasn't very good at his job. He knew how to raise his voice and point a lot. Maybe, that was his job. Well, he was getting kind of annoying.

Tara looked up at him "Yes" she said.

"What did you say?" the detective asked. He seemed a little slow.

"Yes. I said Yes." She repeated. She spoke more slowly this time.

He had laid all the photos of the crime scenes in front of her. It was one thing to see them live, but it was almost like looking at an amazing piece of artwork to see them displayed in front of her like this. It was a pity a few were under or over exposed. When they put them in the books, TV shows and movies she hoped they used only the good ones.

"You're admitting this was you?" the detective interrupted her reverie.

God, he was slow she thought and went back to looking at the masterpieces in front of her.

Hat ~ Rage ~ Silver

"Why is he in a rage right now?" Mark asked Tess as she leaned against the wall of the gym.

"Whatever do you mean?" she asked in a voice that dripped with sarcasm.

Mark pointed out onto the middle of the court where most of the basketball team had backed away from Kevin as he was storming around yelling at something in his hand.

"Oh, you mean him" the pointed to Kevin now stamping on the hat with his feet. "He started this about five minutes ago for no reason and nobody has seemed to be able to stop him." She pulled a lollipop out of her pocket, unwrapped it and placed it in her mouth.

Mark looked back towards his friend who had now picked up the hat and began throwing it, screaming at it, chasing it, picking it up and throwing it again. Mark tried to make out what Kevin was yelling but the only word that seemed to come through clear was "Silver".

"Did he just say Silver?" Mark asked looking back at Tess who was now looking more bored then when he walked in. "Yep" she replied shrugging, "No idea what the heck it means and I think the rest is Klingon or Elvish, but who the hell knows. I'm sure he'll pass out soon."

"Is he even on the team?" Mark asked, "Nope" was all Tess replied.

~~*~~

Desiree Matlock

Avulsion ~ Mug ~ Eternity

"So, what's Avulsion Therapy?" The next test case walked into the doctor's room, where I, as today's nurse on rotation, was to take his vitals before he saw the doctor.

"Well, the part of you that's causing the problem is going to be removed. I know it sounds bad, but it quite painless and effective. You'll be totally cured. It's a new therapy for cases such as yours."

He sat on the edge of the table in his gown, swinging his legs a little, smiling nervously while I took his blood pressure, and a specimen of blood. He was staring at the mug on the counter top with a picture of a kitty on it and the words "Hang in there!" printed cheerfully below.

"Well, I've been signing up for everything lately, in hopes it'll help, but what part could possibly be removed that would cure schizophrenia?"

"Well, from what I understand, it's nothing you need. Just your eternal soul." I grinned at him, and the smile faded slowly from his lips.

Strap ~ Shower ~ Burn

I still had razor burn from last week, but I wasn't going on a date with my legs in this condition. I climbed into the shower, letting the water pour only onto my legs, so I didn't have to disrobe – still in the yoga shorts and top from my workout earlier. Basically, I just wanted to lather up and shave. I still had the blowout from the day before, no reason to wreck it. A friend had bought me a fancy razor with a strap to sharpen it, but I was sticking to the throw-away lady venus ones, thank you. Knowing me, I was more likely to cut my leg off than shave correctly with a razor that required even more maintenance. I just had such a hard time believing her when she said it was less likely to cause razor burn than the disposables. While I was working on leg one, I got a text from my mom, which I saw buzzing on the counter. ON MY WAY OVER. Okay, I texted back. She always texted in all caps, like she was yelling. If I ever got a text from her with proper case, I'd know that she'd been pod personed.

Dammit, I was bleeding slightly, and just got water on my mascara. Crap. As I was working on leg two, the doorbell rang, and I yelled "COME ON IN, I"M IN THE BATHROOM."

The bathroom door squeaked slightly. "Oh for pete's sake, just come on in. I'm only shaving."

The hottest guy I'd ever seen looked around the door, perplexed. Then he walked in. "You sure?"

"Um, sorry. Excuse me." I scrambled out of the tub and stared at him. "Who are you?"

"I'm your new neighbor? Jack?"

Not the best first impression, but I've done worse.

Criminal ~ Blurt ~ Donkey

I was getting worried. This donkey did not want to move, and there were four people watching me now, and one of them was in uniform. Today had already been hell. I'd just totally ruined her birthday, and now I was trying to make it up to her by fixing the fall out.

"Hey, there is nothing wrong with walking through here with this donkey!" The state trooper – I realized by his boots – looked at me dubiously, and then pulled a pad out of his pocket and walked over.

"Okay, well, yeah, it seems a little weird, but why did you feel the need to blurt that out? Are you engaged in anything criminal here, sir?"

"No! I just got left with this damn donkey because the lady running my nephew's birthday party petting zoo on the other end of the park ran out without taking it with, and now I have to take it home. That makes sense, right?" After today's craziness, I was at my rope's end. The trooper seemed to be able to tell how wild my eyes were getting and looked a little worried.

I left out the part about hitting on her in a totally inappropriate way.

"You can't bring that creature home with you. It's a farm animal. You live here in Brooklyn, right? You'd need a permit."

"You mean I would be allowed to have a donkey IN MY APARTMENT if I had a permit?" I squeaked.

"Um, with about a three week wait time, but yes."

"What the hell do those people do with their animals while they're waiting?" The donkey started eating my shirt. Was that safe? That couldn't be safe.

"I don't know. I really don't."

"Damn it!"

"Look, I'm going to have to take you in."

"The donkey too, right?"

"...Sure." He shrugged.

"Thank GOD."

~~*~~

Rhiannon Matlock

Gold ~ Coconut ~ Evil

The gold pocket watch sat in the palm of the man's hand, ticking quietly but steadily. Looking up from it, the man glanced around the square. Currently it was near empty, the brick walkways and coconut colored walls, of the buildings and circling it appeared peaceful. Little would an uninformed passerby know of the evil that lurked within its quarters. In the center the bell tower chimed once, twice and then a third time. It was the top of the hour. There was one last thud of the bell as it reverberated out and danced along the airwaves of the enclosed space. He looked at his watch to confirm. It was high noon. People dressed in pretty clothes and fancy suits poured out of the buildings and circled around the bell tower in anticipation. The man closed his watch and shoved it inside the pocket of his vest. Withdrawing his gun he cocked it and held his breath as the quartermaster made his way through the crowd.

"Crow," the big burly man called out.

Crow's palms slickened but he nodded at the quartermaster.

"What will it be," he called out, "the girl or your soul?"

Placate ~ Sharp ~ Crystal

He stood over the hot steaming fire pit. Waves of sticky heat undulated from the coals beneath and slightly boiled his outstretched hand. He dare not move it though for he had to placate the One Almighty.

The sharp crystal bit into his skin, adding pain on top of pain. It had to be done though. He opened his hand and reached with the other to grab the red stone. One drop of blood is all it would take. He took the jagged rock and was about to slice his finger with it's deadliest edge when he was suddenly interrupted.

"Jimmy, what in the hell are you doing?" Erica said as she walked into the kitchen, her mild irritation plain on her face.

The boy jumped at the sound of the One Almighty's voice and looked up.

"Nothing mom," he said, "Just playing around."

"Well I suggest you stop that and get on with dinner before I have you for dinner instead," Erica said playfully.

Jimmy nodded, not so sure she didn't mean it.

Stuff ~ Crypt ~ Hat

His hat was tall and distinguished, recognizable amongst the sea of otherwise dull head apparel.

Brent signaled from the top of a nearby tower to the spotter below. Once he was sure that he had Angie's attention, he mimed the coordinates to her.

It should be enough. She was the best shot in ten counties and if her bullets that were dipped in all sorts of stuff didn't put that bastard into a crypt, nothing would.

There was a return signal from Angie. She'd gotten the message. Brent's heart beat kicked up a couple of notches and his palms began to sweat. The moment was finally here. It was almost surreal. After 5 years of tracking that mons-.

Brent straightened. No. No. No. The man in the yellow hat turned and peered directly at him.

~~*~~

JM Paquette

Tinkle ~ Spatula ~ Kettle

"Clearly, one of us has overestimated the other," Sam said, looking at his adversary across the linoleum tiles of the small apartment kitchen. The demon held two swords in a ready stance, the curved blades glinting in the gleam of the fluorescent lighting.

He looked down at the spatula he held in one hand, the end still coated in brownie batter. Deciding to brazen this thing out, as if sword-wielding demons appeared in his kitchen all the time, Sam raised the spatula to his lips, tasting the batter, wondering if this was really going to be the last time he ever tasted anything.

The demon grunted, then spoke in a low voice, "You know why I am here."

Sam nodded, savoring the chocolate in his mouth, brain frantically running through anything that could have conjured such a creature. He hadn't been into any of the hard demon summoning for months now. He was clean, over that phase of his life. Now he just hung out and made brownies and drank things.

Like tea.

He glanced over at the kettle, steam just starting to trickle out of the spout. "Of course," he said, taking a casual step to the stove and laying down the spatula on the counter. It left a greasy chocolate smear that would have made his ex-girlfriend crazy. He picked up the kettle instead, gesturing with it at the stranger. "Tea? I think I want some."

When the demon shook his head, Sam sighed. "Everyone likes tea."

The water in the metal pot made the smallest tinkling sound as the spell triggered. Steam came spilling out of the spout, formulating into a huge shape. Sam picked up the spatula again, taking his place next to the hulking beast he had freed. "Now this seems more fair."

Milkshake ~ Cobalt ~ Practice

"Is the milkshake supposed to look like this?" Tabitha asked, gesturing at the bubbling contents
of the shaker. "Why did it turn that color? Is it cobalt?"

Henry glanced over, wrinkling his nose, and said, "You clearly need some practice." Without losing a beat, he whisked the shaker, which was starting to look a bit melted, the metal warping at the sides, off the counter, and dumped the entire thing into the red biohazard container against the wall. A few seconds after the lid snapped shut, there was a dull whump and the container lifted off the ground a few inches.

"Sorry," Tabitha said, running her hands through her hair in a nervous habit. "I just wish I knew what I'm doing wrong!"

Henry stared blandly at her, then his face focused, eyes staring at her hands, now fingering the material of her shirt, and flicking upward to the crown of her head.

Tabitha looked down, surprised to see a small trail of purple smoke wafting from the bottom of her shirt. She reached down to investigate, but paused as a smell suddenly overwhelmed her senses.

Oh crap, she thought. My hair is burning.

Clip ~ Gypsy ~ Word

"Oof!" the gypsy gasped as she hit the floor, rolling with the motion as she tried to get her feet underneath her. The dungeon, she thought frantically, the dungeon, they threw me in the damn dungeon, don't freak out don't freak out don't freak out--

"Dear gods, woman, stop that cursed whining," snapped a voice above and to her left. "You are clearly already freaking out."

She rolled to a stop, shooting to her feet and turning to face the voice. A tall man stood there, his face pale, his hair coiffed, his clothing perfectly unmarred and complete with a clipped tie at the neck. The vampire lifted his cloak in a dramatic bow in greeting, teeth clearly marking his identity.

She took a step back... and hit something solid. Like stone. She felt behind her, expecting to feel the wall of the cell. Instead, she heard someone gasp and then giggle as a breath of hot air hit the back of her neck. "Now, now, love," the gargoyle told her, "we don't need to get fresh quite yet. Besides, you haven't said the magic word yet."

She tried to remain calm, but her voice still stuttered, "The magic word?"

"Please," the statue breathed at her. "You can't just go pawing at people as soon as you drop in. At least you could ask first."

"It's only polite," the dragon in the corner added, a ring of smoke rising above its head into the darkness.

It's just like that old gypsy woman said, the gypsy thought. *My mother was right.*

~~*~~

PART III

The Faery Story came to be when we, the ISG, were invited as a featured speaker for the Halloween addition of an open mic night.

We decided to write a story each giving the next writer a word they had to include in their portion of the story.

It was a blast! Please enjoy.

~~*~~

The Faery Story

Nicole DragonBeck #1

It was that time of year again. The ghosts and mummies had come out and tombstones had sprung from yards like toadstools. Leering pumpkins took their places beside doors and tattered webs adorned the shrubs and eaves of the neat, respectable houses of Harpersville.

Melinda Black watched the transformation take place, wondering if the people of Harpersville understood why they were doing what they were doing, or why it was so important. Of course, they didn't, but she wondered anyway. She also wondered what her life would be like if she didn't know the things she knew.

She turned and walked inside her house, done up in the same manner as the others, but with more attention to the important details of things. The ghosts were placed in front of the windows, to prevent the things they represented from peering inside. The jack-o-lanterns had faces carved on two sides, one happy, one not so happy, and were placed strategically to disorient any creatures of ill-intent. The tombstones in her yard were arranged in an ancient pattern to create a vortex that would send anything they ensnared back to where it had come from. At each corner of the house was a pentagram in Melinda's own blood, and the other symbols of Melinda's craft that would make her house uncomfortable, to say the least, for any creature of the dark to linger long. She was well prepared and protected, for Melinda Black was a witch and those were the things she knew.

Black was from one of the oldest lines of witches, and she took great pride in that. The witches of Harpersville had a very important function, and at no time was it more important than All Hallows Eve. For what Melinda did to her home, and what others tried to do with theirs, the witches had the responsibility to do for the whole town. All over the world, covens would be doing the same for their cities, towns, and villages.

This year Melinda had the honor of hosting the gathering, and that meant further work. She went back into the kitchen where the brew was simmering and checked the timer. It was almost done.

At that moment, her husband Rob came into the room. He wrinkled his nose at the smell and Melinda smiled apologetically. Little Sarah, Jared, and Andrew followed their father into the kitchen. They were all dressed up, Sarah as Dorothy of Oz, and Jared as a space pirate, with a few invisible witchy touches to their costumes. Eight-year-old Andrew was a cowboy and had refused to let Melinda help him, so she just had to hope the crude disguise would be sufficient protection on this night.

Rob gave the 5-gallon pot on the stove a wary glance. "I'm glad I'm not a woman and cursed with the need to do crazy cleansing diets," he commented.

"Men do that, too," Melinda said. It was true in both senses, she thought to herself. Warlocks were few and far between but they did exist, just as men who did cleanses.

"If you say so," Rob said, kissing her. "Have fun tonight. We'll try to be home before midnight."

Melinda smiled and bit her tongue to keep from telling him there was no rush. This year the appointed day fell on a Saturday, which made her life easier. It wasn't so easy to think of excuses to get Rob and the kids out of the house for long enough on a weekday.

"Have fun at the party. Don't let them eat too much sugar, please."

"Of course not." He gave an exaggerated wink to the children, herding them out to the garage.

Melinda watched through the front window as the car drove off, then began to prepare in earnest. The ceremony had to be done out of doors, in view of the sky and in contact with the earth. In olden times, it was done at midnight in forest glades. Nowadays, in civilization, with kids and work, that was not practical. The back yard would have to suffice.

Laura Jenkins #2

Ever punctual, Norman arrived first. He would be performing the role of High Priest, representing *The Hunter* aspect of the male, or God role, as appropriate for this ceremony. Melinda needed to cleanse herself of this world, to prepare, and pointed Norman toward the back yard.

He stopped dead and turned to look at her quite seriously. "There is no more magical place than a witch's garden. This is well for us, as the winds are breathing into town, and not breathing the same breaths back out."

Melinda watched him go out the door and began to measure the area outside before she herself breathed again. Then she took stock of the time again and grabbed the pot off the stove, rushing to the downstairs bath. The coven would arrive soon, bringing breads, potatoes, baked apples, and all the trappings of the circle and the night. They would come into this bathroom and cleanse themselves, returning to her hearth as sisters with secret names and a shared vision that contained those vague portions of reality just below and above the normal spectrum of vision. Tonight, that vision was crucial as the veil thinned between the world of the living and the world of the dead.

Melinda opened the door to enter the world cleansed, and immediately heard the quieted and somber voices of her coven. Meredith, her older sister and the "mother" of the coven, smiled reverently at her before ushering the younger maidens into the bath with her. She would teach and assist them to prepare, as their mother had done. The ritual tonight, however, would not see Meredith as the High Priestess. Samhain requires the wisdom and power of the *crone*, Gizella.

As the giggling subdued into silence in the bathroom, Melinda turned back to the night. She went to the modified kitchen island, ran the tip of the coven athame across her fingertip, and squeezed her blood into the inkwell. From a homemade sheet of paper, she made a strip for each of the dead she would call to her aid and wrote their names on them with the blood of the coven.

Scrawling the last letter of the last name, Melinda felt a chill run down her spine, not as if she were spooked, but as if a cold breeze had blown into the kitchen. Norman was right. She could feel the dead arriving before they were called. Looking up to see if the other women could feel it yet, she saw that Gizella's eyes were already locked on her--the old woman's expression nothing short of terror.

Alanna J. Rubin #3

Melinda didn't need to turn around to know what was behind her. The look on Gizella's face told her everything. The summoning of spirits was a dangerous task even if those called forth were of good intent. There was always the risk that an unwanted spirit would take advantage of the bridge created between the worlds and arrive uninvited. These were visitors to be feared. Never were their intentions of a pure nature and Melinda had to act fast to prevent the spirit from completing its transition to the world of the living. Preparing for her next move, she gripped the athame still close at hand. Its tip was stained crimson with her blood, which was fortunate. Her blood had created the bridge and her blood could force the unwanted spirit back into the darkness from whence it came.

Melinda mouthed to Gizella, "on three" and the older woman nodded her understanding. "One." Gizella began an incantation that stirred the air in the house into a gust as the power of the coven was called forth to hold the spirit in place. "Two." Melinda adjusted her grip on the athame as the spell took hold. "Three." She whipped around and threw the knife, piercing the spirit where its heart would have been.

The spirit shrieked in agony, and they watched as it angrily pushed and pulled against the bonds that had been cast in an attempt to break free and secure its foothold in this world. Gizella's nose started to bleed as the effort of maintaining the incantation began to take its toll, and Melinda could see the bonds weakening. She locked eyes with Meredith and they lent their voices to Gizella's, sharing the burden of the spell and buying the precious extra seconds they needed for the purge to be completed. They watched as the spirit's form bent and warped. It gave one final ear piercing shriek, shattering all of the glass around them as it was sucked back into the world of the dead.

The athame clattered to the ground and they were left in eerie silence. The younger maidens were still clutching each other in shock, and some in tears. They had hidden behind Meredith during the ordeal, but were now by Gizella's side, the old woman about to collapse from the effort she'd exerted. Norman rushed inside, worry creasing his brow as he took in the scene before him. He hesitated before picking up the athame, then handed it to Melinda and said in a hushed tone, "I couldn't get in. Whatever that was, it sealed the house."

Melinda grimaced. "That spirit shouldn't have been strong enough to withstand the wards I have in place, let alone do something like that. This doesn't bode well. This year, something appears far too eager to push its way through."

"What should we do?" Meredith asked.

"Complete the ritual as planned," Melinda responded. "That will be the best way to safeguard against whatever this might be and judging by what just occurred, we don't have any time to waste."

JM Paquette #4

Meredith nodded, face settling into the commanding role Melinda remembered from their childhood. "Ladies," she ordered, gesturing to the younger members of the coven. "Take your places." As the women hurried outside, Meredith paused, hands on Gizella's arms as the older woman regained her strength. "Take my strength," she insisted. "I have plenty to spare."

Gizella smiled, but pushed Meredith gently away. "I'll do for now," she replied. "The ceremony will restore me." She focused on Melinda. "That was no normal spirit," she told her.

"I know," Melinda agreed, hands reaching to the counter to pull forth the strip of paper she had just completed, "and it's worse than we thought." She held up the paper, her blood the bridge the spirit had tried to use to enter the physical world again.

"Nicholas," Meredith breathed the name. Norman's younger brother, a member of the coven until he had died eight months ago. Norman had taken his brother's place, even becoming High Priest when Lucius had died two months ago. "Why would Nicholas want to come back?"

"Wrong question," Melinda corrected, eyes resting on the framed photograph on the wall: a group shot from the Holiday Party last year, all the members grinning with the joy of another year come and gone. Nicholas was happy there, the sickness that killed him not visible yet in the lines of his face, the creases near his eyes. Melinda had often marveled at how quickly her childhood friend had succumbed, but not nearly so much at how devoted his older brother Norman had become in those last desperate weeks.

Norman had come home for a visit when Nicholas first found out he was sick, and stayed to help, abandoning what everyone said was a promising career in the big city, to take care of his kid brother, and even staying on to take his place in the coven. When Melinda had sat with him in those last days, Nicholas hadn't been angry; he had accepted his illness with the same aplomb that he accepted everything else in life--even the fact that Rob had won Melinda's heart despite Nicholas's best efforts to claim it.

Nicholas had never been angry in life; he had joked right up until the very end.

"What would make Nicholas so angry that he would try to force his way back to this world?" Melinda asked, but she saw her own thoughts reflected on the faces of the other women. As one, they turned to look out the kitchen door to the garden, where Norman stood close in conversation with the other women.

"Norman said the house was sealed against him. He couldn't get back in," Meredith recalled. "Why would the house suddenly keep him out?"

"Maybe the house wards finally recognized the true enemy," Melinda guessed.

"Our destinies are woven on the loom of fate," Gizella commented, her face dark in suspicion. "I know this. And I accept it." She paused, her head cocked in thought. "But Lucius too was filled with life. Not a sign that he was unhealthy."

"Died in his sleep," Meredith said, voice cold. "And Norman was here then, too. Still here." She turned to her sister, tears welling up. "I convinced him to become High Priest." She took in a deep breath, a tear escaping her eye as she glared through the lacy curtains. "It seemed like such good timing, that he was here when we needed him. That he had stayed for a purpose."

"He did stay for a purpose," Melinda said. "To face our justice."

Desiree Matlock #5

Meredith reached her hand over to her sister who took it, and they nodded in unison before turning to walk out into the garden. Tonight's task was now deepening, with no time to forewarn the coven.

They exited the kitchen door, and felt the air pressure change. Melinda's toes felt cold against the soil as she wiggled them. The sisters took in the comforting scents of the herb garden, hands clasped.

Beyond the garden gate, a formlessness sighed through the town alongside the breeze, struggling to lift those of the fall leaves that were still alive enough to temporarily bear form. Children wandered from house to house, unaware of ghost, ghoul, and abominations just beyond reach tonight. Hopefully, if the witches did their job, they would remain unaware.

The remainder of the ladies were finding their positions, stretching, preparing for the dance, but Gizella stood stock still. Any other year her wizened gaze would have been skyward already, instead of focused on the high priest. He seemed not to notice.

Melinda released her sister's hand, tightening her grip on the athame, as the sisters strode to their places. Meredith was just on her left, Gizella to her right.

The two sisters formed the strongest bond here, but had their own agenda, and just as she half-expected, their arrival brought a unique change to the strength of circle. The ladies of the coven felt it and all breathed in unison as the bond formed. Norman made no sign of noticing, although his brow furrowed. And was that a slight hitch in his step as he walked to the center of the ring?

Melinda reminded herself that if he meant to do harm, the ring was more powerful by far. The crone lifted her chin skyward, began a hunched rhythm, her chanting grew audible, and the sisters began to dance and chant along. The maidens followed suit, all the witches dancing awkwardly at first, then more smoothly as the motions grew more intentional. The sky darkened further, and the garden gate swayed and creaked.

She thought to herself that so far nothing seemed unusual about this particular incantation, this particular year. Shortly, the dance began to form within them, needing no thought. The murmur of the women grew louder, as the chant formed on their breath.

Melinda struggled not to abandon herself to the dance. She needed to be logical and ready. But, she had always loved this. The circle was more familiar and comforting than the womb, more loving than any friendship, any marriage. She knew Rob would never understand it, even if she tried to explain. Here, in the circle, the women moved, breathed, thought as one. The spirits of those they loved whipped through their hair, danced alongside them, swept around them, some familiar to Melinda, some new. The chant became everything, and the tingle in the skin overcame her as the words formed and strengthened the incantation. Her mind grew calm, her body frenzied.

Lisa Barry #6

Even as their dance flowed like a curious sea around the enchanted yard, Melinda could feel her mind linked to Meredith and Gizella, awareness spreading over the neighborhood. It was a more difficult task than she ever imagined, protecting the city as far as they could reach while also watching their High Priest.

He knelt on the ground; head bent to his chest, hands caressing the minerals and life of the soil, and then elegantly rose as the dance increased. Slowly he raised his arms to the sky, his head falling back as he gazed at the heavens and joined their chant.

Begging protection for the human world from evil spirits in exchange for this night of freedom and joy, they danced. They laughed, and they were one. Melinda started to feel peaceful, found herself worrying less of their leader and more of their incantation. She laughed and smiled as she twirled around and around with her coven.

When the darkness touched her bare feet, she stumbled, Meredith and Gizella missing a step at the same time. The others continued, oblivious to the alarming intrusion.

It was *his* incantation that had altered.

Not wanting to be noticed, Melinda continued to dance, though her eyes, as well as Meredith and Gizella's, watched Norman. His stance had not changed; he still reached to the sky, chanting softly. But his words brought vile corruption to their sacred circle.

A darkness, blacker than ink, seeped from the ground beneath the High Priest's feet. It crept into the air, but even more horrifying, it oozed onto Norman, creeping up his legs.

A screech came from one of the younger girls, her eyes wide, staring at their leader.

The dancing faltered and Melinda found herself face to face with Norman. His eyes were dark as night and his lips were parted in a smile that chilled her neck and froze her feet in place.

It was Meredith who whipped out her athame and sliced her hand deeply. She drew a symbol of protection on her forehead and another for strength on her chest. A foreign spell began to roll off her tongue like a sweet syrup, as power vibrated from her body and her eyes glowed with the moon.

Picking up the words quickly, Melinda pulled out her own athame, protecting herself and joining the new chant, trusting her sister to do the right thing. Gizella and the other practiced witches soon followed as the younger ones joined hands and lent their strength.

Norman screeched, his black eyes angry, but he couldn't seem to move. The darkness that had reached his neck writhed. Melinda gasped when Norman's eyes suddenly cleared and were instantly overcome with a panicked confusion. The inky mass rose up, and as Norman began to scream, it dove into him, shutting out any further sound.

Dee Rea #7

Melinda watched as the fear and panic turned into a look of pure evil. The newer members of the coven were screaming and looking toward their leaders for guidance. Gizella continued to chant, though the words were different. She looked quickly from Norman to Gizella, then to Meredith in time to see her sister had picked up the new chant, looking at each girl in turn to encourage them to join in. Melinda looked back to Norman. His head moved left and right. Whatever it was that had entered him was testing his body.

The darkness continued to ebb and flow within the circle, testing the boundaries. Melinda's voice joined the chorus of her sisters. She knew it would take the combined strength of the coven to keep the darkness at bay. The original plan of protecting the city had taken a turn she hadn't expected.

Norman took a hesitant step toward Melinda. The smile that crept over his features was chilling. It didn't even reach his eyes, void of any sign of life, just dark pools resting in his pale face. The rhythmic words that flowed from the mouths of the coven members held Norman, but for how long?

Melinda's voice caught in her throat when the darkness wrapped around her ankle. She looked around frantically and watched in horror as one of her coven sisters opened her mouth to scream, only to be filled with the darkness. The girl fell to the ground, writhing and twitching. Gizella's voice resonated within the circle as she continued her chanting more forcefully. Normally, the confidence that Gizella radiated had a calming effect on the sisters. Tonight was different. Melinda watched the writhing girl rise from the ground to join Norman in the middle of the circle.

"Come to me..." Norman's gruesome smile never faltered as he walked the inner circumference of swaying bodies. He paused before another of the newer sisters and held his hand out to her. When she opened her mouth to speak, he gestured, and the darkness began to swirl up her slender form and disappear into her mouth. He picked a few more of the newer sisters before one broke to run.

"I...I didn't sign up for this!" she shrieked as she turned to run. She didn't make it far before the darkness wrapped itself around her ankle. She fell forward and was encased in darkness. Melinda looked to Gizella. The older woman shook her head and simply continued the melody of words.

When Norman reached Melinda, he paused. Turning his dead eyes to her face, she felt as if she couldn't breathe. His hand lifted to caress her cheek and she shuddered. His touch was cold. She felt his hand settle at her throat and her heart began to race faster.

Erika Lance #8

His grip tightened and she closed her eyes. Trying to calm herself, she listened for the sounds of her sisters. They were distant, but there and she found her center. She took a moment of stillness, knowing the darkness was reaching into the soil, into the town, and into the hearts of the people, her people.

It was then she knew what she must do. Tears began to roll down her face as she silently called to him...to Nicolas. She hoped he was still close.

The chill began at her feet, and moved up quickly, suffocating her, spots forming in her eyes from the lack of precious air her mortal body so desperately needed. At first, she had the urge to push out the cold, but realized it was *him*, he was there, and for this to work she would have to make the sacrifice. Death for life, she let him in.

As she felt herself pushed back into the torrent of air surrounding them, she watched Norman's wicked smile began to falter. Her neck was still clasped in his hands, but it was the eyes of his brother, the one he betrayed, staring back at him. It took only a moment of his uncertainty for Grizella's spell to take hold. Norman's body fell to the ground with Melinda's, both now empty shells.

Melinda watched as Grizella ripped Norman's spirit to shreds. There would be no afterlife for him.

When the torrent died down and her sisters began the spell to ensure the cleansing took hold, Grizella looked down toward the bodies that lay crumpled and said only a few muffled words, then raised her gaze up and with a small nod, it was done.

As the loss of what happened threatened to overwhelm her, Melinda felt something warm touch her hand. She looked down and knew it was Nicolas, still by her side. He smiled when her gaze met his, a silent understanding.

They were now guardians, bound, the sacrifice had been made. Only a few hours were left before the veil would seal again. Melinda, with Nicolas at her side, would watch until the next All Hallows Eve.

~ The End ~

Thank you!

Thank you for taking the time to enjoy our creative works. Look out for more books from the Ink Slingers Guild, both as a group and as individuals!

If you enjoyed any or all of the stories in this book, we would love it if you could take a few minutes to share it on Amazon or Goodreads. Your opinion really does make a difference!

May your world be filled with adventure and the stuff that dreams are made of.

Cheers!

The Ink Slingers Guild

www.InkSlingersGuild.com